INDIGO

Also by Graham Joyce

Requiem
The Tooth Fairy
Dark Sister

INDIGO

Graham Joyce

POCKET BOOKS
New York   London   Toronto   Sydney   Singapore

POCKET BOOKS, a division of Simon & Schuster Inc.
1230 Avenue of the Americas, New York, NY 10020.

Copyright © 1999 by Graham Joyce
Originally published in the U.K. in 1999 by Michael Joseph

Library of Congress Cataloging-in-Publication Data

Joyce, Graham.
   Indigo / Graham Joyce.
     p. cm.
   ISBN 0–671–03937–7
   1. British—Travel—Italy—Rome—Fiction. 2. Inheritance and succession—Fiction. 3. Fathers and sons—Fiction. I. Title.
   PR6060.O93 I53 2000
   823'.914—dc21   99–053123

First Pocket Books hardcover printing January 2000

10 9 8 7 6 5 4 3 2 1

This one's for the incomparable Tam and Jo Tansey

ACKNOWLEDGMENTS

A special thank you to my editor, Jason Kaufman; to Meg Hamel for Chicago information both architectural and general; to Mike Goldmark, barefoot art dealer nothing at all like the monster portrayed in this book; to Tim Howlett, Luigi Bonomi, Chris Lotts, Sam Hayes, Dan Gudgel, Pete Crowther, Jonathan Lethem, and to all my writing colleagues and students at Nottingham Trent University.

AUTHOR'S NOTE

Ask scientists how many colors comprise the visible spectrum and they will answer: six. Ask any artist, and he or she will answer: seven. In seeking to resolve this conundrum, I plundered some extraordinary books along the way, including Aldous Huxley's *The Art of Seeing*, Steve Richards's *Invisibility*, Mahendra Solanki's *What You Leave Behind*, and Christopher Hibbert's *Rome*. A thank you also to members of the Indigo Society for opening my eyes; even to those of you who remain implacably opposed to the publication of this book.

Graham Joyce
Rome, 1999

INDIGO

PROLOGUE

OSPEDALE SAN CALLISTO, ROME, OCTOBER 31, 1997

A WHITE GRECO-ROMAN WEDDING CAKE OF A BUILDING, THE OSpedale San Callisto commanded spacious grounds in the suburbs some fifteen miles to the west of Rome. Jack parked his rented Fiat, courteously opened the passenger door for Louise, and together they walked through the avenue of slender cypress trees to the portico of the building.

As they climbed the marble steps, Jack said, "You know, you don't have to come in. You can wait in the car."

"It's my business as much as yours," she answered. It was true: It was why she had come back to Rome with him, and why she'd left Dory looking after Billy back in Chicago.

Their footsteps echoed over the immaculate polished floor of the admissions area, and after presenting themselves to the white-uniformed receptionist they were invited to sit on hard plastic chairs. Sunlight flooded through a floor-to-ceiling window, flaring on sterile marble surfaces. They waited in silence.

A doctor carrying a clipboard emerged from shadows at the far end of a long corridor. His approach was interminable and his shoes

1

squeaked at every step. He greeted them rather solemnly, motioning them to follow him all the way back along the immense corridor and up an impressive flight of marble stairs. The doctor sniffed once or twice as if trying to clear one of his nostrils. A couple of patients who were chatting on the stairs stopped conversing abruptly and stared at the visitors.

Guessing Jack's thoughts, the doctor said, "It's not a secure hospital. We don't restrict the patients. We have a kind of solarium, a sunroom. She likes to sit there. All day if we let her."

At last he opened a door to the sunroom. At first Jack thought the room was empty. The south-facing window was a gallery-style fretwork of decorative iron and glass. White wicker lounge chairs were scattered around the room. Then Jack noticed the young woman. She sat in one of the wicker chairs, on the edge of the seat, peering out the window, wearing Levi's jeans and a white T-shirt. Perhaps he'd expected her barefoot and in a straitjacket.

"*Buon giorno*, Natalie!" the doctor called, suddenly jolly. The woman didn't stir. He approached her, stroking her hair lightly from behind. "Today we got some visitors!" She glanced over her shoulder at them, and stood up. "I'll leave you alone," said the doctor, retreating. "I'll be around."

The young woman stepped forward. "Tim?"

She was skeletallly thin, and her eyes were permanently narrowed, as if to shield herself from too much light. Her brown hair was tied back at the nape of her neck, though she freed it and shook it loose as she faced them.

"No, I'm not—" Jack started to say, but she pressed a finger to her lips and hissed loudly. She moved across the room and, taking Louise's hand, slowly and luxuriously sniffed the back of it. Then she bent down and began sniffing at Louise's knee. Louise didn't flinch as the woman sniffed the length of her thigh and around her crotch, keeping her nose just an inch from the fabric of Louise's skirt. Satisfied, she moved over to Jack, sniffing at his waist, then his flank, and, finally, almost but not quite nuzzling his armpit. Jack could only glance at Louise in desperation.

"My name is Jack Chambers. Tim was my father. This is Louise, his daughter."

"You're drenched in it," the woman said.

"In what?"

"Indigo. Wolf gland. Both of you. Mostly you. Is he coming? Is Tim coming?" She began circling Jack, very slowly.

"Tim died," said Jack. "He died a while ago. Anyway, he left you some money. I'm here to see that you get it."

"Do you know where they all went?"

"Who? Where who went?"

"All of them. There were lots of us. Then there was only me. I thought you'd come here to tell me where they all went. It's been such a disappointment. To be the only one." She blew gently, steadily, on Jack's face. Then she moved over to Louise, and began circling again.

"Natalie," said Louise, "do you know where you are?"

Natalie recoiled slightly, seeming to find the question patronizing and stupid. "Of course. I'm in Indigo. Which is why you can't see me."

ONE

A NERVOUS FLYER, JACK CHAMBERS WAS ON HIS FIFTH SCOTCH AND soda when the plane began its descent to O'Hare. Stewardesses made scissor-like strides up and down the aisles, too fast to be asked for another scotch. Jack drained his plastic cup, wiped his corrugated brow with a tiny lemon-scented paper towel, and settled back to fret about the Birtles matter.

It was a good time for all this to happen, he decided. He'd left behind in London only one outstanding case in a frankly declining business. He had instructed his secretary, Mrs. Price, a lady of pensionable years, to take on any new cases but to stall while he was away, and to process the Birtles case. He had neglected to tell her the circumstances under which he'd left things.

Chicago, then, early October, sunlight like salt and lime outside the terminal. Jack shivered in the crisp, cold air, feeling a little lost. Before the taxi stand was a row of curious kiosks, inside which earmuffed female attendants stared dead ahead, bored into narcosis. Like the cab drivers, they had a chopped, bruised look, as if smarting from the sharp wind. Jack would soon find that all Chicagoans looked as though they'd taken a few jabs in a boxing ring. He tapped on the tough Plexiglas window of one kiosk and a woman minimally inclined her head toward a waiting yellow taxi.

It was a long drive into Chicago, with the taxi meter ticking away to doom. A great canyon, but of glass, steel, and prestressed concrete instead of sedimentary rock, rose gradually on either side; glinting, mercurial traffic formed the riverbed. Instead of caves and hemp ladders in the canyon walls, there would be elevators and carpeted lobbies. In one of those lobbies on West Wacker Drive he met Harvey Michaelson, the man who had originally telephoned him in England.

"When I called, I wasn't aware that you didn't know. I didn't expect to be breaking news."

"We hadn't seen each other in over fifteen years. We were not close," Jack told the lawyer.

Michaelson ushered Jack into his plush, oak-paneled office. He offered him fresh coffee, sandwiches, and pastries, asked about the flight, the weather in England. He treated Jack to an account of his visit, when he was a student, to London. His largesse was so great and his manner so relaxed that Jack calculated he must be paying handsomely for Michaelson's time. He stole a glance at his watch, just to let the attorney know he knew.

Michaelson wore gold cufflinks. "As I told you on the phone, you're more of an executor than a beneficiary." In England, no one wore cufflinks anymore, neither aristocrat nor underclass; here they seemed to signal a status that went with perfectly capped teeth, smooth hair, and a polished beech nameplate on the office door. "Oh, you do get something, conditional on you overseeing the will. There's a lot to sort out."

"Bet I don't get as much as you out of this," Jack said, and Michaelson laughed, even though they both knew it wasn't a joke.

Despite being forthright about the money coming to him, Jack wasn't a callous person. He just hated his father. He didn't have a psychological complaint about this. He couldn't understand why Freud made such a fuss. Jack hated his father and assumed that his father had in turn hated his.

Michaelson said, "Extraordinary man, your father."

"He was a shit."

Michaelson laughed again, but let it die when he saw Jack wasn't rolling with it. "Not the easiest man to get along with," he conceded. "Did he give you a rough time?"

With the lawyer's eyes opened wide in anticipation of an answer Jack saw that the sockets were just a little too red: late nights in dark places. "I don't want to talk about it." Not at these prices he didn't.

But Michaelson wasn't slow. "I can relate to that. Let's check out the paperwork, shall we?"

The paperwork, when it was laid out, was considerable. Jack's role as executor of the will was complicated. In order to receive a handsome executor's fee, he had to dispose of assets and deal with some curious provisions. There was an obscure manuscript to be published with funds made available. The will also required Jack to trace someone called Natalie Shearer, who was the main beneficiary.

"I've made some initial efforts at tracking down Shearer. Want me to keep on it?"

"Please. It's too much like the work I do at home."

"Oh? What is that?"

"I'm a process server." This was close enough to the legal world for Michaelson to understand, but far enough down the ladder for him not to want to ask any more. Jack wished he hadn't mentioned it. It was like a sandwich-board man hinting to an advertising executive that they were in the same line of business.

"Interesting. This is a set of copies of all the paperwork. You'll want to go over them in your own time. Where are you staying in Chicago?"

"I came directly from the airport. I thought you might recommend an inexpensive hotel."

"The hell with that. I'll have my assistant check you into the Drake. You get to draw your expenses from the will. It's provided."

"But if I read this correctly," said Jack, "anything left over after these provisions goes to me. So it may be my money after all."

Michaelson smiled indulgently. "Then you've got to pay inheritance tax, not to mention . . . look here." The lawyer then explained to Jack how he could actually make money by staying in a more expensive hotel, and Jack saw why his father had employed the man in the first place.

"And if I fill the room with call girls do I make still more money?"

Michaelson blinked.

"I'm kidding," said Jack. "Really I am." That's lawyers for you, he thought: If you don't laugh at their fees, they won't laugh at your jokes.

TWO

FOLLOWING MICHAELSON'S SUGGESTION, JACK CHECKED INTO THE opulent Drake on North Michigan Avenue. The Drake had a palm court centerpiece lobby and an air of grande dame gentility reminiscent of a film set. The ghosts of a tuxedoed four-piece orchestra played invisibly and the receptionist treated him like a VIP. Flaking from jet lag, he dined alone in the hotel. The waiters were so attentive he thought they must have him confused with a celebrity guest.

He showered, wrapped himself in a hotel bathrobe, and poured a glass of Dalwhinnie. He left the TV on quietly in the background, comfort against loneliness, and spread Michaelson's papers across the emperor-sized bed. The old man's will was professionally drawn, brief, and relatively uncomplicated. The file also contained a bound manuscript and a collection of typed essays, all awaiting publication. There was a further portfolio of assets drawn up by Michaelson. Jack's father had owned an apartment on Lake Shore Drive, which Jack already knew about, and a house in Rome, which he didn't. There were investments in both U.S. and Italian companies and a decent amount of capital. Jack smacked his lips at the

Dalwhinnie, aware that none of this was coming his way. Perhaps he should have been more persistent, or even patient, with the old man.

But no proportion of the money would have been worth it. It suddenly occurred to Jack that he hadn't even asked Michaelson how the old man had died. That was how much he cared.

· · ·

Jack had last seen his father in New York almost twenty years ago, when Jack was twenty-one. Some months before that, having abandoned Jack's mother when their son was just five years old, Tim Chambers had turned up bearing gifts appropriate for a young man's coming-of-age. Jack, studying geology at the University of Sheffield, was crossing the campus shortly before his final exams. A tall man in a pale suit and wearing a turtleneck sweater had stepped from a doorway. He was carrying a bottle of champagne, a book of poetry, and a sealed envelope. He said, "Jack Chambers?"

"Yes."

"I'm your father."

Jack had blinked at the man. He *might* have been the gray figure Jack remembered from when he was five. In some ways he looked too young. His hair was unfashionably long for a man approaching fifty, silvering, swept back in a leonine mane. The Mediterranean tan suggested a social standing beyond anything Jack's mother experienced. There was something else. Though otherwise expensively attired, he was wearing neither shoes nor socks. Jack looked at the bare feet and said, "I've got an exam in half an hour."

The man looked sadly at the champagne in his hand. "Timing. Never a strong point with me. Can I meet you afterward?"

Jack arranged to meet him on the steps of the examination hall. He completed his exam in a kind of dream. It was as if his head were a helium-filled balloon, floating upward and looking down on the scribbling figure below. Later, he would blame his father's dramatic intervention for his poor results, but at the time he thought he'd done rather well.

When it was all over he came out of the exam room and his father said, "How did it go?" Jack had the distinct impression that the man had been waiting on the steps, champagne and gifts in hand, for the entire duration of the exam. Three hours. Barefoot.

"Not bad."

"Splendid. Spot of lunch?"

Tim Chambers led him to a sporty Alfa Romeo, laid the champagne and gifts on the back seat, and drove them to a French restaurant. Jack couldn't help glancing at the bare feet as the man toed the pedals. The maitre d', too, noticed the bare feet, but chose to say nothing. Jack fingered the heavy silver cutlery and tried to take his cues from the man frowning into the menu. His eyes also fell on a small bone-colored disk hanging from his father's neck like some kind of amulet.

"Bad luck," his father said.

"What?"

"Having an exam on your birthday."

"They've got to fall on someone's birthday."

"How philosophical of you. Geology, did you say? Should have studied philosophy."

"Do you feel guilty? Is that why you've suddenly appeared?"

The wine steward arrived before an answer. Expertly, Tim Chambers ordered. "Guilt is an utterly useless emotion; one that I've cleared from my life. You might think about doing the same." Another waiter hovered, pen poised over his writing tablet, but Chambers ignored him. "Curiosity and concern: the first, naturally, to see what sort of a man you've made, and so far I like what I see; the second to perform at least a vestige of paternal assistance if I can, and if at all you'll let me. Tell the waiter why we shan't have pheasant in almond sauce."

11

Jack looked at the waiter, who only gazed beadily back at him.

"Because," Tim Chambers answered his own question, "pheasant is out of season, there being no R in the month; and if they have pheasant it's been frozen; and we haven't come here to eat frozen food."

Jack wasn't sure who exactly was being rebuked, but when Chambers ordered filet mignon instead, Jack found himself following. Throughout the meal Chambers did the talking. Jack, suspended between simmering resentment and enchantment at the man's urbane and mesmerizing charm, replied to probing questions mostly with monosyllabic grunts.

Before dropping Jack at the university, his father pressed into his hands the champagne, a leather-bound copy of Dante's *Inferno,* and the sealed envelope. The man was long gone before Jack tore open the envelope. It contained a check for more money than his annual student loan.

Jack had disappointed himself that day. He'd tried to remain aloof, but had only managed to be sullen. He'd wanted to appear cool, but had seemed only inhibited. He felt uncomfortable at the thought that, all the time, his father had been able to see straight *through* him.

. . .

That was all a long time ago. Now Jack lay sprawled in his Chicago hotel room fingering the paperwork on the bed, dislocated by memory, jet lag, and a dull headache. He fell asleep.

When he awoke, the TV was showing highlights of the previous weekend's American football game. He stared stupidly at the screen trying to figure the actions of men dressed like comic-book superheroes. It was 4 A.M. and he felt wide awake. There was nothing else to do except make a doomed effort to understand American football.

. . .

Michaelson had arranged for Jack to meet Louise Durrell at his father's apartment on Lake Shore Drive. Durrell had the keys both to that apartment and to the property in Rome. She was Chambers's daughter; Jack's half-sister.

Jack had seen her once before in his life, for about ten minutes. That was also twenty years ago. She'd been lurking in the background, an eleven-year-old with freckles, bad hair, and braces across her teeth. As far as he could remember they had never exchanged a word that day.

Before leaving the hotel he telephoned his office in London and left a message on the answering machine for Mrs. Price. Having read somewhere of the American disdain for walking, he decided to walk to the apartment just to show an important nation that it could be done.

If God created Chicago, He did so with a stiff compass, protractor, and slide rule. In that metropolis of the clean line, the erogenous curve, and the sweet angle, to be of eccentric human proportion is to be freakish, irregular, almost a joke, an affront to the draftsman's art; to be human is to be warm chaos at the heart of cold mathematics.

Jack was energized by Chicago. In its streets he wanted to make some noise, to hear his voice come back off the glass, steel, and concrete canyon. He angled his neck at the monolithic elevation. Sparkling towers huddled at the shores of Lake Michigan like a migrating press of thirsty, leggy white birds; birds who may have forgotten how to fly.

Underestimating the distance, he arrived almost half an hour late. The doorman was expecting him. He rode in an elevator better carpeted, mirrored, and otherwise appointed than his house at home.

Louise Durrell let him in and he instantly had thoughts that were inappropriate for a sister. She wore a well-cut beige suit and expensive-looking low-heeled shoes. The length of her skirt hovered at that magic point, revealing and concealing in equal measure. Jack suspected her of superior taste. Louise exuded the odor of money, as if she'd been around it always; there was a residual whiff of soft kid leather, new banknotes, and sensible restraint. It was a scent that made him aware of the frayed cuffs of his raincoat.

He hesitated, uncertain how to greet a sister he didn't know. She failed to return his smile, seemed impatient with his apologies. Leaning her thin shoulder blades against the wall, her pose almost insolent, she squinted at him. As if he were being measured for something. Right, he thought, an Englishman can match anyone for reserve, so here's some, on the rocks.

Pretending to make a sweep of the apartment, he studied her at the periphery of his vision. Louise Durrell watched him closely in turn. When he caught her gaze, she lifted a stray lock of blond hair from her eye and looked away.

"What will you do with it?" she said.

She's not sleeping properly, he observed. A puckering around her eyes, heavy lids, tired skin, something keeping her awake at night. Something pulling on her.

"The apartment? I have to sell it. Proceeds to be directed in different ways. Not much in the way of furniture, is there?"

The apartment was appointed on minimalist lines. The windows in the den were shaded by electrically operated blinds. A pale wool twist carpeted the floor and three large sofas were lavishly upholstered in turquoise leather. There was a liquor cabinet, an impressive-looking sound system, and the kind of paintings on the walls that Jack took to be an expensive scam. Not a nanospeck of dust anywhere.

Jack couldn't get past feeling rude around Louise, the child Tim

Chambers *did* care for. When he rummaged in the liquor cabinet, she looked as though she wanted to say something. Instead, she compressed her lips, but her eyes leaked provocation. Jack chose to irritate her a little further by slouching on one of the sofas. "Hate this color," he said. "Why don't you sit?"

"Why don't I just give you the keys and I'll get out of here?"

Jack liked her brisk manner. There were a hundred things he wanted to ask. She was ten years younger than he was and as far as he knew she'd been raised by Chambers. He wondered if she'd been useful to him in his work or if she was merely an indulged daughter. "Fine. You run along. I've got things to do here."

"What sorts of things?"

"Complicated sorts of things." Jack had a disarming smile when he was being rude. Something he'd learned from process serving.

Louise opened her handbag and produced two bunches of keys. Each was efficiently labeled. One *Chicago*, one *Rome*. "I just meant maybe there are one or two things I could help with."

"Have you seen the will?"

"Yes."

"Then you already know you do rather well out of it," said Jack.

She thought hard before answering. "He could have treated you better."

"I'm not complaining. I had no respect for the old man. We had no time for each other. I'm not even sure why I got pulled in like this; I only know it will pay better than my work at home."

"You're some sort of court official in England?"

"Not exactly. Look, thank you for your help here. I have your number—is it all right to call you if I need you?"

"Sure."

"By the way—the old man, how did he die?"

Louise lifted her shoulders from the wall. "You don't know?"

. . .

Over lunch Louise started to thaw. Although Jack had been hoping for a cow-sized American burger, after he'd pointed out they were dining on expenses she'd chosen a Japanese restaurant. As it turned out, there was more mystery in the Asian menu than in how Tim Chambers, aged sixty-six, had died; but he'd still been unable to go out without a whiff of impropriety.

"He died in bed." Louise forked sushi into her mouth. "He was with a twenty-year-old girl, and he already had a heart condition. The girl was hysterical. She called me and I went over to the apartment. I got the doctor. He'd had a heart attack—not his first."

"What happened to the girl?"

"She wasn't anyone important. He was cremated, according to his wishes. Hundreds of people came, although I don't think he would have known or liked most of them. I thought you might come. Being his son."

"I hated him. Didn't you?"

Her eyelashes quivered. "No, I didn't hate him at all, but I had less and less respect for him toward the end."

"Anyway, I didn't hear of his death until after the cremation. Not that I would have come." Jack told her the story of their father's brief reappearance in England when Jack was a student. Louise was an attentive listener. There had been more, much more, but he decided not to tell her the rest.

. . .

When Jack graduated he failed to find a job immediately, never straying far from the Sheffield of his university days. One by one his cronies disappeared from the scene, until he found himself the last of the sad ex-students still turning up every night at the student bar. On a desperate whim he decided to contact the man who'd appeared on examination day.

A whirlwind followed. Why don't you come and stay in the

States, his father said. Really? Sure, get an open ticket, we'll show you a good time. So Jack told his mother he was going to spend six weeks in the States with his father. She'd almost become apoplectic. She implored him not to go. Jack had thought people were being theatrical when they talked about getting down on their knees, but his mother's arthritic joints left indentations in the carpet. She'd cried. She'd pleaded. She'd used language that shocked him, saying monstrous things about Tim Chambers.

But Jack, determined to be his own man, took the silver bird to his father's adopted land, where his father, then living in New York, received him like a young prince. Folded dollars were pressed into his hand, as many as he could use. Domiciled in his father's apartment, he was given a Buick—a Buick!—to drive around. He was also surprised to find that his father, an art dealer, was a party animal with access to enticing young women and unlimited supplies of marijuana. And except in extreme circumstances, his father never wore shoes.

"What's with this barefoot thing?" Jack asked.

"What's with this shoe thing?"

Jack left it a week before asking again. "Why don't you wear shoes?"

His father looked nettled. "Let's say I like to feel the vibration under my feet."

Jack never asked again, and anyway Tim Chambers turned out to be the daddy of all dads. Jack could talk to him as a friend. He was wise, witty, sensitive, and a great raconteur. He'd been everywhere on the planet. Jack hardly had to ask before Tim would produce his wallet and roll out the green. He was universally admired by all the young people, mostly from the New York art scene, who hung around his apartment. It was during this time that Jack first spied Louise, who, home from boarding school, was hovering around bug-eyed at the antics of the young adults. But to Jack she was just an uninteresting kid. Six weeks passed in a grass-and-booze-induced fog, during the last month of which Jack saw less and less of Tim. He was having too much of a good time.

Then his father foreclosed on him like a bank.

They were in the apartment. Jack was just helping himself to a beer from the fridge. Tim was putting on his coat to go out somewhere when he said, "You've got to go home tomorrow."

"Tomorrow?"

"Yes." Tim had seemed distracted. His mind, buzzing with internal noise, was clearly elsewhere.

"Where's the fire?"

Tim had stared hard at him for a long time before answering. Fingering the bone-colored talisman he always wore around his neck, he said, "I don't brook arguments. Tomorrow you pack your things, get a cab, and you fly back to England."

"Have I done something wrong?"

"This isn't about anything that you've done. The world does not revolve around your ego. It's home time. Say good-bye." Tim had proffered an upside-down handshake, squeezed Jack's hand, and then was gone.

It happened that no flight was available for three days, but in that time Tim never returned to the apartment. When Jack tried to call some of the hangers-on he'd met, either they were not available or were evasive. The last of the bountiful dollars was spent on a taxi to the airport. Over the Atlantic, high above the clouds, Jack reran events again and again, trying to recall if he might have *said* something.

He didn't tell Louise any of this over lunch. One thing she said to him struck an odd note. "Sure, he was an odd fish. Have you read that manuscript he wanted you to publish?"

"Haven't had time."

"Read it."

"What's it about?"

She shook her head. Jack decided he liked her. She had lioness eyes, and she narrowed them at him. "Just read it. See for yourself what he was." Then she moistened her upper lip with her tongue, and laughed, and Jack thought for the second time what a nuisance it was that she was his sister.

"They did a good job on your teeth," he said. "Last time I saw you, you had braces."

She colored and shrank back. "So you do remember me!"

"Yes. You were only there for five minutes, but I remember."

"You hurt me."

"What? We never spoke!"

"Exactly. Do you know how much that wounded an eleven-year-old girl?" She was being serious. "Let me tell you about that time. Dad told me I had a brother, and that you were coming over from England. England! All the girls at my boarding school were sick with envy. Who knows, maybe I told them you were a kind of prince. Anyway I wore a pretty new dress and got my hair fixed, all to meet my mysterious brother from England, who I knew would be this cool guy to whom I could tell everything and who would treat me like a grown-up and who would love me, you know the kind of thing? And there you were having fun with all these crazy people Dad used to have around the apartment. I tried to speak to you three times. All that came out was a kind of croak. You didn't want to spend a single second with me. I cried for three days. It broke my kiddie heart. I went back to school and told my friends what a swell time we'd had and how you'd brought me a necklace from a London jeweler but it was so valuable I wasn't allowed to bring it to school to show anyone."

Jack recalled the bug-eyed eleven-year-old staring at him, eyelids fluttering weirdly. "Oh."

"It was the worst thing that ever happened in my life. Really."

"Please." Jack had done very few things in his life of which he was ashamed. Now he felt like the kid who kills a pigeon with a pebble from a slingshot.

"There was no way you'd have known. It was just a girlie thing at a time in my life when I really could have used a kind older brother."

Jack forgot his cool. He seized her hand impulsively, kissing her cool, elegant fingers. "Can I make it right? Could you use one still? A brother, I mean?"

Startled, she gazed back at him. "I could use a vodka and tonic."

THREE

LUNCH WITH LOUISE HAD GONE WELL AND HER INITIAL HOSTILITY had vanished before the main course arrived. She still didn't feel much like a sister (not that Jack had another with whom he could effect a comparison)—for one thing, he was too interested in the way she smelled. When he'd impulsively kissed her hand, her scent lingered long after contact was withdrawn. She was sharp and smart and she laughed easily. There was nothing extraordinary in the idea that they should get along, since they had half a genetic makeup in common. But it was odd for both of them to realize they shared the same father and yet were unknown to each other.

Louise left Jack with a telephone number. Afterward, Jack returned to the apartment, letting himself in with the keys she'd passed on. He wanted to be there alone, to get a sense of the place, to tune in to his father's ghost. He stood in the middle of the characterless lounge, still in his coat, squinting at the paintings on the wall. There was a faint smell of incense in the apartment, perhaps sandalwood. Jack remembered the odor from those few days in New York.

The bedroom was neatly furnished; a hairbrush rested on the dressing table, still bearing a few white hairs and the oily whiff of sebum. There was a study, impossibly tidy, with a computer, a wall of books, and a separate writing desk. The blotter revealed the only evidence of human disorder in the entire room. It was scrawled with fantastic doodles: black spirals, conchs, double helixes, cones like wizards' hats, covered in moons and stars, phone numbers all writhed together, and, in the corner, a Latin phrase: *auribus teneo lupum.*

Jack soon found the secret of his father's scrupulous tidiness. A spare room was crammed with junk, as if every unwanted item had been stored there just to maintain the order of the other rooms. While in some places it was stacked high with old magazines and yellowing newspapers, all else seemed to have been flung inside and the door slammed before the contents hit the floor. It would all have to be disposed of before Jack could sell the property.

. . .

Jack spent time downtown before returning to the Drake. He wandered the Loop, passing between the iron struts and riveted girders bearing the vibrating, dirty trains overhead. The street jarred and rattled, scraped by a demon claw. Every time a train passed overhead, Chicago time seemed momentarily to unravel, and then to reform before the wind-stung faces hurrying beneath had time to notice.

Back at the Drake, Jack plumped a few pillows on his bed and opened up the file Michaelson had passed on. He wanted to see why Louise was so anxious for him to read the manuscript. It was neatly bound and sheathed inside a blue plastic folder with a clasp lock. He unclipped the folder and found every page blank. Nothing. He fanned the pages, turned the bound manuscript upside down and back to front, tried shaking it to see if anything might fall from between the leaves. Finally he tossed it onto the bed and snatched up the will.

Rereading the will, he clearly found the reference to the "enclosed" manuscript and directions that it should be published to high professional standards. A large print run was specified, though no recommendations were made concerning distribution or sale of the published copies. The executor of the will was to ensure that no editor be allowed to change a single word of the manuscript, "given the general untrustworthiness of editors."

Louise had been reluctant to explain the contents of the manuscript over lunch. She was enjoying a small laugh at his expense. Jack pawed the thing again, thumbed the pages, and let it fall open on to the bed. Then he got up, ran a deep, deep bath, and climbed in, clutching the whisky bottle.

With the bottle resting on his chest and the water slowly cooling around him, he dozed and started dreaming about the junk room in his father's apartment. Everything started to slide out; Jack, with his back to the door, couldn't keep it in.

He woke and dried himself. Thoughts of Louise gave him an erection. He regretted not asking her out to dinner. But Jack was a shy man who couldn't bear rejection, and therefore rarely asked; and in any event his motives would have been muddled.

The manuscript was still lying facedown on the bed. Turning his attention away from lewd thoughts about his sister, Jack picked it up again, turned it over, and was astonished to see the first page full of print. He flicked through the rest of the pages. All of them bore type, faint and of uneven resolution, but developing even as he looked.

He turned back to the opening page:

INVISIBILITY: A MANUAL OF LIGHT

by Timothy Chambers

There was a short preface. As Jack read it he could hear the ring of his father's urbane vowels:

Nothing more than a schoolboy's trick, effected by specially prepared chemicals in the ink. The words were there all the time, but when you broke the seal on the folder the ink began to oxygenate and react with the room temperature. I apologize for this shameless device in grabbing your attention, but the subject matter of this manuscript is so unusual I couldn't take the risk of you dismissing me. Some discoveries should not be brought before the public at large, and it is only after lengthy consideration that I choose to proceed. In fact, it is not without a degree of fear that I do so now. After all, *auribus teneo lupum*.

Jack wondered whether the preface was directed at the general reader, at the person who first opened the folder, or at him, Jack Chambers, specifically. The Latin quotation at the end of the preface was, he thought, the one he'd seen scribbled on the blotter on his father's desk. Jack had no idea what the words meant.

He settled back with his scotch to read the manuscript. It began with a convoluted introduction couched in self-consciously poetic language. Jack steeled himself to stay with it, but after the first thirty pages he concluded, and not for the first time in his life, that his father was a lunatic. The references to the concept of invisibility were literal; that is, the manuscript was concerned with the task of making oneself invisible to others. Exercises were described, most of which involved sitting in the dark. When he reached a section inviting him to sit in a closet for two hours in order to visualize violet light, Jack snorted and tossed the entire manuscript aside.

. . .

One evening in New York all those years ago, Tim Chambers had thrown a glamorous party, attracting many bright young things. There had been much booze and dope, and in the small hours, when everyone was trying to put their brains back together, Tim, in what Jack had thought was a party game, made him sit in a closet and look for "violet light." Jack, in good spirit, had done as instructed but had fallen asleep inside the closet. When he came out, befuddled and confused, he tried to rejoin the party, but everyone pretended they couldn't see him. They ignored him. At last he grasped a girl's arm and she screamed. Everyone gathered around her.

"Somebody grabbed me!" she insisted.

Then Tim "saw" Jack. "Here he is! Here's Jack! Where the hell have you been, Jack?"

"In the closet," he laughed.

They all looked blank.

"Come on," Jack said. "A joke's a joke."

But they all seemed locked in a conspiracy, no doubt orchestrated by the old man, to deny that Jack had ever been put in the closet. Jack began to speculate about what was in those joints he'd been smoking. A nasty edge of paranoia set in as he looked at their staring faces. Someone offered him another joint and he declined, saying he thought he'd had enough.

They'd all laughed at that, as if he were Oscar Wilde.

· · ·

"Was he psychologically ill?" Jack asked.

"He was a character," Michaelson said. "We need more characters."

The door to Michaelson's office opened and a young Hispanic woman carried in a tray of coffee. She wore a fire-engine-red tunic and a sensationally short skirt. Setting the tray on Michaelson's desk, she poured for them. The coffee bubbled and flavored the air.

"He may have been a character," Jack said, still gluing his eyes to the pouring coffee, "but I think he was barking mad."

"I just love your accent," Michaelson's secretary said. She finished pouring and stood with her hands folded behind her back, as if to push her pelvis forward a little. "I could listen to you talk all day."

"Sally, Jack's over here to sort out the Chambers estate,"

Michaelson said lightly, as if it were perfectly normal to set up clients with his secretary. "He's alone in Chicago for a few days."

"Someone oughta do something about that," Sally said on her way out.

"Great girl," Michaelson said after the door had closed behind her.

"I asked you if you thought he was ill."

"You never knew what kind of mood you were going to catch him in. Let's leave it at that."

"You've got new information on this Shearer person?"

"Absolutely. Natalie Shearer is in Rome. I've been unable to get a telephone contact but we can send someone out there."

"What's that going to cost?"

"Won't cost you a dime. It'll cost the estate whatever we charge. You ever been to the Eternal City? It's a fucking dump. You don't want to go chasing off to Rome."

"I'll think about that."

"It's your call. I'll let you have whatever information we've got. How did you get along with Louise Durrell? Prickly little thing, isn't she?"

"No, she's fine." Jack decided he didn't like Michaelson.

Outside Michaelson's office, Sally provided Jack with further information about Natalie Shearer's whereabouts in Rome. She plied him with questions, shuffled files, and licked an envelope twice before sealing it. Then she said, "Wanna go out some time?"

Jack, who ever since puberty had wanted to meet a woman who would call all the shots, just blinked at her.

"Take all the time you need," Sally said.

FOUR

Great patience is required to achieve the power of Invisibility. Before proceeding further, let me define my terms, if only to give you the opportunity to lay aside this Manual of Invisibility, having decided that you want no more of such talk. To be precise: I am talking about managing the art of vanishing. Not by trickery, conjuring, hypnosis, or other deception. But vanishing by strength of mental force.

I do not propose to show you how to become incorporeal. My own abilities have never extended quite so far. In my own experience of Invisibility, it is not possible to lose one's substance. Thus, what we talk of here relates to optical phenomena. As soon as another sense, say, of touch, impacts on the body, the spell (for want of a better word) is instantly broken. This, of course, can be distressing or alarming for persons suddenly becoming aware of a body they were previously unable to see; and it may foil your purposes in wanting to remain invisible. But then your motives for wanting to become invisible are not my concern.

I offer this information to the clean and the ugly of spirit alike.

At least by now you should be clear that I am not talking of making the corporeal body vanish into some other plane or dimension or other such nonsense. I am specifically talking about making oneself unseeable, and no more or less than that.

This ability has been available to the adept from the most ancient times. It is my belief that such practice has enacted great moments of history. Consider the founding of the ancient Roman empire, a culture contributing more, by means of colonization rather than mere conquest, to the advancement of the human race than any other. Who was the mother of Rome? The answer is Rhea Silvia, mother of Romulus and Remus. Rhea Silvia was a Vestal Virgin, a keeper of the sacred flame, ravished in the grove sacred to Mars by an *invisible* spectre, an adventure attended by an eclipse of the sun covering the heavens in darkness.

I don't claim to have been that spectre (not *completely* insane, you sigh); but I think I know who was, and how the deed was done. But already I am getting ahead of myself. If you wish to follow my instructions, you need patience, practice, and dedication.

There are seven steps (are there not always seven?) to be followed assiduously. Each step must be mastered in turn through diligent practice; and when all seven steps are perfected then they must be applied in sequence. In my experience, any mistake or lack of concentration on one of the steps requires the practitioner to go back to the first. Since some of the steps require several hours or even days of work, a failure of nerve late in the procedure can be deeply demoralizing. But then at no point have I suggested to you that the process of achieving Invisibility would be easy.

The seven key words are as follows: Colour, Light, Cloud (or Breath), Smoke, Darkness, Indigo, and Void. I will disclose the seven exercises in plain and simple language, without mystery or obfuscation. You, in return, must recognize that the exercises are unlikely to produce results on the first time of calling, or sometimes even on the twenty-first time. But rest assured that they will ultimately produce effects that will be so astonishing to you that they will put you beyond all help.

A word of warning. Your skepticism at this point in the proceedings is extremely harmful to the enterprise I am about to propose for you. Not only will any such skepticism ensure that all your experiments in this matter fail, it will also turn back on your mind dangers of a very real nature; real in both a physical and a psychological sense. If you are unable to abandon your rational objections at this point, I strongly recommend that you do not proceed beyond the gate of this closing chapter.

After all, I hold the wolf by the ears.

FIVE

Two messages awaited Jack at the Drake. One was from Louise. She was meeting people in a downtown bar and he was welcome to join them. He called back and left a message on her answering machine, explaining exactly where he was going. The other message was from Mrs. Price, his secretary in London. There appeared to be some complication over the Birtles case. He knew if he called immediately he might just catch her, the time difference notwithstanding. He decided against it.

He would have liked to have joined Louise, but he'd already agreed to meet the delectable Sally after work, in a bar called Rock Bottom. He was doing well, he figured. Only his second night in the United States and he had two offers of dates; one that, with discernible irony, Sally had called hot, and one with Louise, sisterly and lukewarm. It had been more than twelve months since he'd been on any kind of date anywhere.

With women, Jack was a catastrophe-in-waiting. Difficulty sat on his shoulder like an invisible ape, and the worst part of his trouble was that he comprehensively adored women. He spent three-quarters of his life gazing after them with pitiful longing: from the

window of his office as they strolled by; from his car as they over-
took him at the lights; from the top of a London bus as they took a
different route; from the down escalator as they passed by on their
way up. He was consumed by an unfulfilled need to devote himself
not just to one of them but to all of them. From a distance.

Lacking the confidence to make things happen, he waited for
life to come to him. And come it did, usually in the form of women
who wanted to rescue him, heal him, burn him, and break him all
over again.

His trouble with women was that he saw right through them.
Spotted when they lied easily, noticed when they cheated with a
smile, caught on when they were bored and faking interest, saw
when they were hurting but pretending to be happy. This transparency was too much for him. He could read faces. Every muscle,
line, crease, skin fold, pucker, twitch, or tremor on a woman's face
was a letter of the alphabet to him. Especially when making love.
Then they spoke volumes he would have preferred not to have
heard.

. . .

Chicago decanted its entire corps of office workers into the
early-evening bars. Rock Bottom was packed to capacity. High-
decibel music pumped out at heart-stopping volume, but you
couldn't hear it because of the talk. It was like drinking in the bear
pits of the stock exchange, everyone red-faced and bawling,
pumped up by the day's business and the happy-hour booze. Sally
perched on a high bar stool, advertising legs sheathed in shimmering nylons. Her dark eyes glittered and her lip gloss sparkled. She'd
saved him a stool and he squeezed in beside her, blinking.

"You made it!" She flung her arms around him but seemed to
look over his shoulder at the same time. Flicking back her lustrous
black hair, Sally talked just to fill the airwaves while Jack ordered

thin American beer. "This is a great place. Great crowd. Is this like an English pub? Yes? No? It's sort of how I imagine an English pub. You still staying at the Drake? Great place. I stayed there once. One hot night! Why don't you stay at the apartment? I mean your old man's apartment? Do you—"

"It was your boss's idea that I stay at the Drake." Jack suspected Sally needed to be interrupted in order to make conversation.

"That's Mike for you!" She scanned the bar. "He likes to take his mistress there, and if you're running up a bill there he'll shave a few nights on your account. That's why he recommends it, though I must say—"

"He tried to tell me I'd make a saving."

"Aw, he's full of shit." She was still trawling the bar over his shoulder. "Keeps tapping my butt. Wouldn't—"

"Are you looking for someone?"

"Looking? Not especially. I just love your accent. Did I tell you how much I love your accent? How do you like Chicago?"

"It's windy."

"It's not called the Windy City 'cause of the wind; it's—"

"So everyone tells me, but here's a secret: It's still very windy. Sally, are you certain you're not looking for someone?"

A man in a gray business suit came into the bar. He had a hunted look. For a moment it seemed to Jack as if everyone in the place went silent; but what he really felt was the slipstream as lovers spot each other across a room. The man saw him with Sally and, communion over, turned away. Sally's eyes narrowed to tungsten-tipped darts. Then she put down her glass, balanced a manicured hand on each of Jack's shoulders and said, "I'm gonna tell you three amazing things about Chicago. Firstly—"

Over Sally's shoulder Jack spotted a new group of people entering the bar. He put a finger to her lips. "Stop! I came here on a jet with a Rolls-Royce engine. I didn't come on the banana boat."

"I love the way you say banana—" Realizing that Jack had just got her number, Sally dropped her arms. "Okay. I'm gonna explain something. I admit, I did want some company tonight so that guy over there would . . . but I want you *especially* to know I decided not just *anyone* would do for a date, only someone I respect—"

"Stop. Stop talking. You want to make him jealous?"

"—someone who I felt sure I could, like, not *use* but get along with, but who—"

He had to put his hand over her mouth to shut her up. "On the count of three, you have to laugh out loud. As if I've said the funniest thing you ever heard. He'll hate it. He'll think if I can make you laugh that much, I'll get you in the sack. Don't look; I can clock him from here. Then raise your hand to your mouth, as if you're embarrassed to be having so *much* fun in a public place. Ready? One, two, three—"

Sally was good. She had a cackle that bounced off the ceiling. Heads turned to check them out.

"That's good," Jack coached. "Pause for breath and we'll do it again. Let me whisper this one."

"Is he looking? Is he?"

"He's fingering his collar. He's burning up. Ready to go again? One, two—"

It seemed everyone else was looking, too. Sally's laughter was so convincing she almost fell off her bar stool; she waved her hands rapidly in the air, fanning her cheeks; she stuffed a pretty little handkerchief in her mouth. It was quite a performance. Jack began to think maybe he really was the funniest man in Chicago.

Then he felt someone squeeze into the space beside him. "Having a good time?"

"Louise! Imagine seeing you here. Let me introduce you to Sally."

"He's a funny guy," said Sally.

"He must be," Louise said. Then to Jack, "Got your message. There are some people I'd like you to meet."

"Hey! Don't steal my date!" Sally complained.

Jack offered a parting handshake. "Keep that stool free, Sally. Your chum will be along in two minutes. Trust me."

He followed Louise through the crowd of drinkers to join up with her friends. "We just got here," Louise said.

"I know. I saw you come in."

Louise's pals were friendly Chicago naturals; they bought him drinks, they shot some pool; they let him lose narrowly. Louise asked him about "the woman at the bar" and he was suitably evasive. "Didn't seem your type," she said as he hunkered down to line up a shot. "Anyway, she's leaving."

"With a man in a gray suit."

"What's going on?"

"I'm just playing pool."

Then one of Louise's friends soured the evening for him by saying, "Hey, hear you used to be an English cop." He looked up from his shot at Louise and her eyelids fluttered. He wondered how much else she knew about him.

"Bobby, not cop," Jack said. "In England we say bobby."

Outside it was pouring, and Louise drove him back to the Drake. In the car Jack asked her about their father. "What do you know about this Natalie Shearer in Rome?"

"I know nothing about his life there. He kept things separate. I suspect there was stuff he didn't want me to know."

"What kind of stuff?"

Louise lit a cigarette and smiled. "Did you take a look at his manuscript?"

"Gibberish, masquerading as gibberish."

"I had to type it."

"Did you know about the ink trick?"

"Yes. He wanted to know if it was possible to publish it that way. You could, but it's insanely expensive. Wanna know what that little trick cost, just for your entertainment?"

They sat in the car for a while longer and Louise said, "Sorry about mentioning the cop thing. I didn't know it would embarrass you. Dad told me you only became a cop—sorry, a bobby—to annoy him. Is that true?"

Jack laughed that off. "Not everything was about him."

He wanted her to come to his room for a nightcap, but he couldn't ask. Even though she switched off the ignition. Even though she lit up a cigarette and wound down her window to stop the windshield from fogging. Even though they chatted inconsequentially for several minutes before he finally hauled himself out of the car and said goodnight. He was furious with himself. The fact that she was his sister made it all right to invite her in; but then again it didn't.

After she'd driven away, Jack stood in the portals of the Drake looking out at the rain-slicked Chicago night. It was like an oil canvas, blurred, streaked with the ember-red reflections of taillights and the acid-blue light-strike of neon signs. Darkness snapped to the city tower-blocks like crafted joints. Something new, something cold was coming off Lake Michigan. This rain was just a lick of it.

. . .

The next day, Jack checked out of the Drake and moved into the apartment. Alone inside, he prowled, knowing there must be a ghost in all the compulsive tidiness. Jack believed in ghosts, whether they drifted on a whiff of hair oil or floated in a swirl of dust motes lit by the morning sun suspended over the vast lake. Something triggered a memory, an impression, a fear of the old man. But it was like trying to sniff out and isolate pheromones, or

35

the one scent in a complex weave that invokes fear or provokes desire. Jack always thought of it as a signal between odor and white noise; a signal his father broadcast only at certain times. It was a warning.

After Jack had been summarily dismissed that time in New York, he had spent many hours puzzling over what he might have done or said. He let some months go by before writing a letter asking for clarification. When the letter went unanswered, he telephoned. Tim Chambers had made light of it, told Jack he was being too sensitive, invited him to come back again for "more great times."

Taking him at his word, Jack pulled some money together and arranged to return to New York. When he called to give advance notice, he found his father vague, distracted, almost as if he didn't know who Jack was. But he went anyway. This time he found a very different person. Their initial conversation was conducted through a crackling intercom.

"Who?"

"It's Jack."

"Jack who?"

"From England. Your son, for God's sake."

"What do you want?"

"What do I want? I want to see you, that's what I want!"

"Why?"

"Can I come in?"

"It's not a good time. Come another day."

Jack dropped his backpack on the sidewalk and sat on it. After a while he pushed the buzzer again, determined to give the old man a piece of his mind. This time the intercom went unanswered. Baffled, dismayed, Jack fell back on a friend he'd made on his previous trip, but returned the next day.

He found the scenario played out all over again. Hot with anger, near to tears, he said, "If you don't let me up then I'll smash the door." The lock dropped and the buzzer sounded. He let himself in.

His father stood in the middle of his apartment with his arms folded. He was wearing a Chinese silk dressing gown, and was barefoot as usual. He didn't take his eyes from Jack. "I don't take kindly to threats."

"So why did you invite me here if you didn't want to see me?"

"Invite you?"

"On the telephone. You invited me to come."

The old man cocked his head. That was the very first time Jack picked up the warning signal, the white noise, the odor, the metallic taste coating his tongue, all of it emanating from Tim Chambers. The old man's mind seemed to move like greased machinery on steel rails. "As a person you lack precision. You heard me make some encouraging and friendly remark to you. This you interpreted as an invitation to come to my door."

Jack was bewildered. "What about all the other stuff?" Meaning the gifts, the parties, the high times.

"Again you lack precision."

"So you just wanted to be my dad for a few days, was it?"

Chambers stepped briskly toward him and Jack jumped aside as his father picked up the phone, tapping out a few numbers. Someone answered quickly. Jack heard his father say, "Look, there's a young man here who claims to be my son. Yes, from England. Yes. Yes. Thank you." Chambers replaced the receiver on the cradle with incredible delicacy, turned to Jack, and said, "It seems you are correct in your claim. In which case you have my sympathies. But I'll say this: I'm not a number on your jukebox. You can't punch out a sentimental and fatherly tune on me whenever you feel like it."

Jack felt his scalp flush. "Why are you talking to me like this? I don't understand the things you say."

"Who are you? Yes, I know you're Jack, and I know where you

come from." He moved to the door, holding it open for Jack to leave. "I want you to come back. Really. But not until you know who you are."

Jack was shamed and humiliated by the withering impotence of his position. He wanted to hurt his father at that moment, but more than that, his voice was fracturing with rage and pain for the abandoned little boy who'd at last been beckoned forth only to receive a stinging slap. He left the apartment without a word, went home, and got back to find that his mother had died while he was away.

Twenty years later, Jack stood in his father's antiseptic apartment, raging that his mother's last thoughts were of her son returning to the despised father. And somewhere in that apartment he could scent him—detect that loathed and lingering presence, the odor and the echoing white noise of him.

· · ·

Jack made a serious assessment of Tim Chambers's estate. He called a realtor to come and pin a price on the apartment. Given its location on the golden mile of Lake Shore Drive, he guessed at a value of $600,000. About the value of the furniture and the artwork hanging on the walls, he would need some help from Louise.

He began unscrewing paintings from the wall to see if any information was pasted behind them. The first to come down was a black background with an eel of nightblue daubed in the middle. It was called *Invisibility 1* by an artist named Nicholas Chadbourne. Jack didn't need a degree in fine art to guess that two similar efforts still hanging would be called *Invisibility 2* and *Invisibility 3*; but he would have liked to know what his father had paid for them Each painting left behind it a light rectangular patch. When he'd finished lifting down a dozen paintings, he was no wiser, but it felt like a start.

The junk room had to be faced. Jack opened the door on the pile of trash and shook his head. Then he found some black plastic garbage bags and began to fill them.

He was methodical. There were piles of clothes; designer labels on items that would have fitted him nicely—but the thought was repugnant to him. Instead he filled bags for charity, always checking the pockets first but warming to the idea of Chicago's homeless dressed in Armani and Gucci. There were women's clothes, too, jeans and underwear slung carelessly, worn shoes—never a pair—leather gathering mildew. There were piles of art magazines, obviously on subscription and unread. These he would dump.

There were photographs, mostly so old that the chemicals were unfixing; a standard lamp; African masks; unspooled cassette tapes; paperback novels; ski gear; an old hi-fi unit; obsolete computer hardware; empty wooden frames; dozens of empty vitamin jars; withered house plants still in earth-filled pots . . . all carelessly tossed into the room. And underneath all of this were still more paintings—undistinguished, to Jack's eyes—horizontally stacked.

Jack found a newspaper article inside a transparent plastic sleeve. The headline caught his attention:

PAINTER VANISHES

The brief article described the disappearance of a young artist who had gone missing on the eve of being presented with a national award and cash prize. The article alluded to the *Marie Celeste*, claiming the artist's friends had found an unfinished meal and a half-empty bottle of wine in his apartment. This had all happened two years ago. There was a picture of the twenty-seven-year-old artist: a sultry and intense young man peering haughtily at the camera through wire-rimmed glasses and wearing a pretentious goatee. His name was Nicholas Chadbourne.

Jack took the report back to the living room and checked behind one of the paintings to confirm that the artist was the creator of *Invisibility 1*. He placed the cutting with his other papers and resumed the task of emptying the room.

By the time the realtor arrived it was late afternoon, the lake was still, and Jack had filled fifteen bags. The woman with the clipboard, her hair lacquered into an edge on which you could have sliced your finger, addressed him as family, as though he were someone who finally had the good sense to sell this old place. Jack's estimate of the value of the property had been conservative. She was out in less than half an hour, assuring every possibility of a quick sale, but before leaving she advised Jack to screw the paintings back on the wall.

Jack phoned Louise, asking her advice about the paintings and the furniture, hoping to steer the conversation around to dinner. She gave him the number of a dealer for the furniture; she also told him that most of the paintings on the walls were by unknowns to whom Tim had taken a liking, and agreed their only real value was in remaining on the walls to enhance the apartment. At last Louise said, "Jack, I have to go. I've got to think about eating."

"Eating. Hadn't thought about that since moving out of the hotel."

"Want to come over? You could eat with Bill and me."

Bill? Jack's heart murmured. He hadn't heard anything about Bill. "I couldn't do that."

"Sure you could. Bring some wine." She gave him an address, told him to take a cab, and put down the phone while he was still writhing and protesting. Given the choice between making small talk with some unknown Bill while secretly wanting to woo his wife naked—a wife who happened to be his sister—and a lonely evening chewing a two-pound T-bone in a sad downmarket restaurant, he'd opt for profound loneliness any time.

He was in a sour mood by the time he climbed out of the yellow cab in a district close to the University of Chicago.

Something was cooking. Louise let him in, relieving him of his carefully chosen wine and ramming it in the freezer without looking at it. "Where's Bill?" he couldn't help asking.

"Other room." She spoke in a hushed tone, indicating he should do the same. "You staying? Take your coat off if you're staying. I mean, you look like you might not want to."

The apartment was small, but, like Tim Chambers's place, it was uncluttered. The living room was also a dining room; Louise had lit a candle at the table, but hadn't yet laid a third place for Jack. Etta James purred smoky and blue in the background, with the volume turned down low. On the sideboard Jack noticed a familiar bone-colored disk on a leather strap. It was the talisman his father always used to wear.

"I was just telling Bill all about you. I lied and said you were a famous soccer star. Okay?"

"Why? Does he like soccer?"

"Don't be ridiculous. You want to meet him? Follow me. He might be asleep."

Jack wasn't sure he wanted to meet a sleepy husband in an undershirt, but, brushing aside his protests, Louise led him through to the bedroom. Bill was indeed sleeping. In a crib. His baby lips were like a slice of strawberry. He slept with a tiny fist clenched outside the blanket.

"You can stop looking at him now," Louise said.

"I can watch a sleeping baby for hours It's like looking down from a bridge onto a river."

She had to tug at his sleeve. "Let's eat."

She'd made jambalaya, and the hot spices made him perspire. "How old is Bill?"

"One. And a half."

"Beautiful kid. And the father?"

"I'm thirty-one. I wanted a baby, but I hadn't found the right guy. So I picked out one I liked the look of and got myself pregnant. I figured he'd done his job; he didn't know anything about Bill until later. Does that shock you?"

Jack was shocked, but because this was Chicago and cool seemed to be the local virtue, he said, "Not at all."

"Really? It shocks a lot of people."

"I'm lying. Yes, it's very shocking. Very modern. Very American."

"American? You think that's American? That's interesting. Would an English woman be unlikely to do something like that?"

He thought about it and decided the answer was no, women anywhere were likely to do that if they wanted to. "Sometimes I just burble to cover up my surprise, that's all. Wow, this dinner is hot!"

"Like it?"

He hadn't said he'd liked it, he'd said it was hot, but he scooped another forkful to show he wasn't complaining. "Who is the father?"

The smile withered on her lips. "I'm not telling you that. If I do, then you'll know something that Bill doesn't."

"I shouldn't have asked."

"It's a normal question." She got up, remembering his wine in the freezer. "I'm just not a normal person."

She was right. She wasn't a normal person. Louise sat down again and poured wine for both of them, with the unwavering candle flame spinning light from the yellow-green wine—the same color as her eyes. He saw again that some anxiety was pulling on her, leeching at her, and he knew it was more than the fatigue of raising a small child alone.

"You okay?" she asked. "You look distracted."

"I was thinking about all the stuff in our father's apartment."

"I told you: The pictures were all by unknowns. Maybe one or two have appreciated slightly, but that's all theoretical until you find someone who wants to buy them. Anything really valuable he used to sell immediately. I know because I did all the paperwork."

"I found a newspaper cutting about one of the artists represented on the wall."

Louise glazed over slightly and put down her fork. "He was typical of the young people Tim used to have around him all the time. He had all these young followers. Never people his own age: He needed them to sit at his feet with damp eyes. And they were like him. They saw themselves in him."

"I don't understand."

"They were all very unstable types. It was like a mental ward at times. Manic depressives, victims, loners, all kinds of strays. Tim would build them up and help them to see themselves as suffering artists. Buy their pictures, hang them in his apartment. They thought he was a god."

"Why do you say they were like him?"

"Something you should know about Tim. At different times it was difficult to believe you were talking to the same person."

"Oh, I've seen some of that."

"You think so? You didn't see the *haf* of it."

"I love your accent."

"I don't have an accent." Watching Louise smile was like watching a match burst into flame. "This is America. You're the one with an accent, buddy." Then her brow wrinkled. She drained her glass and rubbed her eyes with forefinger and thumb. That strain he'd noticed. Now he knew for certain it was more than the effort of being a single parent. *Switch off,* he told himself, *switch off the bobby eye.*

"You know, I'm really tired," she said. "Would you mind if I called you a cab now?" In England, Jack noted, people would be glancing at their watches, fiddling with the strap, yawning, "Gosh, is that the time!"

As they waited for the cab, Louise asked Jack if he was still going to publish the Invisibility manuscript.

"I have to or I don't get my fee."

They talked for a while about the terms of the will. "The funny thing is," Louise said, yawning again, "that Invisibility thing. It works."

The door buzzer sounded. It was Jack's cab.

"Not in the way you'd think. But in a surprising kind of way. About seeing things."

"How?"

"Try it." She held his coat for him as he slipped it on. Then she surprised him by cupping his jaw with a cool elegant hand and pecking him on the cheek. "Thanks for coming by. I enjoyed the company." He looked deep into her yellow lioness eyes. "Cab's waiting," she said.

SIX

"HI, MOM." LOUISE KICKED OPEN THE BACK DOOR, LAYING A bag of groceries and gifts on the kitchen table. Louise's mother lived in the suburbs of Madison, Wisconsin, far enough north to get away from Chicago without crossing into Canada. As a matter of some principle never actually explained, she always kept her back door unlocked.

"Hi, darlin'!" Dory Durrell—she'd dropped her married name after splitting with Tim Chambers when Louise was three—swept through the kitchen, planting a kiss on Louise's proffered cheek and relieving her daughter of Billy.

"Why, look at you! Look at you! He's growing some, Louise."

It didn't matter that Dory had seen Billy only a few days earlier; Louise visited her mother at least once and sometimes twice a week. Dory doted on the child, was a great baby-sitter, and a wellspring of maternal wisdom and comfort. Louise and she had a robust mother-daughter relationship. The best. So long as they steered away from one subject.

"Didn't expect you today," Dory said to Billy, stroking back his hair.

"We smelled the coffee." Coffee always meant home-baked

45

cakes and cookies in Dory's house, though she was a dreadful cook. "Just thought I'd surprise you."

"You can surprise me anytime, hon. Let's see what Grandma's got in the cookie jar for *you*."

Billy sniffed at the cookie in Dory's hand and accepted it grudgingly. They went through to the living room. Dory dug out some toys for Billy and worked up a head of steam about a new system introduced by the garbagemen. She told Louise about a telephone confrontation she'd had with a telemarketer. With Dory it was not always easy to break into the monologue, and though Louise laughed and took a few potshots at telemarketers on Dory's behalf, she had a difficult time focusing on what Dory was saying. She'd arrived today with an agenda beyond the usual small talk.

Dory was overweight and gray-haired, though she always wore black slacks and a black vest to remind herself of what she called her "bohemian youth." Dory had met Tim Chambers soon after the Beatles first arrived in the United States, and Louise was born a year later. "Englishmen," Dory had once said pointedly, "were very much in vogue, and I just damned well had to find one, didn't I?" Though she was only twenty-four when she'd first met Tim Chambers, she was way beyond screaming herself hoarse at mop-head Liverpudlians. Her tastes instead ran to jazz and the dying beat scene, to folk cafes and existential poetry and the art circuit.

Now she hated any "art." Though she'd had a fine eye herself, she'd managed to adapt all of her artistic talent to domestic space. Louise picked up a patchwork quilt lying on the sofa. It was "Billy's quilt." Dory had started it the day Billy was born eighteen months ago. She hoped it would be ready when Billy was three.

Louise studied an individual square. "This is fine work, Mom. Really fine."

"It gives me something to do nights."

Dory's modesty was misplaced. The quilt was exceptional. "It's a real work of art."

"The hell with that. If it looks pretty it keeps Billy warm, that'll do for me."

But that was nonsense. The idea of the quilt, in Dory's eyes, was to make a patchwork of bedtime stories. Each square contained embroidered figures in a scene from a particular tale. In no special sequence, there were Bible stories, Greek myths, Aesop's fables, Native American legends, Chinese parables, fairy tales, folk yarns, and family anecdotes. Dory collected the story, figured out a design, and hand-stitched it in multicolored glory. It did away with bedtime books, she said. All you had to do was to pick a square and tell the story. Both sides of the quilt had thirty-five squares.

Louise knew Dory had been stitching that quilt almost every single evening since Billy's birth, give or take a few nights when she was feeling groggy or had been away on vacation. If she finished it for Billy's third birthday it would be the work of a thousand nights. It was a Sheherazade comforter and a flying carpet; a lullaby and a dreaming suit. So much love had been stitched into that quilt that just the thought of it could make Louise want to weep.

"I've decided to leave one square *abstract*," Dory said.

"Oh?"

"I have this Islamic tale I'm working on, and I read about how these Muslim carpet makers put a deliberate flaw into the weave, on account it's a sin to try to imitate the perfection of Allah. Well, I can't speak to that, but I did figure Billy ought to see there are stories still to be told. Right?"

Louise knew something else: the abstract was the Indigo square. "You've got it all figured out, Mom."

"Louise, have you got something on your mind? You're not listening to a word I'm saying."

47

"Sure I am. The quilt—"

"The hell with the quilt. I can hear your brain, chug chug chug. Like some guys drilling a hole in the road outside."

"Okay. It's about my brother."

Dory snatched up the quilt and folded it to put it away. "*Half* brother."

"Whatever. You've never actually met Jack—"

"Don't want to, either."

"You don't have to like him, but—"

"Damned right I don't have to like him!"

"Will you shut up, Mom? Will you just shut up for *two seconds?*"

Louise stopped. She stopped when she saw a weird cast come over her mother's eyes. It lasted no more than a second or two, but it was a trait Louise knew with absolute familiarity. Dory's eyes would shift, set, and glaze, as if she'd suddenly spotted something startling in the upper corner of the room. Whenever Louise saw that look, she backed off.

Two people could not have loved each other more, but it often happened that within ten minutes of their being together voices were raised. Dory compressed her lips, stowing away the quilt and her needlework box in a chest behind the sofa. It was invariably the same topic that brought on their bouts, or straying close to it, that produced a puff of heat.

Dory would never talk about Tim Chambers, and she'd never answered any of her daughter's questions about him. In turn, she never, during the times Chambers had reasonable access to Louise, wanted to know where they'd been, what they'd done, or what they'd talked about. It was not possible to deny his existence, since the courts had awarded paternal visiting rights and holiday arrangements. But he existed on another plane; in a world inhabited by wraiths; at a corner of hell exclusively his own.

"So whatever you think," Louise persisted, "he's my brother and although I only just met him I think you should too."

"He'll have too much of that man in him, that's for sure. Here, Billy, come sit on my lap."

Billy didn't want to sit on Dory's lap. He started hollering for Louise, but Dory wasn't letting him go.

"Mom, I have a feeling he's going to ask me to go to Rome with him and—"

"Rome? You keep yourself away from him *and* there, you hear me?"

"And if he does ask me I wondered if you'd look after Billy."

"The hell I will. I told you—that man's got too much of his father in him, whoever he is."

"So what does that say about me? And whatever you think, I can see Jack is a victim of his father too. Like you. Like me."

"Victim! I'm not a goddamn victim." Dory hoisted Billy onto her shoulder and carried him through to the kitchen.

Louise followed behind. "You can't even bear to have his name mentioned in your presence."

"Just speaking his name pollutes my house and the air my child and grandchild have to breathe." With Billy still screaming and struggling on her shoulder, Dory kicked open the kitchen door and marched out into the garden.

"Mom!" Louise shouted after her. "What did he do to you?"

. . .

Winding up Tim Chambers's estate—at least the American part of it—was easier than expected. On the realtor's advice, Jack rehung the paintings to cover up the sooty rectangles they'd exposed when he'd taken them down. The bags of junk had been disposed of, and a furniture dealer waited in the wings. The only things Jack kept were some photograph albums.

All that remained unsettled in Chicago was the publication of the Invisibility manuscript. Then there was the question of Natalie Shearer. And Rome.

Whoever Natalie Shearer was, she had a lot of money coming. After Louise had taken her share (a handsome endowment, much more than Jack stood to receive) and the manuscript was taken care of, Shearer got most of what was left. There were a couple of donations to obscure charitable foundations; and then there was Jack's generous fee.

He glanced wistfully around the apartment with the paintings restored and gazed out the window at Lake Shore Drive. He wondered how long an executor might be allowed to languish in this property before selling it. He thought of his own property and business in Catford, London.

It was a dismal thought. His office, a single room shared with Mrs. Price, looked out onto a busy thoroughfare. After quitting the police force, he'd become a process server because it was a job at the soft end of the law in which he could still use his police experience. At first, business had come to him easily. Solicitors hired him regularly to deliver court summonses and he took a particular pleasure in serving papers on wife beaters and those defaulting on child support. But his heart was no more in it than his tongue enjoyed licking stamps.

A small psychological revelation one day made him realize why he took inordinate pleasure from cornering the absconding fathers, the useless dads, the violent husbands; and he'd understood with a wave of self-disgust that Tim Chambers had gotten to him again. He'd lied to Louise: It was true, he'd originally become a bobby because of something Chambers had said about detesting the police; and after extricating himself from that, here he was, still working out personal grief on any sap in the street who'd failed the minimal demands of fatherhood.

50

He'd begun to take longer and longer lunch breaks, given over to solitary drinking in sluggish London pubs. Mrs. Price had warned him. She'd seen the caseload shrinking. And then when this Chicago matter had cropped up, he'd done an unforgivable thing over the Birtles case.

He was sorry that he'd failed to get back to Mrs. Price after she'd tried to contact him. But anyway, he knew he couldn't stay too long in Chicago, even by pretending there was more work to be done on the estate. Everything here was contaminated by the carrion whiff of Tim Chambers. The apartment still reeked of him. Everyone he knew in Chicago was connected to Chambers. All conversation inevitably came back to the man he loathed, like roads leading to Rome.

Even before Chambers had turned up at the university on that examination day, Jack had blamed his father for anything awry in his life. Now that Tim Chambers was dead, who was Jack going to blame?

. . .

Jack spent the day trying to make sense of the Invisibility manuscript, and it was a nightmare. He knew nothing about publishing. The manuscript was hardly a page-turner. No commercial publisher was going to take on the ravings of a madman. He called Academy Chicago Publishers, where an editorial assistant on her lunch break was kind enough to take his call and pass on the name of a vanity publisher, pointing out that any number of people would publish the thing if he paid them to do it.

The vanity publisher, an outfit called Brace, salivated before gnawing Jack's hand. A man named Joseph Rooney asked if Jack could come by the offices, located on Chicago's South Side. Jack got out of the cab uninspired by the neighborhood, and after climbing three flights of stairs was none too impressed by the Brace offices either.

Rooney was a huge and lumbering bear, instantly likable. He guided Jack through a room stacked high with cardboard boxes to a small glass-partitioned office at the rear of the building. Jack thought he was in Al Capone territory; he knew he should walk out, go for something more upmarket, but when Rooney revealed that the company comprised only himself and an old lady who copy-edited for him, it reminded him of home.

Rooney smiled all the way through the interview, mopping his huge face with a handkerchief even though the offices weren't particularly warm. "We publish crap," Rooney growled. "All kindsa crap. Fact, if it's any good we send people a rejection slip. We specialize in volumes of crap poetry. Some of the shit we publish would make a horse bite its own ass."

"Aren't you supposed to pretend it's all great stuff?"

"Naw. They do that in England. Vanity presses. Tell people they're giving a service. We just say make it as bad as you like, give us the money. Here's some examples of what we do."

Jack was impressed. There were a couple of biographies of obscure men who had served in World War II, and some anthologies of poems. They were neatly bound, had nicely designed glossy covers, and the typeface was clean and readable. Despite everything the man suggested to the contrary, he obviously took pride in the finished product.

"Poetry's where we fleece most people," Rooney said candidly. "Get 'em to stump up the dollars to have two or three sweetheart verses bundled in with a load of other saps. Nice moneymaker for us. I fuckin' hate poetry."

Jack took out the Invisibility manuscript. Rooney leaned over and grabbed it, tossing it into an in box. "Fine," he said.

"Don't you want to look at it?"

"Nah. I pay someone else to do that. An' if I can squeeze enough cash out of you, they'll make it spell right and take a pen to your bad grammar. I told you I don't care what it is, we'll do it. On the phone you told me cost is no object. Far as I'm concerned I'll treat this as if it was the confessions of the shah of Persia's concubines. How many copies are we talking here?"

"The will states two hundred thousand."

Rooney snapped to attention and then jumped out of his seat. His eyes bulged, like eggs frying on the grill of his huge red face. "You're putting me on!"

"No. Can't you handle it?"

"Handle it? Look, *I* can handle it; *you* can't handle it."

"I don't follow you."

Rooney danced from behind his desk, flapping a hand at Jack. "Come on. Come with me. C'mon, c'mon." Jack followed him back into the warehouse space. "Normally I deal with numbers of about five hundred. But this is a big run I did for someone last week. They're waiting to go out. Look at all these boxes. How many do you think are here?" Jack surveyed a wall stacked high and deep with cardboard boxes, and shrugged. "Fifteen hundred."

"So?"

"So where you gonna put two hundred thousand?"

"I'm not planning to keep them." Jack was thinking on his feet. "I'll be distributing them."

"*Distributing* them. Ha! You're a fucking comedian from London, England, Jack. Come on, sit down again." Back behind his desk, Rooney rubbed his hands. "Look, I'm talking my way out of work here. If you want a coupla hundred thousand I'll give 'em to you. Heck, if you want a million, it's only a fuckin' forest in Canada. But here's the thing about publishing crap. You can make as many copies as you want. But you can't *give* them away."

"Obviously I haven't thought this through."

"No you haven't, but I have. Bookshops won't take 'em off you, even for free. You can stand in the street trying to push 'em into people's hands, they won't take 'em. The only thing you can do with these books is mail 'em to people you hate."

Jack hadn't considered for a second what he was supposed to do with all these books. He supposed he might rent a warehouse somewhere, but for how long, and what then? He shook his head. He appreciated that Rooney could easily have gone ahead without warning him.

Rooney seemed to read his thoughts. "I'm telling you now, so you don't have a big problem later," Rooney said.

"It's just that the terms of the will are absolute."

Rooney hitched his trousers halfway up his rib cage. "Go home. Think it through. If you want that number, you've got it. If you want a more modest print run, let me know. Here, take your manuscript. I'll still be around."

As he walked Jack back to the door, Rooney pointed out more boxes of books he'd been stuck with for years. He claimed to have taken to sneaking them out with the garbage a hundred at a time. Jack thanked him for his candor.

"I'm an honest guy," said Rooney. "I publish all this crap, and honesty is all I got. So I tell people it's crap and it keeps me straight. How long you in Chicago? Come have a beer with me some time."

"I might."

"I like to have a beer and look at nude girls." He pronounced the word *nood*. "That's what I like: *nood* girls. Fat guy like me, the girls don't want you to touch 'em. Okay, that's the way it is, I just look. I know all the places in Chicago where you can drink beer and look at *nood* girls."

"I'll remember," said Jack.

Rooney smiled and waved. But Jack thought he looked sad, pained even by his own honesty.

SEVEN

THE TRIBUNE TOWER ON NORTH MICHIGAN AVENUE BRISTLES with irregular rocks and stones like barnacles fused to the hull of a ship. Pillaged from around the world, each stone is identified with a famous or historical structure. The first stone Jack's eyes fell upon was a boulder, lodged in the buff masonry, from the Colosseum in Rome. Adjacent to that was a nugget torn from the Holy Door of Saint Peter's Basilica. Roads, stones, and the imperatives of his father's will, all leading him to Rome.

After meeting Rooney, Jack called Louise for advice about publishing the Invisibility manuscript. She, too, had no idea what he would actually do with two hundred thousand books. His encounter with Rooney had depressed him. He'd thought it would be a simple matter to commission some printer. He did consider the possibility of producing and instantly pulping the books, but it seemed wasteful and perverse. In any event, it would violate his position of trust as executor of the will.

His lunatic father's will.

He owed nothing to his father. But in another sense he was grateful for a very different legacy. Jack had shaped, entirely out of his contact with his father, a scrupulous integrity in his dealings with people. He configured his father as a model of how *not* to be-have. Often, if he was confused or uncertain about what to do in a given situation, he would ask himself what his father might have done; and since he always imagined his father in the worst possible light, an opposite—generous, sympathetic, or kind—alternative al-ways presented itself.

It bothered Jack that he hadn't fulfilled his duty in the Birtles case. This rectitude, or the anger encased in this rectitude, had al-ways sustained him in his work at home. As a police officer, his scrupulous honesty insulated him from the people he had to deal with, and also from some of his colleagues. In English process serv-ing, all that was required—usefully, in the case of slippery eels like Birtles—was for the appropriate papers to be "touched" against the body of the servee. The papers might then slip to the floor or be blown away by a stiff northeaster so far as the courts were con-cerned. Indeed, the server might lie (as the servee often would) for all the difference it would make, since it was often only one word against another; but there existed that ethical code in the mind of a process server like Jack that somehow prevented the entire business from slithering into the morass of bluff and counterbluff. Jack had to touch Birtles; otherwise Birtles was not real.

Jack needed to contact Mrs. Price as a matter of urgency. He had to figure out a way to give Birtles what he had coming to him.

He turned his attention back to the publication of the Invisibil-ity manuscript. He'd started to read the thing again after returning from Louise's place, intrigued by her claim that the trick actually worked. Something like that would certainly be useful for serving papers on Birtles one night in the back room of the Haunch of Veni-son public house: *May the lord strike me dead if I lie, but something just crept up and touched me on the ear!*

Jack returned to the manuscript with a skeptical eye.

. . .

The band playing behind them in the Tip Top Tap Club was so tight Jack wanted to keep swinging around to have a look at them. He guessed Chicago must be spoiled for jazz and blues if quality musicians slummed in a joint like the Tip Top Tap. A black man blew a lazy, dirty Harlem Nocturne on sax, while organ, bass, and vibes rumbled along with sleepy, almost contemptuous virtuosity. Jack sipped beer from a bottle and stole another guilty glance at the band.

"Whaddya keep lookin' at?" Rooney barked, never unfixing his gaze from the stage. "Want another beer or somethin'?"

Six feet away, a nude girl shimmied and arched her back. Rooney's vast bulk slumped in his chair, his arms dangling at his side, one fist scraping a beer bottle along the sticky floor. He was eye-locked. There might have been a steel brace connecting his unblinking eye and the pudenda gyrating on stage in a shadowy puddle of blue light.

Jack would have preferred a less blinding seat a little further back from the action, but Rooney had insisted on getting in close. The proximity made Jack feel slightly queasy. Perhaps that was why he wanted to turn around and look at the band; but he couldn't, because he didn't want Rooney to think he was gay.

Fact was, he would rather have been in Louise's company. He'd tried to invite Louise out that evening but failed to find an opening in their telephone conversation. She'd chatted happily about Billy, about what a stormy day she'd had with him, and the subject never seemed to round on prospects for this evening. So after he'd hung up he was left with the desperate remedy of a night out with his prospective publisher. Rooney cheerfully dragged him along to the Tip Top Tap, where, he said with pride, he was a member; though Jack didn't detect much of a door policy, and the price of a single beer was so high it would have made an astronaut blanch.

The girl on stage didn't engage him at all. No connection, no desire. He began to study the dancing girl, observing how she looked straight through her audience. It was probably a trick, like a ballerina "spotting" to avoid dizziness, to get her through the performance. She smiled, even made eye contact, but she might have been doing all this in a mirror in the privacy of her bedroom. She'd found a way to render her audience invisible.

At last the act on stage finished (although there was no denouement, as in a conventional striptease, since the girl came on naked and left the same way). Rooney surfaced, mopping his brow with a tissue and smiling happily at Jack. "Told you you'd have a good time."

"Really cool music," said Jack.

Rooney jerked his head around very fast to look over at the band, who had paused for a cigarette break. He frowned at them as if trying to figure out how they'd got past the door policy. "Yeh."

"Do you publish pornography?" Jack asked.

"That what your book is?"

"No. I just wondered."

"I publish whatever people give me. I told you before, I don't read it myself. Personally, I think reading is an unhealthy activity."

"Right."

"Thought any more about your old man's book?"

Jack had. "I started reading it again last night. I wouldn't bother with all this trouble; but if I don't publish it then I don't get my fee."

"I did a bit of checking on your old man. Friendly research." Rooney summoned a waitress and ordered a couple more beers. The waitress was topless. Jack thought her nipple looked sore, and the veins on her swollen breast stood out so prominently that she had to be a nursing mother. "I don't come here too often. This is not my favorite place in Chicago. But your old man did. Yeh, he used to come here."

58

"You're kidding." Jack looked around as if seeing the room for the first time. "Did you know him?"

Rooney turned his gaze on him. "No. But I know people who did. In between the pornography I've published a couple of art books. Full-color plates. All bullshit, fuckin' zigzag lines or things that look like microbes. Another thing your old man did was to import Renaissance artifacts from Italy and eastern Europe. Unlicensed, you might put it." Rooney was telling Jack not to underestimate him. "Seems he had a particular habit, your old man. He used to come down here. Some of the girls, they do more than just dance . . . not treading on any toes, am I, Jack?"

"No. Please go on."

"Seems his favorite thing was to get a girl and have her tattooed. On her shoulder here. Little wavy spectrum. Seems this would really get it up for him. Strange guy."

The waitress returned with two long-necked bottles. It was Jack's turn to pay. He tipped generously. Rooney must have finished his speech because he turned to face the stage. The band settled to their instruments again, and the saxophonist hit a note so low it vibrated Jack's testicles. A new dancer came on, a slender girl with her hair dyed blue-black. Jack was relieved to see, when she turned around, that she had nothing tattooed on her shoulder. He wondered if Louise Durrell did.

He turned to say something to Rooney, but Rooney was incommunicado.

EIGHT

ROME, OCTOBER 9, 1997

As the aircraft began its descent into Fiumicino airport, Jack got a bad case of the sweats. He tried to stand up but a hostess gently pressed him back into his seat. "Where are you going, sir? The plane is coming in to land."

Billy was screaming because the decompression had given him an earache. Louise, nursing the boy in the window seat, turned from Billy to ask Jack, "You okay?"

"I told you I'm a terrible flier. And here I am, being a terrible flier." Jack rubbed the back of his neck.

Louise reached across, placing her cool hand on the back of his wrist, letting it rest. Other than a greeting or farewell peck on the cheek, it was the first time she had touched him. Strange balm. Jack looked into her eyes. Billy stopped screaming and looked from one to the other of them, wondering why he'd suddenly ceased to be the focus of everyone's attention. Then he started screaming again.

Jack didn't mind at all that Billy was screaming. He was just happy that Louise had agreed to come to Rome with him. After his beery night out with Rooney, Jack had decided that the only reason he was still hanging around Chicago was Louise; and since nothing could possibly be allowed to develop between them he might as well go to Rome to settle with Natalie Shearer before returning to England.

So he'd put Rooney on hold, notified Michaelson that he was on his way to Rome, and stopped by at Louise's apartment to say good-bye.

"Rome," Louise had sighed, taking his coat. "Guess you won't need any help there, huh?"

"Pardon?"

"No, why should you? Wishful thinking, Jack."

Jack heard himself speaking a mint-cool language not his own. "Now that you mention it, there might be sense in that. I mean, you knew my father's business inside out. I could use some administrative assistance. Of course I'd pay you, whatever he used to pay."

"Pay me? Are you kidding? I was just hustling for a plane ticket and a pizza on the Spanish Steps."

"No, of course I'd have to pay you. From the estate. I'd have to."

Delight lowered her jaw. "Hey! Don't you think I'm a mean hustler?"

"Is that a yes?"

"Aw, it's a great thought. But there's Billy to think about."

Jack then heard himself assuring her that it would be no problem taking Billy, that he was at a portable age, that she should bring her laptop and they would work around the boy. He talked about how they were family, after all, and how they should spend as much time together as they could to make up for lost time. In fact, he said too much and Louise began to eye him strangely. But she was never going to say no to Rome.

. . .

From the airport they took a train into the Termini, and from there a taxi directly to Chambers's property. The terraced house was located on an ocher-colored block on a tree-lined avenue on the southeastern side of the city, between the Colosseum and the Appian Way. Dusk was falling on Rome, some elusive color between blue and violet. It was a color you could scent.

They let themselves into the building. Operatic music was playing loudly, contralto soaring from one of the rooms, drifting through the house like an evening mist. "Is someone living here?" Jack said, setting down the bags in the hallway.

"Not that I know of," Louise said.

Jack looked up the stairwell. The house had three floors; it was creaking and smelled damp. It was in a poor state of repair, and there was little evidence of the obsessive tidiness of the Chicago quarters. The banister was rickety. Blue-and-gold wallpaper suggestive of heraldry was peeling at the corners. There was stucco everywhere, and gold leaf, and ornate framed mirrors, and massive banks of half-melted candles in ironwork stands. There were no paintings on these walls.

The loud music emanated from the front downstairs room, the sitting room. Still in his coat, Jack went to investigate, but pulled up abruptly. Someone was standing in the corner of the lounge. The bobby eye flared on instantly, but in a split second Jack perceived that there was something amiss with the figure.

Jack understood from habit the power of visual field. The human eye moves fast, too rapidly for the brain to compute all it observes. But when it moves, it does so in strict hierarchical order. Assuming all these things to be in a room at any one time, the eye picks out a female before a male, a man before a dog, a dog before a cat, a cat before a plant, and a plant before any inanimate object. All in strict sequence within a splinter of a second.

This was what alerted Jack, arresting him in the sitting-room doorway. The figure in the corner was wearing a tuxedo and bow tie, and it was the last thing he'd noticed. The figure was also wearing dark glasses and a beret.

"Creepy," Louise said, pushing past him into the room with Billy in her arms. "For a second I thought it was a real person standing there."

It was a tailor's mannequin. Louise fingered the Savile Row material of the tuxedo and Billy grabbed at the beret, pulling it away. The exposed head of the mannequin was fractured, with underlying fibers showing through. "Hell of a conversation piece!" Louise said.

Jack didn't answer. He sniffed. There was a smell of recently melted candle wax, but more unsettling was the residual odor he'd noticed the moment he turned the key in the door and let himself in. Mingled with the whiff of dampness was the olfactory warning, the scent he always associated with fear and his father. He looked at Louise.

She hugged Billy closer to her as she stepped over to the audio system to turn down the music. "Mahler. *Das Lied von der Erde*. One of Dad's favorites."

"Wait here. I'll check upstairs."

Jack was only gone a couple of minutes. "No one around," he said when he came back. "Lights don't work up there."

She seemed to read his mind. "Maybe a cleaner left the music playing."

"Maybe. But it doesn't feel right."

"Let's get some heating going in here."

Billy's excitement alone was almost enough to drive away ghosts. As there were elaborate candleholders everywhere, Louise lit them, fortifying the dim electric lamps. The candles charged the place with soft orange light as Louise and Jack unpacked a few things. Soon the odor of thick black Arabic coffee made everything seem all right. Jack found a full wine cupboard in the kitchen. The Mahler was still playing very low.

"Ich suche Ruhe für mein einsam Herz," Louise said of the music. "I seek rest for my lonely heart."

"How come you know so much about classical music?"

"One of the things he gave me, I guess."

"One of the things he *never* gave me," Jack said ruefully. "Have you noticed something about both of his apartments? No television. Neither here nor in Chicago. Who doesn't have television in this day and age?"

"He objected to TV. Anyway, we're in Rome. Who the hell wants to watch TV?" She scrambled to her feet. "Can't we do something achingly predictable? Colosseum at night? You said it was close by."

He didn't want to go out while there was the possibility that someone else was still using the place. But as he looked at her in the orange light he was burned by his own incapacity to resist even her smallest requests.

. . .

"Can a thing be the brighter for being looked at so often?" Louise said. She was awed.

The Colosseum, Rome's biggest and sweetest confection, half-chewed by age, still bearing the teeth marks of history. Jack had seen so much film footage of the monument with traffic speeding along the adjacent highway that the two things had become grafted; it was certain that gladiators had arrived for the games in a Fiat.

They'd expected the monument to be jammed with tourists, but there was no one else there. Closed for the evening, the building was washed by golden floodlights and it was still possible to wander among the outer arches. Jack carried Billy as Louise swayed around the perimeter with her arms held curiously, like an airplane or a soaring eagle.

"It looks bigger," said Jack. "Bigger than I remember." He'd done an obligatory European tour as a student, in days when he was too busy looking at himself to look at buildings.

"These things always look bigger"—Louise was still soaring under the arches—"when you're with someone you like." Jack looked back at her but she winged her way into a puff of dark shadow. In an involuntary reflex Jack hugged Billy closer to him and kissed the boy. All the way from Chicago airport he'd been playing father; now the role flashed perilously close.

"When I was very small, my father used to tell me about the lions and the Christians," he said when Louise returned. "And then he would say he was on the side of the lions."

"Me, too," said Louise. Jack didn't know whether she meant she was also on the side of the lions or whether the old man used to say it to her too. But he didn't get a chance to clarify because she said, "It's dizzying. The thought of just being here. Rome. I feel high."

He knew what she meant. He could sniff the river Tiber on the breeze. You didn't look at Rome, you slipped into it and it parted around you like warm water. History lay everywhere, like mineral mud on a riverbed or glistening as it broke the surface of the water. Antiquity waved vast anemone clusters and drew your attention to submerged treasure, or to a sunken rock that on closer inspection proved to be an artifact. There was no more pristine, native rock. Everything had been mined, carved, sculpted, worked, improved, discarded, reworked into a lustrous flow. In Rome you needed a set of gills to move through history, and if you tried to come up for air you found that even the sky was seeded with the dust of ancient brick. It was cloying and sweet and pearly with reference. Every evening the city crumbled under the weight of its own memory; each morning it was rebuilt with the fresh hot brick of making the past anew.

Too much history, a narcotic pellet. A pearl-gray gas. Jack looked about him, at the Via di San Gregorio bearing fume-belching buses and honking Fiats past the vibrating Arch of Constantine, and at the sable sky over the ocher brick, feeling the dank and languid breath of Rome on his collar, and was afraid he might be falling in love with his sister.

"I'm ready to go back," Louise said. "I've taken in all I can in one night."

Billy had fallen asleep in Jack's arms. It was a twenty-five-minute walk back to the apartment, but he insisted on carrying the boy, even though his muscles prickled with the effort. At some point along the way, Louise slipped her arm through his, and they walked quietly back through the shadowy streets under weak lamplight, like a real couple returning home.

This time there was no music playing. Jack fixed the fuses for the electricity on the upper floors, but Louise suggested he leave the downstairs lights off. She preferred the candles. While prowling the house, he was startled by three more mannequins. One stood in a recess on the landing of the first floor, wearing a greatcoat and a World War II gas mask and respirator; another, its head also dented, wore a toga and stood in a bedroom; the third, dressed like a ballerina and wearing heavy army boots, lurked in the bathroom.

When Louise had made a bed and laid Billy down, Jack opened a bottle of wine while Louise put on some more music. Louise took her glass to the window, dividing the window blind with two fingers, gazing down at the tree-fringed avenue below. She'd pinned up her hair and Jack's gaze rested on her tanned neck. He wanted to move to the window, to stand right behind her, very close.

"This place," she breathed, "just being here . . ."

"We haven't scratched the surface."

She turned from the window. "But it's not just the ancient buildings, is it?"

"No. It's not. It's like some . . . I was going to say some *invisible* force at large in the city. Perhaps I've been reading too much of that crazy book my old man wrote."

"You've been reading it?" She moved to the sofa and scattered a pile of cushions on the floor near his feet, refilling her glass, and his, before kneeling there.

"Only because you told me the thing worked. But it reads like the ravings of a psychopath."

"I only said it works in a surprising way. What would you do if you could make yourself invisible?"

"Follow you around. Watch you do things."

Jack saw her neck flush, up to the lobes of her ears. "What things?"

"I'd watch you pour a glass of wine. I like the way you do it. I'd watch you put Billy to bed. Things like that."

She squinted into her wine and he wished he hadn't said it. She was ready for sleep, she said. She'd already put her things in one room with a giant, creaky bed. Jack asked if he should carry Billy through to that room, but she said thanks, she was fine, it would be better if she did it herself. She said goodnight, but didn't kiss him.

There were a number of bedrooms to choose from. Most of them looked as though they'd been occupied until quite recently. Jack settled on a room overlooking the main street. He stood at the window. He'd forgotten to turn off the music downstairs. Soft contralto drifted from the floor below, beyond which he could hear the faint, steady drone of midnight traffic across the arterial roads of the Eternal City.

NINE

In order for you to master the art of Invisibility you must first develop the capacity to see a certain colour; and that is the elusive colour Indigo.

You have never seen the colour Indigo. You may think you have, but you have not. There may be some adept or a freak of human nature to whom the foregoing does not apply, but I would be very surprised if more than one person in five million could by accident or defect of birth arrive in this world equipped with the wondrous capacity to see the elusive shade.

Certainly the name of the thing is invoked often enough in the casual and standard description of the colour elements of the spectrum. To the skeptic I say go now and find a spectrum of refracted light. Study it for yourself. Point out to yourself the grades of red, orange, yellow, green, blue, and then feel your heart skip—almost imperceptibly, but skip it will—as you realize what you have always known. That your eyes move through blue to violet without genuinely registering a gradation of colour in between. Where is the missing Indigo? Point to it. You cannot. Isolate it. You never will. Pretend that fine gradations of either blue on the one hand or violet on the other constitute the mysterious property in question. Delude yourself, by all means. You've done so all your life; why change now?

I take it you have now returned from this exercise having satisfied yourself that I speak a surprising truth. The more sluggish amongst you will, I am afraid, find the strictures and disciplines that follow in this Manual of Light rather more daunting than your more scientific co-readers.

If in these pages I tell you to do a thing, and you fail to do it, you will have no success. I personally have journeyed the seven continents in search of the hue, guided by other adepts, occult manuscripts, and arcane clues. In all this time, I have found only three places on this globe where the colour is easily accessible—at any rate, to the adept or to the person who follows my instructions to the letter—and one of those places is currently out of bounds, with political and military events generating chaos in that particular country. The other two places of which I speak exist in Chicago, in the United States, and in the Italian capital of Rome. You can go to both of these places and see for yourself, though you will find the presence of the fugitive Indigo mentioned in no guidebook other than this one.

There is a further possibility available, one that I assume to be beyond both the means and the endurance of most people. I only mention it out of a sense of completeness. The shade is instantly available, and not merely to the adept, at either polar extreme.

Directed by other travellers, I joined walking expeditions to the North and South Poles. On both occasions, the expeditions failed to reach the Holy Grail of the polar positions and we had to turn back; but on both occasions I was the only member of the party who was not dismayed. I had stumbled across my own grail object; and had on both occasions seen and embraced the elusive matter.

Let me add that it would not be possible to jet in and out of Arctic or Antarctic terrain expecting to return with this particular chalice. The discovery depends upon subjecting oneself for days and days to an unrelenting environment of White Light. In the polar extremes, one experiences no natural colour. The ground is white, the sky is white. After a while, even one's colleagues come to represent no more than a line of grey wraithlike figures trudging ahead or behind. The early conversation between friendly colleagues soon gives way, and even becomes an irritation. Silence, broken only by the rhythmic trudge of one's boots on snow, becomes the only acceptable condition. At this point, the eyes begin to drop, mirrors to the soul, glazed by the inward stare. Day upon day of terrifying whiteness.

And then at night one dreams. Inspirational dreams of swirling, lavish, and exotic colour. Just as it is possible to dream of warmth, it is possible to dream of rich imperial crimsons, aristocratic sapphires, gem-like greens and yellows. As if in antidote to the unyielding white of the landscape, dreams flourish and bloom and threaten to overwhelm. On many days I found it possible to wake, rejoin the column, continue the trek, and to instantly fall back into my dream state while on my feet and marching. And it was there, within the kaleidoscopic majesty of dreaming, that I would find the mystical Indigo.

Once seen, this colour is never forgotten. For just as it chooses to make itself in most situations utterly invisible, it is itself the very secret of the attainable condition of Invisibility.

But let me assume you have neither the capacity nor the stamina nor even the resources to visit the polar regions merely to get a glimpse of this awesome phenomenon. Therefore you must follow my instructions exactly as I lay them down. Earlier, I hinted to you that no guidebook would lead you where I intend to take you. Neither Baedeker nor Fodor's has supped in the palace of Indigo. Yet it is as a guide that I must lead you; as if I were saying, approach this place on a certain day of the year, at a certain hour of the twilight, from a specific street, and view it from across the river when the light is just so. Though you appreciate that this is merely a figure of speech, there is a fixed route leading to the doors of perception. And only if you follow that route, never deviating, staying out of danger, observing precise instructions every step of the way, will you be delivered into the hands of the miraculous.

TEN

NOW THERE WAS TENSION BETWEEN THEM. PLANS HAD BEEN fluid, Rome at leisure, eyeballing the antiquities, the piazzas, and the monuments before getting on with the business of tracking down Natalie Shearer in order to execute the will. But it wasn't possible to do that after the events of their first evening in Rome. They didn't discuss what had happened. Jack could have asked, "What did I do?" but didn't. Louise could have broached the subject by saying, "About last night . . ." but didn't.

"You're up early," Louise said, slipping out of the bedroom in a silk dressing gown she'd found hanging on the back of the door. Azure blue with a writhing Chinese dragon on the back in violet, it ignited her mild tan. The light from the window went spinning on the silk.

"Thought I'd get on with the Shearer thing."

"Good idea. Get to it."

"I'm going to start with all the obvious places. I've sorted out a couple of phone numbers for you. Maybe you could try this morning."

"Sure."

"I'll be back sometime this afternoon." Jack skipped down the

71

stairs, blowing out his cheeks, realizing he'd been holding his breath throughout this brief but paradoxically long conversation.

He failed to get on with the Shearer business at all. Retracing his steps from the previous evening, he returned to the Colosseum. When it started raining hard dozens of Arab peddlers appeared on cue selling umbrellas, so he bought one and paid his way into the Colosseum. Not even the rain kept the tourists out of that place, but he found a sheltered seat on an upper tier. With his umbrella cocked at an angle, he could stay dry enough.

What bothered Jack most was that he didn't know whether he was in Rome because of someone called Natalie Shearer or because of someone called Louise Durrell. If Shearer really was the subject, then he'd taken his eye off the ball for a fraction of a second too long. Now he couldn't pretend to remain interested in his role as executor of a maniac father's will. Although Louise was here on the pretext of assisting him over Shearer, he still had too many inappropriate thoughts about her. He berated himself that he hadn't made a clean escape from Chicago. Then, at the last moment, against all his best instincts, he had managed to engineer the further complication and torment of Louise's presence here in Rome.

Naturally, when she'd agreed to come to Rome, she had no idea he was harboring a romantic attachment. The notion of her coming to Rome hadn't occurred to her until he'd pressed it. Why did he lacerate himself over women? He didn't even know who she was, this Louise Durrell, or why he couldn't shake her from his thoughts, or why she (and other women like her) always had this power to make him sit in the ruins in the rain.

He was chained in the arena, hearing the roar and scenting the lion-smell of female concupiscence as it prowled and waited for the handler to trip the bar and open the cage. And how the citizens of Rome would rock back and forth, until the arena rang with laughter. Because she was his sister.

The rain subsided, the sun came out, and the umbrellas, except for Jack's, all went down. He didn't move from his spot, and after a while he saw, between the pillars in the gladiatorial runs under the base of the arena, a woman with a small child. It was Louise, pushing the buggy he had lifted from the luggage carousel. Her instinct to return to the scene of that first-night magic had been identical to his own.

She couldn't see him, but he angled his umbrella further, watching and hiding. Even from this distance, Louise cut a lonely figure, lost in the vastness of the Colosseum, wandering through tunnels, looking for a way out. She pushed her hair from her eyes, seemed to frown, unsure of which way to go. He had to choke back an instinct to scramble all the way down to join her.

He despaired at the power women had over him; that his every thought was governed by his need to be with them; that he was so helplessly magnetized by women that he would lie to himself about his own motives in order to draw up next to them; that he couldn't trust his judgment about them; that he was like an addict after a fix of some unholy substance; and, here, that he could languish in the undisputedly most romantic city in the world, a city full of beautiful women, aching to walk side by side with one in particular: this one, the wrong one, the one trying to flick hair from her eyes and looking lost and lonely and pushing a battered buggy between stones that trumpeted like a fanfare of history.

Louise moved out of view, and something inside him squeezed, that he should get after her quickly. But chaining him to the ancient stone was a fear greater than the gladiatorial desire to be with her, and that was the fear of her rejection. So he let her pass on, allowing her time to get well clear of the Colosseum before getting up to leave.

But not enough time, and that was the point. There he sat, knowing that if Louise made a direct exit, she would have been away; if she dawdled, on the other hand, she might still be around. So he allowed enough time to convince himself he wasn't chasing her, but not enough time to be certain of her departure. And that's how he ran into her coming out of the Colosseum.

She squinted at him, pushed a stray hair from her eyes, and said, "Can we start again?"

. . .

They spent an afternoon gorging on more great sweet cakes of ancient Rome, even though they knew it was displacement feeding. They entered the Forum from the Colosseum end and did the standard tour backward, Louise reversing everything in her guidebook. They talked about architecture. *Architecture.* While really wanting to talk about what was going on, Jack found a voice inside himself, like a museum tape recording, talking about elaborate relief panels on the Arch of Titus and of the spectacular vaults of the Basilica of Maxentius and Constantine. Louise took her turn at this game, speaking of the balanced proportions of the House of the Vestal Virgins and of the soaring, elegant columns of the Temple of Castor and Pollux. Throughout this tour, Billy in his buggy was oddly silent. Occasionally, he took to twisting his neck to look up and back at his mother, then at Jack, as if he, at the age of one and a half, couldn't quite believe what these two people were discussing.

Then Louise, apropos of nothing in particular, said, "Do you think marriage is a kind of architecture?"

Jack didn't take his eyes from the massive Arch of Septimius Severus. "I've been married twice, and neither remained for a fraction as long as these things have been standing."

Billy vibrated his lips at that. "I think he's hungry," said Louise.

They found their way to a *pasticceria*, where the waiter exuded Latin charm, fetching Billy a high chair and warming to them as if they were the season's first customers. Billy jabbed his finger at the waiter and said, "Dada!" The waiter blushed. Louise blushed. Jack ceded a jaw-aching grin. They had small Neapolitan rice cakes and cappuccino. Rome was proving to be unbearably sweet. It produced, for Jack at any rate, a novel kind of toothache.

Jack never assumed that Louise's ambitions for a Roman experience were identical to his own; he reminded himself frequently that there had been no such understanding. He lamented the fact that he'd made the city itself an instrument of torment.

Rome was responsible for his predicament. The problem with Rome was that it placed you on a stage. It didn't matter where you were in the city, your backdrop was flaming and operatic. Roman ruins, medieval cobbled streets; Renaissance churches; baroque fountains; it was all interchangeable. Scene by scene, it made you speak into an echoing auditorium, so that you hardly dared utter anything banal. And in every situation you felt posthumous, as if great events, the rise and fall of empires, the lighting and fading of golden ages, had passed you by, and yet you had, miraculously, survived. And what had delivered you from history? It was love and the state of being in love: That was the only currency in Rome these days. Love put you outside of events and history. It diminished the howl of mortality. It was the only antidote to the passage of time attested to by these lavish backdrops.

This is why Romans didn't care about the antiquities on which they trod every morning en route to work. They cheerfully littered and polluted great monuments and streets, and the *menefreghismo*—the Roman disease of don't-give-a-shit—was a condition of the need to step aside from the roaring tide of history. Those Romans not delivered by the weightlessness of love flung themselves around the city with mobile phones, paying agencies to call them on the half hour, frantic to be hip, to be street-smart, knowing all the time that the effort was as self-defeating as it was desperate. Otherwise, the fashion had just changed; you missed the trick; you were mugged; because in Rome only one condition is acceptable, only one story will clear you from the debt of history. If you could love with fervor and were loved back with equal fervor, then you could soar above the accelerating crumbling decay. If not, you were dragged along the dirty earth by the *retiarius* Mortality, to the howls and derision of the crowd.

"Why are you frowning?" Louise asked. "You are always frowning."

"Am I? I was just thinking. More coffee?"

Louise was about to say something. She thought better of it. "Shall we go?"

"You want to see some more?"

"I'm kind of drunk on bricks right now."

"We could walk down to the river. Take a look at the famous Tiber."

"Sure. Then we'll go back, huh? Take a nap? I'm a bit lagged. We could get some things, put a meal together at the apartment. How's that sound?" She searched his eyes as if it were the most soulful question she could ask him.

"Sounds good."

They walked down to the river. Billy fell fast asleep in his buggy. They ventured a little way along the two-thousand-year-old Fabricio Bridge, peering down into the swollen gray-green waters. Jack read something out loud from a guidebook, about the river being full of corpses and hissing snakes in the days of the empire's decline; and of kings, emperors, popes, antipopes, and political officials all being killed and thrown in the Tiber. Almost ritually.

"Not thinking of throwing me in there, are you?" Louise said.

"Not yet," said Jack.

ELEVEN

LOUISE SURPRISED JACK THAT EVENING, BECAUSE AS WELL AS PASTA and an angry, spicy sauce with salad and wine, there was candlelight and a made-up face with a smear of pink lipstick. This confused Jack. They were staying in and there was no one but him to see it.

They kept the opera music on and the electric light off. Candles flickered throughout the house. "Kathleen Ferrier," Louise said, inserting a compact disk. "Dad adored her."

Jack was learning not to hate things simply because his father had loved them. The woman's voice, flush with integrity, made the hairs on his arm stand up. "He liked soprano, huh?"

"Contralto," Louise corrected, and Jack felt stupid.

This all happened after she'd prepared a meal for the two of them. "Does Uncle Jack get a kiss goodnight?" she'd said to Billy before taking him through to the bedroom to settle down for the night. Yes, Uncle Jack got a kiss goodnight and he felt his heart contract, again. But he did like being called Uncle. It included him in the core of things.

Louise had asked him to look for some napkins and to set the table. The living room was furnished with an ornate walnut sideboard, which he began to root through. Unlocking a cabinet drawer, he found a pile of papers: correspondence, bills, and a set of newspaper clippings. The clippings were all from Italian newspapers and carried a photograph of one AnnaMaria Accurso, a raven-haired, doe-eyed Italian beauty. He didn't need to be able to read Italian to deduce the story from the reports. The word *suicida* was splashed over each clipping. His eyes strayed to the publication date: February 17. Making a mental note to ask Louise about the matter, he put the papers aside and rummaged through the drawers until he found napkins.

Some time later he heard the shower running, and later still Louise appeared in lipstick and eye shadow and ready, he thought, for an assault on Rome's nightspots. He blinked, but said nothing. All thought of newspaper clippings went out of his head.

Louise made straight for the red wine, and though he thought she was putting it away fast, again he said nothing. He had to open a second bottle before they sat down to eat. They speculated over the personality of Natalie Shearer. Jack made a disparaging remark about his father's associates but was surprised to hear Louise defending the old man.

"I know you have reason to hate him," she said, "but in many ways he was a remarkable person."

Jack wasn't having any of that. "You know why I think he liked Rome? He liked its fascist associations. I heard him talking once about the beauty of fascist architecture."

"So what?" Even I like the train station. "Did you ever hear him express any truly fascist opinions?"

"Plenty." Jack thought about it. During the time he had spent in New York he could never figure out his father's political allegiances. Sometimes there were rabid right-wing statements; at other times he sounded like an anarchist; and once he had said he was Republican in the United States and a Communist in Rome. Louise drained her glass and took the plates out to the kitchen. She was weaving; she had to stop to negotiate the narrow doorway to the kitchen. While she was serving a caramel dessert, Jack heard a crash.

A dish had shattered on the terra-cotta tile floor. Jack cleared up the slivers and recalled a broken glass at one of his father's parties in New York. "You remember he never wore shoes?"

"Sure. He hated shoes."

"Well, one time—ow!" Jack sliced his finger on a sliver of crockery. Instinctively he put his finger to his mouth.

"Let me see." She took his hand and examined the wound. She put his finger in her mouth and sucked. He felt her tongue slide along the cut. Then she dropped his hand and turned to pick up the desserts. "It's nothing. Get a tissue. And open another bottle of wine."

Jack uncorked a third bottle and returned to his seat. Louise, flushed, asked him what he'd been saying. He had to think for a moment. "So. There was a party and a glass broke. At that time I worshiped him, having known him for a full three weeks. Aware that he was barefoot, I immediately got down on my hands and knees and started collecting up bits of broken glass. He stopped me. 'What are you doing?' 'Saving your feet,' I answered. 'Never mind that. Skin just sucks up glass,' he said, and he demonstrated for me by treading the entire area with his full weight and brushing all the bits of glass from his feet into a bin. Then he showed me his feet. There wasn't a mark on them. No cuts. Nothing."

"He traveled the world just learning tricks like that. He went to Borneo or somewhere to walk barefoot over hot coals. He tried to teach me when I was little but I was too scared. Pour me some more wine, please."

"Are you out to get drunk?"

Her eyes misted and a slight cast came into her gaze. She grabbed the bottle and took it over to the sofa, falling back heavily before refilling her glass. "You staying at the table?"

He made a move to sit in the seat across the room from her, but she pressed the cushion beside her with the flat of her palm. He sat, but a little away from her. She smiled and stretched, and relaxed back into the sofa. The candlelight lit the downy hairs on the backs of her arms, invisible by ordinary light. "Why don't you like to talk about your time as a cop?"

"Bobby. I've told you before, we say bobbies in England. At least on the inside. I'll talk about it as much as you like."

"Did something bad happen?"

"You mean did I see dead babies? Drug wars? That stuff wasn't why I quit."

"So why'd you quit?"

"Bobby-eye."

"What?"

"What yourself."

She looked quizzically at him, making a slight shake of her head. Miraculously, Louise seemed to sober up. She hauled herself to her feet. "I shouldn't even be here. I've got a zillion things to do in Chicago."

"Sit down," said Jack. "Relax."

"No; I'm going to bed. My head hurts. I drank too much wine." She accidentally kicked over the unfinished bottle.

After she'd gone, Jack waited up a while longer. Finally, he went to his own room, leaving the bottle and the spilled wine.

. . .

The following morning, Jack rose deliberately early and got out of the house before Louise was awake. He walked very quickly in the opposite direction of the Colosseum, not stopping until he reached the Gate of Saint Sebastian, still thinking about blood.

Blood, he figured, was the accident that located children at the same hearth, growing together, fighting and playing until familiarity (and he'd never previously understood that word before) hardened into a lifetime bond. But did blood call to blood, did blood recognize blood? For this attraction was mutual now, if he understood her correctly.

Who said it was forbidden? The white-caped pontiff in the Golden Dome across the Tiber, for one; the gilded polyp, the swollen cyst of guilt and fear on the north bank of the river. Plus, of course, the *polizia* in their headquarters at Questura Centrale. The police in Rome wear different uniforms according to their function, summer white and winter blue, light blue, black-clad *carabinieri*, and gray. He wondered which ones came for you when you lay down with your sister. And who told them to come.

Perhaps it didn't count if you didn't know she was your sister, the innocent act without the guilty mind. What if he'd accidentally turned up in Chicago on some other errand and they'd met in a singles bar? And was she really your sister if she spoke with a wild accent and didn't understand any of your jokes, and thought trouser turn-ups were some kind of vegetable? A real sister wouldn't do any of that. He looked at his hands. They trembled very slightly.

The Gate of Saint Sebastian loomed overhead. Rome was beginning to take on a rotting hue to match his feelings and the monument was a dirty papier-mâché imitation of an ancient arch. Suddenly Rome's operatic backdrop was built by shoddy and obdurate sceneshifters, whistling bad luck in the wings.

Jack reminded himself of why he was in Rome, and made his way to the agency. While in Chicago he'd hired an Italian agency to work on tracking down Natalie Shearer. They had an office located in the San Giovanni district. He hailed a cab. A large second-floor office in a modern block was single-handedly staffed by a tiny young woman with heavy spectacles called Gina. Gina looked no older than thirteen but wore gash-crimson lipstick. Jack mentioned his name and she recognized the case instantly. She made a few key-strokes at a computer and printed something out for him.

"We have an address for you. We made contact. This person is living here."

It was easy enough, but then Jack knew that tracking people down usually is. He squinted at the address.

"Trastevere," the young woman said helpfully. "West bank. Can we be of any further service to you, Mr. Shambers?"

"No," Jack said, but then had a second thought. Her English was very good. He took out his wallet and withdrew one of the newspaper clippings he'd found while hunting for napkins. "Actually, there is one thing. Could you translate this for me?"

She took the clipping from him. "You want a written translation?"

"No. Just tell me what it says."

She shrugged, read the thing to the end, and said, "Well, this girl in the picture was an artist. Sculping?"

"Sculpture?"

"*Si*. Sculpture. And she kill herself. AnnaMaria Accurso. They don't know why. It was a mystery because she had make many prizes. And she didn't leave any informations why she do this thing. And she make this on February fifteenth, exactly at midnight, they know this. And they ask why, but they have no answer. She was twenty-three years old and living also in Trastevere district of Rome." She took her glasses off and looked at him with sympathetic brown eyes. "This story I think is very sad."

"Yes. Yes. It's very sad. You've been a big help to me." He took out a credit card. "Can I settle my account while I'm here?" She shrugged again, scratched some more keys with her elegant, painted fingernails, and an invoice slithered out of a printer. Jack looked at it and said, "You didn't include the translation service," whereupon she made a timeless Roman gesture. "Thank you once more."

"You're welcome. Let us know if we can help you again."

"I will." He went out of the building desperately trying to remember the name of the young Chicago artist who had disappeared. Was it Chadbourne, Nicholas Chadbourne? He was also trying to remember the date on which his sudden disappearance had been reported. He made a mental note to quiz Louise about it; but first he had to visit Natalie Shearer.

TWELVE

JACK CROSSED THE PONTE GARIBALDI AT NOON. CANNON FIRE boomed out the hour from the hill. He found the address off the Viale di Trastevere, locating it in a narrow street of pepper-gray buildings. Overhead, an old woman leaned on a windowsill between her winter geranium pots, sucking her cheeks, observing his approach. At another window, laundry hung motionless in the still air. A caged canary, invisible to him, stippled the brickwork with its song.

He arrived at a huge door under an arch, its ancient wood mildewed and split, its leprous green paint blistering and flaking. A vertical strip of doorbells offered no indication as to which sounded in which apartment. Jack floated a finger to the highest and waited. From the window above, the old woman gazed down at him, sucking her cheeks. He pressed all the other buttons in turn.

No one came, so Jack prodded at the door and it swung back, admitting him to a narrow passage that led, in turn, into an open courtyard bounded by the three-story apartments. There was activity in the yard; a cascade of acid-blue wormlike sparks as a figure in an industrial mask crouched over a welding torch. As he approached, the torch arced with a sudden crack, and Jack had to blink away the aftervision of violet shadow. He averted his eyes, waiting for the welder to finish. The welding torch sneezed and snuffed out, smoking like a gun in a movie. The welder became aware of Jack's presence, turning slowly, a pair of dark eyes blinking behind the dirty tinted glass of the mask.

The mask was torn off and dropped to the floor and Jack was surprised to see that the welder was a woman. Her long dark hair was scraped back from her face. A fiery red scarf drew attention to her ivory neck. Her face, smeared with carbon, gleamed with per-spiration.

"Speak English? I'm looking for Natalie Shearer."

"Who wants to know?" Though she looked Italian, her accent was as English as afternoon tea.

"You knew Tim Chambers."

She made a hard, straight line of her mouth as if resisting a smile. Scooping up her mask, she ignited her torch again, and re-turned to her work. Jack was left cooling his heels until the smoking torch was laid aside.

"What does he want?" she shouted from behind the mask.

"He doesn't want anything. He died."

The mask came off again. "So?"

"He left you a lot of money in his will."

"Good. When do I get it?"

"You don't seem at all dismayed to hear he died. Yet you don't seem surprised he left you some money."

She cut a tall, willowy figure in her oily, frayed denims. Jack set her in her early thirties. Easy to see why the old man had gotten mixed up with her, though her loveliness was slightly eroded by too much experience. Most women managed a reflex smile on a first en-counter, but not this one. "If you've come to give me some money, good. If not, then I'm a busy girl."

"Not that simple. There are one or two conditions. For example, there's a book to publish."

"Don't tell me. Invisibility. Shit." She pulled cigarettes from her breast pocket and lit one, wedging it deep in the V of two long, elegant, but dirty fingers.

"Heck of a lot of money left over for you."

Natalie Shearer surveyed her welding operation moodily, as if making a decision. All Jack could see was an arrangement of pipes like spokes in a wheel. Then she looked up, squinting at him hard. The whites of her eyes were a little bloodshot, maybe from the weld shower, but there was also something wolflike and silvery in her gaze, unnerving and provoking. Jack felt a tiny trickle of dampness under his collar. "Let's go inside," she said.

"Inside" was a gutted work space with naked pipes, bare boards, and exposed areas of plaster and lath in the walls. The studio was a preposterous imbalance of orderly working area on one side and a jumble of barely figurative sculptures tightly packed at the other, as if a giant hand had lifted the floor by the corner and shaken everything down to one end of the room. As they walked in, two doe-eyed Italian boys looked up. They squatted on sleeping bags, sharing a cigarette. The air stank of hashish and foot odor.

"*Vattene!*" Natalie snapped, as if they were cats in a kitchen. "Get out!" Like cats, they vanished smartly. "These Italian boys are good-looking," she said to Jack, sprinkling coffee in a pot before slamming it on a stove, "but you just want to use 'em and throw 'em away."

She had an aggressively sinuous way of moving her thighs as she crossed the floor, as if they were a sensuous burden to her. Her eyes raked him, snagging on detail, measuring coldly. She was out to make him feel self-conscious, set him on his back foot. He'd seen it before in people with something to hide.

86

There was nowhere to sit, not even an upturned orange crate. He remained standing even after she'd pushed a cracked cup into his hand. Their entire conversation was conducted in the uncomfortable upright mode.

"Did you know Tim?"

"He was my father."

Her brow wrinkled. "He never said anything to me about having a son."

"He never said much to me about it either."

"So you'll know why I don't weep, right?"

Jack snorted. She had the same hauteur and cold beauty as a statue in the Forum, and would as soon shed a tear. "How well did you know him?"

"He helped me. He arranged an exhibition for me here in Rome. Though I had to sleep with him to get it."

Coming on whore-tough; but now he could see it was all evasion. "You're an artist; can I ask you a question? Ever seen the color indigo?"

"Ha!" She put her cup down on a paint-spattered work surface and drew his attention to a picture on a wall comprising gradations of color between blue and violet, roughly textured. "I've mixed everything on the planet. There's menstrual blood, semen, all kinds of things in there. Poppy juice. Blue curaçao. Everything. You can't see indigo 'cause it ain't there to see."

"He believed in it. My father."

"So does everybody. The whole world believes there's this color called indigo until you ask them to point to it. I believed in it once. When I was young and impressionable. I spent a long time trying to get it on canvas. There are two colors in that painting representing the dye from the plant we call *Indigofera*. Tell me they're not blue."

"In order to qualify for my father's legacy we have to publish his book about Invisibility; plus there are other conditions. Are you prepared to do it?"

"Maybe."

"I'm not here to persuade you. It's yes or no and pardon me but you look like you could use the money. I'll be here perhaps two more days. I'm staying at his house. The address is—"

"I know his house. If the answer is yes, I'll call you." She took the cup from him and tossed the dregs into a sink in the corner. Then she led him outside, snatching up her welding mask in the yard, ready to resume work. The two Italian boys sat in the yard, blinking at them.

"What are you working on?" Jack asked.

"If you can't see what it is, there's no point me telling you." She pulled on her welding gloves, donned her mask, and ignited the torch. Jack left the courtyard. Out in the street, the old woman watched from the windowsill, still sucking her cheeks.

THIRTEEN

You may think when I refer to the genius of Invisibility or to the capacity to see the colour Indigo that I am referring to some trick of the mind. In all cases, what I have to say relates to observable optical phenomena. The scientific difficulty is that you will only be able to repeat the demonstration satisfactorily to yourself. It will not be possible for you to draw aside a colleague for a repeat result unless that colleague is also adept in the skill of seeing.

People are passive receptors of the visual world. They see only a part of what is put before their eyes. They merely react, missing, even on a superficial level, the figure in the carpet, the shadow on the lawn, the serpent beneath the flower.

Then there is the proactive or scientific observer, straining his eyes with twisted lenses, with telescopes and microscopes and magnifying glasses trained on objects massive and minute. Yet it is a truism of modern science that an object closely observed is changed by the very act of observation. The figure bleeds, the shadow eclipses, the serpent slithers for cover.

There is a third alternative, though it requires practice. It involves the capacity for indirect seeing. Only in the apprehension of the colour

Indigo have I found direct access to indirect seeing. But how to capture it? Unstitch the figure from the carpet and you are left with loose threads; trap the shadow with nets and weights, see where that gets you; grasp the serpent by the tail and it sloughs its skin.

Before proceeding with the seven steps of seeing, I am first concerned with preparation of mind. These exercises are not for the feeble-minded. If you suffer from any nervous disorder, psychological infirmity, excitable imagination, inability to complete tasks, excessive introversion, melancholia, drug/alcohol addiction, or other softness of will, then you should replace this book on the shelf. It is not for you. If, on the other hand, you remain confident of resolute mental faculties, the risk of losing everything stands counterbalanced with the opportunity of experiencing the miraculous.

You must be entirely free of the influence of drugs and alcohol for a period of at least six weeks before attempting these exercises. Failure to observe this directive to the letter will result in your illness.

You must watch no television during the course of these experiments (and I suggest not for two weeks before their commencement). This is not due to any inherent evil in the contents of television shows, but because of the flickering nature of televisual presentation through the cathode-ray tube. The training of the eye on the brightly lit television screen results in an optical disturbance that will blur your indirect vision (see the appendix for a more technical discussion of this problem).

To begin a process of focus before the commencement of the experiments proper, set aside a period of twenty minutes twice daily, during which you will need quiet and privacy. Simply settle yourself into a comfortable armchair and spend the time contemplating the missing colour of the spectrum. You have already established that the colour Indigo is not available: Therefore, simply focus your thoughts on the gap between the blue and the violet flare of the spectrum. You will find that your mind drifts away from this focus. Don't fight the drift; merely remind yourself of your purpose on discovering that you have indeed drifted, and begin again.

The last act of mental preparation is a kind of purification. I am not talking here about the lighting of incense or describing magic circles in the air or other mumbo jumbo. I am talking about confronting the demon of Skepticism.

If you have friends or acquaintances who are indeed skeptical, then do not attempt to discuss these exercises with them in any way. (You may even consider if it is time to free yourself of friends who may not eventually prove their worth—that is your business.) Having drawn a line in the sand regarding your friends' demons, you must now deal with your own. The demon of Skepticism is cunning. I have met him and looked upon him. From a short distance he does look attractive and seductive. He is modern and fashionable, streetwise like a young Roman, and he is intelligent, amusing, and friendly. But on closer inspection, he is, I assure you, quite the ugly brute. His skin is pocked and peeling. His hair is falling out and his fashionable clothes are poorly tailored. The amusing gleam in his eye is none other than the glimmer of hoarfrost. And his embrace is as cold as liquid nitrogen.

Having discarded your whisky and your ganja; having spent twenty minutes twice daily in contemplation of the missing color Indigo; and after finally having overcome the demon of doubt, you are now ready to proceed to the first step.

Step one concerns the matter of Colour.

FOURTEEN

"**Y**OU LOOK DIFFERENT, SOMEHOW. SOMETHING CHANGED.**"** Natalie Shearer lit a cigarette with a Zippo and poured her third glass of wine, though they'd only just finished the antipasto.

They were in a trattoria called Da Giovanni, which Natalie said was nicknamed The Poisoner by people who kept coming back. Natalie knew all the staff and half of the clientele, most of whom were relatives of the prison inmates living almost next door. The other customers were a collection of Fellini grotesques.

Returning from his encounter with Natalie earlier that afternoon, Jack had found a note from Louise saying she'd gone with Billy to take a look at the Vatican. Fine, thought Jack, I don't want to look at no Vatican. It wasn't true. He'd wanted to stand under the index finger of God in the Sistine Chapel, touching fingers with Louise, listening for static. He was crackling, spitting, sparking with repressed yearning. It had to discharge somewhere.

Late in the afternoon, he had called his office in London, but there was no answer. Mrs. Price, for some reason, had disconnected the answering machine. Jack furrowed his brow, thinking about why she might have done that. Then Natalie had called and asked him to meet at The Poisoner, so he in turn left Louise a note.

"So?" Natalie said, blowing smoke vertically. "Did something change?"

"Can't think what," Jack sniffed, looking around him at the Roman faces.

While preparing to come out that evening, he'd cranked up the volume of the stereo; he'd had operatic voices soaring throughout the house and dozens of candles burning while he shaved. It was an eerie dwelling and as he scraped his face before the mirror he felt a deep disquiet about the house, what with its three dusky stories, its mysterious doors, and its brain-crumbled mannequins ghosting the stairs. But while he was developing a taste for managing without electric light he was, more importantly, resolving to put away all inadmissible thoughts about Louise.

Natalie had done some preparing too. Given their first meeting, Jack was surprised to find her groomed, manicured, and fragrant. When he'd thought about Natalie—and in the few hours since meeting her, he had—he'd imagined her with dirty fingernails. He was almost disappointed, in some odd way, to see the polished pearls at the tips of her slender, elegant fingers. There were, however, traces of some violet substance ingrained in the palms of her hands. She traced the rim of her wineglass with her index finger, regarding him steadily. "I'll get it out of you. By the end of the evening. Do you like black-and-white films?"

"Not especially."

"Good. I hate them. I hate people who watch them. Give me your hand."

"Why?"

"Just do it. No, the right hand."

Natalie drew his hand to her lips and began licking at the cusp between the fingers. She had no care for who might be watching.

Keeping her eyes fixed on him, languorously, sensuously, she inched his finger into her mouth, sucking gently, lashing it with her silky tongue. Then she bit hard.

"Ach!"

Other diners looked around. Jack held his hand under the table. Her teeth had left two white imprints in his finger.

"That's good. You didn't get angry. I wanted to see if you're the kind of man who gets angry easily."

The next course skidded across the table as the waiter arrived. Natalie barked something at the waiter, who yapped back a reply; but it was Natalie, Jack noticed, who had the last word. "You look like a woman who is used to getting what she wants."

The remark made her turn that strange wolflike gaze on him. Her eyes seemed to be in a condition of permanently dissolving. What he'd meant was that although her skin was like porcelain there was clearly nothing fragile about her. Her long brown hair was still pulled back, exposing an elastic white neck. He wondered what she would do if he leaned over and bit that neck in return. Jack felt his erection quicken below the table, and forked his pasta.

"This afternoon you were tense, preoccupied, giving off a strange energy. Tonight relaxed, resolved. Your aura is different."

"Is that wine very strong?"

"I'm not drunk. When I see I can see auras. I mean I *feel* them. Then I visualize them. Is that cheating?"

"I wouldn't know. What does my aura say."

"It says you want to fuck me."

He tried not to stop chewing his pasta.

"Let's have another bottle, pussy-man. Let's get wasted."

Jack looked around, perhaps for help from the waiters or the criminally connected other diners, but he didn't get any. "Is this how you made a play for my father?"

"Christ, no. I made him work for it. He hated sluts. You, on the other hand, prefer to recognize such women as generous. You're nothing like him. Though you do have his good looks."

The subject was getting a little cramped. Jack suddenly remembered the names of the two young artists, the one who'd vanished and the other who'd killed herself, and asked Natalie if she'd known either. "Sure. I knew both. Your father had his followers, and they were two of them."

"But did he have anything to do with what happened? The disappearance? The suicide? Seems to me odd things happened around him."

She shrugged. "Your old man was a dangerous person to know. Dangerous ideas. But always trying to get other people to put his ideas into practice, you know? And he liked to collect unstable kids. He liked their energy, and they flew to him, iron particles to a magnet. You can't entirely blame him if they were already mentally ill."

"Were they good artists?"

"They're dead, so they might be," she said bitterly.

"Don't make much of a living, eh?"

"I'll be honest, I didn't want anything to do with your father's will. But I've swallowed my pride, because it means I can go on working for a few years without having to worry. Can we leave? You're paying."

Outside it had turned cold. Jack stopped to button his coat and as he did so he saw in the gutter a thin skin of gas or oil floating on the surface of a black rainwater puddle. He peered into it. The oil swirled slowly, bleeding its spectrum. Along with the other four colors there was an iridescent blue and an intense violet.

"I know what you're looking for," Natalie said. "You won't find it there."

"Is it to be found at all?"

"Maybe. But not there. Come on. Let me make you some coffee in my studio. You said there were some things I have to know."

Natalie pushed open the door to her studio, catching the same two young Italian boys lounging there, smoking hashish. "Out!" she said sharply, and out they went. Then she summoned one back and made him part with a tiny nugget of cannabis, handing it to Jack along with tobacco and cigarette papers. While she lit the stove to make coffee, Jack sat on the floor and did his best to roll a joint.

"Don't get the wrong idea," she said. "About these boys, I mean. I let them hang around to keep out the burglars. They sleep here sometimes, but *never* with me. If I bring someone home, the deal is they get out."

Jack looked up from his messy rolling. He wondered why she was suddenly concerned about what he might think of her.

"I allow myself one man every two years."

"You're kidding."

"You can tell when I joke, because I laugh. You're different in that regard. You laugh when something hurts. I'm due my biennial conjugal rights about now, as it happens."

"I don't know whether to feel flattered."

"Slow down. I never said it was going to be you." She handed him a tiny espresso and snatched away his poorly constructed joint. "What's this? A dog's hind leg? Where did you learn to roll these?" She lit the thing, puffed at it, and blew a funnel of smoke.

"In the police force."

"Now you're kidding me." She leaned against the wall, smoking, squinting at him. "No, you're not, are you?"

"Nine years on the force. Then I quit for an easy life as a process server for the courts."

She shook her head, preferring not to think about it. "So what's the difficulty with this will?"

He explained the complication of distributing two hundred thousand free books, a problem she dismissed airily. "Tell me something," Jack said. "When I asked you about the color indigo, you lied, didn't you? You said you'd never seen it. Were you lying?"

"What a question. What I told you was that I can't reproduce it on canvas or in any artwork. Though I have seen it. I saw it in a dream, and I knew what it was immediately. It's not blue and it's not violet. It's unmistakable. Once you've seen it you spend the rest of your life looking for it."

"Science declares the color not to exist."

She made a steeple of her fingers, becoming serious. "The scientists are partially correct. Color is electromagnetic vibration, right? Well, indigo doesn't vibrate in the same way as the other colors." She gave up on the effort to explain. "Anyway, what does science know but half of every story?"

"Have you followed the instructions in my father's book?"

"Ha!" At last she slithered to the floor, drawing her knees under her chin. She had long legs, like a ballerina. There was something simultaneously thrilling and repulsive about her overt sensuality. When she leaned over to pass him the joint she didn't take her eyes off his.

"The problem with your father is sorting the chaff from the bran. He was so full of traveler's tales no one knew when to believe him. Once he told me he'd made love, in Sumatra, to a woman with indigo eyes; and that when he went back to find her a year later the tribe she belonged to had blinded her, put out her eyes because they thought she was demonic."

Jack looked again at Natalie's eyes. Not indigo, but disconcerting. Steel-gray flecked with dissolving yellow. Despite her sensational magnetism, something about her gave off a chill. She seemed unlike other women, who defined themselves by the quality of the relationship at hand. She was different. She was someone who walked alone. She could go alone to the warm desert or to the snowy wastes, and she liked it that way.

He got up to leave. "I'll get some papers drawn up for you to sign. I have to dispose of his property before any money can be transferred to you."

"How long are you in Rome?"

"Couple of days."

"Pity."

"Why?"

"You want to find indigo, this is one of the best places in the world to look. But you have to know where to start."

"You said the old man was dangerous. But I think it's you who's dangerous."

She followed him to the door. "You're only saying that because you know it's what I want to hear. You're a charmer."

Jack turned on the threshold to offer a parting shot, but she took his face between her hands, letting her gaze settle on him for a single beat. Then she abruptly closed the door on him. He heard a muffled "Bye" from the other side, and was left with his nose butting up against the panel of the door.

When he got back, the house was silent. Louise and Billy's bedroom door stood ajar. He looked in on them, watching for a moment. Billy flashed open his eyes, saw Jack, and sat up. Then he lay down again and went instantly back to sleep.

FIFTEEN

Louise, Billy, and Jack sat at the breakfast table. Jack was feeding Billy eggs and bread. Billy was more interested in taking the half-masticated eggs and bread out of his mouth and offering it back to Jack, when the phone rang.

It was Natalie. "Can you meet me in an hour?" When Jack hesitated, she added, "It's important."

"Where?"

"Inside the Pantheon. Do you know where that is?"

"I can easily find it."

Louise's face was upturned toward him. Two minutes earlier, they'd just agreed to spend the morning sightseeing together at the Villa Borghese. Now here he was breaking plans. "What's so urgent?" Louise said.

"She didn't say."

Louise took over with the eggs. Billy resisted with a strong protest babble. "What's she like?"

"Natalie? A little weird."

"Is she beautiful?"

"Oddly unsavory."

"Dad's women were invariably beautiful, intelligent, sensuous, strong women. Does she have a tattoo on her shoulder?"

"How would I know, Louise? I'd better get going if I'm to get there within the hour."

"Hey! Where's the fire? It's just ten minutes by metro. Can't Billy and I come too?"

Jack obviously hadn't considered the idea. He hesitated before answering. "Of course. Why not?"

Louise smiled. "Nah. You've got business to discuss. We'd just be in the way."

Billy pointed a finger at Jack and minted a bright new word, "Huddock!"

. . .

Tourists in guided groups sheltered under the slick wet portico of the immense Pantheon. Arab hawkers drifted between the red and gray granite columns peddling umbrellas. There was a whiff of wet coats in the air and the babble and the warmth of human stock rose in a mist into the roof of the portico. Jack moved beyond the portico to stand under the miraculous vault.

Taped Gregorian chant played softly in the background; the rotunda was vibrant with chattering visitors but the dome flattened the sound. The effect was of a hundred people whispering excitedly. Rain cascaded through the oculus in the center of the dome. The gleaming wet marble floor directly beneath the aperture was roped off. Jack found a bench. He looked up at the shimmering rain, silver-black, suspended in a cylindrical column in the space between stone ceiling and marble floor. Something happened to the rain as it passed through the hole. It was buoyed up by the light, slowed in its fall.

Someone eased onto the bench next to him. Her trench coat carried the whiff of rain and leather, and of her body warmth inside it.

100

She said, "He told me this was one of the only places where the untutored might see indigo. But only at a certain time of the year, and
under exclusive conditions of the light."

"Have you ever?"

"No. Though I've sat here many times."

"Why did you ask me to meet you here?"

"Look at the rain. In future, every time you hear Gregorian
chant you will think of the Pantheon and of soft rain falling through
the roof. Your father came to me in a dream last night. He was wearing a suit of indigo. It was electrical. All other colors were muted. He
came to remind me."

"Remind you?"

"Not to give up. Not to give up looking for the fugitive indigo."

Her eyes were upturned to the water sloughing in through the
aperture of the dome, irises dark and inspired, like a mystic's. He
saw that deliquescence in her eyes and with a start he realized he
was already *fixing* on her. Different from falling in love, he'd decided, this fixing. It was a psychological dysfunction by which
he could instantaneously convince himself that he needed this
woman's intimacy like he needed oxygen. "Why did he leave you
the money?"

"Because I'm pretty damn wonderful. Because he believed I allowed him access to seeing indigo where no one else could do it for
him."

"And how did you do that?"

"I only said he believed it. I have no way of knowing if it is true.
Come on, let's go."

Outside the portico, Natalie produced an umbrella and drew
him under. She linked arms, pressing her leather trench coat against
his flanks. He could smell the shampoo on her hair. They drifted
through side streets, with the wet cobbled stone hissing underfoot

and the buildings on either side of them crumbling like biscuit in the rain. He was content to let her lead, and not to ask where they were going.

Perhaps it was the soothing effect of the Pantheon, or the rain, but Natalie was subdued. "The other day you asked me about those young artists. I wasn't completely honest with you. Your father brought about their demise. And that of other young people."

"What do you mean, brought about their demise? Are you saying he killed Accurso?"

"Not exactly. But if you train a puppy to fetch a stick, and then you throw the stick into a lime pond, who is responsible? The puppy, for being stupid?"

"But what did he do, exactly?"

"I don't know all the details. When I realized what was going on, I got out. I used to argue with him all the time. He assembled people around him to manipulate them. It was his God game. He'd see two people falling in love and find a way of interposing a third, just for the fun of watching a jealous passion develop."

The rain had stopped, but Natalie showed no inclination to lower her umbrella. They moved down to the Tiber, crossing by the Fabricio, pausing halfway to gaze into the river. It was swollen with fresh rain, churning, flowing very fast, the color of mold on leather. Sharp new mineral odors streamed the air. "In Rome, one is always crossing bridges. Your father thought bridges were sacred places. Places of possibility. Doors to other worlds."

As she spoke, a heron breasted the water, following the current toward them. Before it reached the bridge, it began to climb, laboring impossibly with its cumbersome wings. Finally it drew itself above them, its strong beak mere inches from their faces, motioning with its wings but still failing to ascend. Jack had the thrill of eye contact with the creature at shuddering proximity, and the beat of its wings caused his skin to flush. Then the giant bird caught an air current, banked, and wheeled away. Natalie followed the curve of its flight, but Jack caught sight of something floating in the current below.

Whatever it was in the water, it surfaced for a moment and then went under. It was difficult to see. The water was chopped by turbulence into violet and cinnamon chevrons. The object appeared again, moving very fast in the muddy stream. A face flashed briefly. It was a corpse. Then it was gone again.

"Auguries," said Natalie. "Do you think the appearance of that bird was an augury?"

Jack wasn't listening. He leaned far out over the side of the bridge, trying to catch a glimpse of the corpse again, but he knew that the current must have swept it under the arch. He hurried across to the other side of the bridge, to watch it emerge. It was difficult. Choppy little waves in the water created shadow play. His eyes made bulky shadows out of every swirl and crest in the muddy flux.

"What is it?" Natalie wanted to know. "What did you see?"

Jack stared into the water for a long time. If it had been a corpse, it was long gone. "Nothing," he said.

"You look strange."

. . .

This time the cat boys back at her place got up and left without having to be ordered out, though Jack heard one of them complaining bitterly about the rain. Jack poked about in Natalie's chaotic studio while she brewed coffee. Her paintings and sculptures were wildly abstract; they had no resonance for Jack at all. "What exactly are you trying to achieve with all this?"

"I never discuss art," she said, lighting first her stove and then a cigarette with a blowtorch.

That at least was a relief for Jack. He found a hatch at the back of the studio. Thinking it was a toilet door, he opened it. Inside was only blackness, though he caught a flash of light as the door swung open. The walls within were painted black, and the shimmy of light was merely a mirror reflecting back. A light cord dangled. He tugged at it and the tiny closet was suffused with ultraviolet light. A hard-backed chair stood in the middle of the space, facing the mirror.

Natalie came up behind him, gently closing the closet door. Hiding something. "What's in there?"

She didn't answer. "If you're looking for the loo, it's out the back."

They sat on her mattress, drinking coffee and smoking hashish. "Your father never really approved of this stuff. He was very intolerant."

"Were you in love with him?"

"Please!"

"I think that's why you're interested in me."

She squirmed slightly. "Partly true."

"Why did you leave him?"

"I told you. I had to get out. Or I would have gone the way of the others."

Maybe it was the strength of the hashish, but Jack was beginning to feel persecuted by the power of his father's ghost. Was he not here in Rome because he had been directed by his father's corpse? He recalled what Natalie had said about God games, about interposing a third person between two lovers. Natalie was ambivalent about the old man; hating his vices but still clinging to some memory; marked by him, on the shoulder, probably. His father's presence lay on the room like a dead hand. That warning, the signal odor: Jack took a slurp of strong coffee and felt his heart scudding,

104

like the moon going behind clouds. His instincts gathered to defy his father and go home at once, back to England; to forget about the will, forget about everything.

But he didn't have the capacity to do that. All roads led back here. He wondered if in engineering the will his father had made a shrewd assessment of his son's character, knowing this would be the case. Had he deliberately steered Jack into Natalie's arms? A lick of paranoia on the smoke.

Natalie leaned forward, her face a bright moon, and he thought she was going to kiss him. Instead, she drew a lungful of smoke, pressed her lips around his, and blew the smoke back into his mouth. He inhaled it deeply, tasting the crackling heat of the hashish and the sweet undersmoke of her own breath. Something made his blood fizz, and he didn't know whether it was the drug or her used air. The mix was potent and for a second, as he accepted the rush, he had a premonition that he might not easily get away from this woman. The stuff he was smoking was too strong. He was finding it hard to focus. Natalie's face was slipping like a malfunctioning vertical hold on a TV set.

This time she did kiss him, very deeply and for a long time. Her long tongue was deliciously slippery, a saddle of wet silk; a smooth melting texture. She probed his mouth with long gentle stirrings, her tongue carefully curling under his palate. It smacked like a first, virginal kiss. His lips tingled.

Suddenly she pushed him back roughly. She sat back on her haunches, observing him, then got up and stood against the window, looking out at gray skies. "Can you leave now?"

Jack was actually grateful for the opportunity to gather his thoughts. He felt as though a flame had just rolled over him. He reeled slightly on his way out, paused to say something, but thought better of it.

The courtyard was smoky with shadow. The two boys loitered. One of them hissed at him and said something derogatory. Jack stopped and returned a baleful stare. He walked toward the boy and stood over him, a millimeter separating their two eyeballs. Jack remembered an Italian expression meaning, "Fuck your mother on a dark grave." He made certain no reply was forthcoming before he turned his back on the boys and left the courtyard.

SIXTEEN

Late that afternoon, Jack got back to the house to find Louise drinking coffee with a handsome, bespectacled Italian man in a linen jacket. Billy was asleep on the couch. The man nursed a clipboard on his knee. Looking slightly guilty when Jack arrived, he mumbled a greeting, made his excuses, and left. Jack looked at Louise.

"The realtor," she said.

"Estate agent. We say estate agent in Europe."

"Whatever you say, I thought someone ought to get on with the job of why we came here."

"Get a price?"

"Not yet. We had a good look around the house. I've been everywhere. Some strange rooms in this house."

"Find anything new?"

"Some weird smells. But there are no secrets hidden away. Except maybe one."

Louise beckoned him to follow her down the hall. There was a closet built under the stairs. A wood-paneled door, previously unnoticed, slid back with a whisper. Louise reached inside to tug a cord and an ultraviolet light snapped on.

They stepped inside. The closet was surprisingly spacious. A high-winged armchair commanded the center of the floor, resting on a kilim-style rug and facing a large mirror. A second cord was suspended from the ceiling immediately above the chair. The walls were painted with a swirling design, a color difficult to identify under the UV light, which appeared to scintillate very softly.

Louise slid the door behind her and it was sucked into position with a perfect seal, shutting them in. She stood before the mirror, her skin an opulent amber under the UV light. Her eye cavities shadowed purple, as did the area under her nostrils and the cleft under her lower lip. The whites of her eyes and her teeth shone with demonic brilliance. Jack felt uncomfortable to be in the closet with Louise. "But what was it for?" he asked.

Louise just slid back the door and stepped out again. Following her, Jack had to blink back the woolly haze generated before his eyes by the normal light. They returned to the sitting room, where Billy slept on.

"Natalie has one too," Jack blurted. "I saw it earlier today. Same thing. Light, mirror, chair."

"Did you try it out with Natalie? Just kidding. Don't look so sheepish. How did it go today?"

So he told her; some of it. He neglected to mention certain things. He didn't know why he held part of it back, or whom he was protecting, but a doped kiss and a corpse in the water were not for speaking about. The phone rang. Louise went out to the hall.

She came back and said, "It's Alfredo."

Jack looked blank.

"The realtor—estate agent. He wants to take me to dinner. Tonight."

"Only married men move that fast."

"I mentioned you were my brother. He's still waiting on the phone. To see if I can find a baby-sitter."

Jack glanced about for candidates. "Oh! Sure. By all means."

"Really? It's okay?"

"Go ahead. Me and Billy will have a great time. Go on; the man's waiting."

"Don't rush me. I figure any serious guy can wait on the phone for at least a minute."

They used up another few seconds gazing at each other before Louise confirmed arrangements with Alfredo for an evening out.

. . .

"Baby-sitting? I don't go anywhere near babies," said Natalie.

Jack squeezed the phone under his neck while bouncing Billy up and down to stop him from screaming. It wasn't working. Billy had started bawling two seconds after Alfredo picked up Louise.

"Okay. It was just an idea."

Seven seconds of empty but active line before Natalie said, "But in your case I'll make an exception. Give me an hour."

She arrived on a Vespa scooter, honking its feeble horn and revving the hand-grip accelerator. Parking the scooter under the front window of the house, she bounced inside and through to the kitchen as if she knew the layout of the place all too well. She'd brought pizza in a cardboard carton. She went directly to the wine rack, aggressively clinking bottles until she found one to her taste. Billy, in Jack's arms, stopped bawling long enough to stare.

"So this is Tim's grandson. Cute kid."

"Billy, say hi to Natalie."

"Huddock," said Billy. "Melb poin!"

"Looks like Nick, too," she said, expertly uncorking the wine.

"Nick?"

"His father."

"You know the father?"

"Well, Tim told me Nick was the father. Who really knows who their father is? Can you say for certain who your father is?"

Jack accepted a glass of wine as it it might contain a virus. "Nick? Who is Nick?"

"Nick," Billy chimed in. "Nick nick nick nick."

"Are we going to eat this? Nick was one of the kids I told you about. He went walkabout. Maybe he's dead."

Jack suddenly tumbled to the fact that Natalie was talking about Nicholas Chadbourne, the young artist whose paintings still hung in the old man's Chicago apartment. His recall started tracking on why Louise didn't want anyone to know about Billy's father. "Look, if you meet Louise, you'd best not say anything. She thinks no one knows."

"Have you fed the kid?"

"Fed him?"

Despite her original protests, Natalie was adept with Billy. After they'd shared the pizza, she picked up the boy, chucked him under the chin, tickled him, tossed him in the air, crawled around on the floor with him, played boo with him, and changed his diaper. Her expertise was commensurate with Jack's incompetence. "I used to be a nanny," she said. "But I was always getting fired because all the daddies wanted to fuck me."

Natalie took Billy on a tour of the house, which Jack suspected was a pretext for checking out what had changed since she'd been there last. Jack was surprised to find this was as recent as four weeks ago. She saw what he was thinking. "I have a key. This kid's half asleep; shall we put him to bed? Louise commandeered this room, did she? Your father asked me to keep an eye on the place, and from time to time I do."

"I thought you despised him."

"I did. But it's a good house for throwing a party, or to put guests in. You've seen my place. Actually, a few other people have keys. You should watch out for uninvited visitors."

They stood over Billy for a few moments to see if he was going to settle. He pointed at Jack and said, "Dad-dee!" Jack felt his eye-lids fluttering uncontrollably. Natalie nudged his arm and they crept out of the room and returned to the lounge.

"Uninvited visitors? I thought one or two of the bedrooms looked lived in."

"They're probably waiting for you to leave."

"I suppose I should care. But then I just have to sell it and give you the money."

"I certainly don't want the place. Look at these fucking man-nequins everywhere. Too many bad memories."

"What bad memories?"

But Natalie just lit a cigarette and let the question hang in the air. Jack asked instead about the under-stairs closet with the mirror and the UV light. Natalie called it a smoke cupboard and said it was just another of Jack's father's crazy ideas.

"If it's so crazy why have you got one, too?"

"There was a time when I believed everything he said. I just haven't got around to dismantling it yet."

"How does it work?"

"It doesn't work."

"So how is it *supposed* to work?"

"Read the book if you really want to know. Have you found the headset?"

Natalie was shifting the subject again. Conversation with her was too often like switching horses mid-canter. "No."

"Wait here. It's probably at the back of the smoke cupboard."

Natalie went out into the hall and Jack heard the paneled door slide open. After a few moments, she returned carrying a grotesque contraption. It was a helmet constructed from a lightweight metal frame and leather straps, complicated by metal tubes, mirrors, and distorted glass lenses. "Try this on for size."

111

Jack looked doubtful. The contraption looked gothic, evil. The leather straps were stiff and smelled new. "Tell me what it is first."

"It's just standard Stratton optical headgear," she said, casually unbuckling the straps. "It rotates your visual field 180 degrees, reverses left and right, and makes up down. It's a real head-fuck." She held it for him to try as if it were a slice of melon.

Natalie instructed Jack to close his eyes while she buckled on the headset. Straps tightened under his chin and at the back of his neck, pinching a fold of flesh. The thing had an uncomfortable weight, making his head nod. Natalie told him to open his eyes. What he saw shocked him. He thrashed his head right and left, up and down, and began hyperventilating. He reached to drag the contraption from his skull but his hands sailed down through air.

"Don't panic. Take a deep breath. Don't try to take it off."

Jack was disoriented. He tried again to grab the headgear but his hands floated the wrong way. His grasping fingers entered his view from above instead of below, like frenzied wings. Just a tilt of his head caused his field of vision to swim wildly. He moved his right hand but saw a flutter from his left.

"Get me out of it, Natalie!"

"Try this. Put your hands where you think your groin is." Jack tried to move his hand slowly to his waist, but felt his palm brush the headset instead. Natalie laughed. "No; start thinking with your dick!"

"Get it off me! I'm going to throw up!" He felt her elegant fingers brush his ears as she unbuckled the straps. To his relief, the headgear was lifted away. He blinked at the restored room. He felt hot and nauseated. "I need a drink."

"What you would find," Natalie said, laying the contraption on the floor and topping off his glass, "is that the initial nausea passes quickly, and then after a few hours you'd become accustomed to what you're seeing."

112

"Sure. Who's going to wear that skull-cracker for a few hours?"

"Your father researched it. He found that if you wear it for a week things start to seem normal. After several weeks you adapt completely."

"After several weeks! But it's pointless."

"Nothing your father did was ever pointless. It demonstrates human plasticity. The bedrock of our perception can be altered and we can go on to function normally."

"I can't imagine him wearing *that* for several weeks."

"I never said *he* wore it. He would get some other sucker to do it."

"One of his young artists?"

She nodded sadly. Another inward stare possessed her, as if remembering something. "This topic is making me depressed. Can we talk about you?"

But after exhausting his standard police anecdotes he became stuck when talking about himself. Natalie watched him like a hunter. Though she stretched languidly on the couch, lazily advertising her hips, she balanced his every word. She asked him what was the worst thing he'd ever done, and he said, "I lied and said I'd touched a man, when I hadn't."

"What?"

So he explained the Birtles thing to her.

"But that's nothing," she said. "So you didn't touch him. So what?"

"People like you don't understand. It's everything."

He was in danger of becoming morose, so she kept him talking. She asked about Louise, and despite Jack's throwaway answers she picked up everything. She yawned to pretend indifference, but she was stalking him. That strange deliquescing in her gaze. She narrowed her eyes at him, and the dissolving yellow wolf-fleck in her venereous stare unsettled him.

. . .

113

Louise arrived back in the house well before midnight. She brought Alfredo in with her and they were flushed and ebullient from the delights of a successful meal. Clumsy introductions were made; Jack introducing Louise and Natalie to each other, and then Louise introducing Alfredo to Jack, even though they'd already met briefly. Somehow in the shambles Natalie and Alfredo were left to introduce themselves to each other. They did so in Italian, trading the usual greetings, and, while everyone seated themselves, continued their conversation in what was at first a genial tone.

"Good time?" Jack asked Louise above the mellifluous exchange of Italian pleasantries.

"Terrific. He's so sweet. So this is—?"

"Yep."

"Seen her tattoo yet?"

"Nope."

"And I give you all this opportunity! Slow mover, buddy."

"That's me: slow." He fixed her for a second too long; then they both became aware that the tempo of the other conversation had gone wrong. Natalie sounded aggressive, Alfredo petulant. Realizing that Louise and Jack had now trained their attentions that way, the other two stopped talking. There was an embarrassing hiatus, in which the room seemed to tilt.

"So where did you eat?" Jack asked.

Alfredo was charming again. His English was impeccable. "I took Louise to my favorite restaurant in all of Rome. On the Via di Monte Testaccio. I mean real *cucina romana*. You like it, Louise?"

"What just happened?" Louise wanted to know. Natalie, arms folded and legs crossed, gazed out of the window. Her bottom lip pushed out.

Alfredo laughed. "I forced Louise to try hoof-jelly salad and sweetbreads in white wine."

"Did I miss something?" Louise tried again.

Jack wasn't letting her in. "Did she resist, Alfredo?"

"Very strongly. At first. But I worked on her. Slowly—slowly."

"Catchee monkee," Natalie muttered.

"Sounds wonderful," Jack said. "I'll have to try it myself."

"Very expensive," Natalie said.

"Not too expensive," Alfredo cooed.

There was an uncomfortable silence before Alfredo got up and made to leave. He made a fine point of kissing Natalie goodnight, in addition to Louise, before pumping Jack's hand and expressing the hope that they might eat all together at that very restaurant. Louise saw him out. Jack had liked him and said so while Louise was away.

"I hate that," said Natalie.

"What."

"Married, and chasing other women."

"So he's *chasing* Louise, is he?"

"I despise men who haven't got the integrity to leave their wives," Natalie opined, "if they want to be with other women."

"You have a tough set of values."

"What's that?" Louise said on returning, pointing at the Stratton headset. She stooped to collect it, fingering the leather straps, unable to guess its function.

"Try it on," Natalie suggested cordially.

"Don't," Jack said. There was too much urgency in his voice. Louise looked surprised. "What I mean is that," Jack recovered himself, "it will make you feel sick."

"Really?"

"He exaggerates," said Natalie. "Try it for size."

"I put it on earlier and I still feel a bit nauseated," warned Jack.

"What the hell is it?"

"One of our father's fun toys."

115

Louise surveyed it at arm's length as if it was fizzing. "So what did he do with it?"

"Oh," Natalie said casually, "he'd get someone to take a tab of acid before strapping it to their head for six hours. Or he'd get a pretty girl naked and—"

"We don't need to hear this," Jack said.

"Sure we do," Louise insisted. "What would he do?"

Natalie disregarded her and turned to Jack. "Something I've noticed about you, that you prefer to ignore things. Keep things under wraps. Speak in code. Why do you do that? Or are you just protecting Louise?"

"Protect me? Protect me from what?"

"Nothing specific," said Natalie.

"I don't know what you mean, either," said Jack.

Natalie got up. "Hey, Louise, you and I have got a guy in common."

"Oh?"

"Yeh, you remember Nick? He and I go back a way." Louise looked stunned. She looked to Jack. Jack felt his cheeks flame with anger. He'd specifically asked Natalie not to mention Nick.

"Hey, it's late, and I'm going," Natalie said. "Good to meet you, Louise. Give Billy a kiss from me."

Jack tried to get up but Natalie pressed him back into his seat. "I'll see myself out." She planted on him a full-lipped kiss, one which lingered for a beat too long to be ambiguous to Louise. Then she was gone. They heard her Vespa stutter into life under the window, move off, accelerate, change gear, and accelerate again until it became a diminishing insect whine swallowed by the clamoring beak of the Rome night.

"Give Billy a kiss from me," Louise mimicked, unnecessarily heavily.

"Don't," Jack said, looking tired. "Don't say anything."

SEVENTEEN

While you contemplate, for twenty minutes twice daily, the gap between the spectral colours of blue and violet, let me remind you what science has to say about the colour Indigo.

Nothing.

You and I have been taught since childhood that the spectrum consists of seven colours. No doubt you learned some mnemonic: Read Only Your Great Books In Venice, indeed. So who, since time immemorial, has been assuring us that there are actually seven distinct colours in the normal spectrum of light? Not science, which admits to only six. Turn to your physics books and to your encyclopaedias and you find a strange aversion to mentioning the fugitive Indigo. A member of the family we no longer talk about. The colour that dares not speak its name. To science, taboo.

Scientific apprehension of colour is based on the concepts of hue, saturation, and vibration. All visible light is electromagnetic vibration. The differing wavelengths of some of these vibrations are seen subjectively as hues. The hue of red and the hue of violet are at opposite ends of the visible spectrum because they have different wavelengths. The hue of red vibrates at a wavelength of 0.000030 inches; violet at

0.000014 inches. Between these extremes are four clearly spaced wave variations, or bands (orange, yellow, green, blue). If there were five other bands, making a total of seven, then we could shout *Indigo!* But there are not. What is going on?

The colour of light in a single wavelength is known as pure spectral colour. These colours are said to be fully saturated. You are unlikely to see these colours outside a laboratory, but the sodium-vapour lamp used on highways is an exception and constitutes an example of almost fully saturated yellow. Most colours we see every day are of lower saturation—in other words, mixtures of wavelengths. This is precisely what every artistic rendition of Indigo turns out to be: a disappointing variation of the blue vibration.

There is no Indigo. There never has been an Indigo.

So much for science. But what of art and artists, vibrating at the opposite end of a different kind of spectrum? What have they to say on the matter? Ask them, if only for the recreational laughter it will afford. Though I confess to having a soft spot for artists, to hear them stammering and blustering over the question of the elusive Indigo makes me want to throw them all into the canal (and I once did, with one irritating young man). They will, with eyes moist, cite famous paintings and present you with a richly concocted array of exotic varieties of blue, blue, blue.

Scientists and artists. Knaves and fools. There is an alternative, and I can lead you there. The perception of Indigo is a doorway to Invisibility. (You may need at this moment to alter your concept of Invisibility. The idea purveyed by science fiction is of course quite absurd: If you were invisible in the sense suggested by H. G. Wells, why then even your eyelids would be transparent. You would not be able to close your eyes. You would not be able to sleep.)

On the other hand, I do not mean that if I point you to some shadowy corner or to some other camouflage you might be able to pose unnoticed. That is merely disguise, or conjuring. True Invisibility can realistically be likened to a crack in the material world through which, after having made an envelope of yourself, you may be posted.

Is this what happened to the fugitive Indigo, that it slipped from the world through such a crack? Clearly, historically, the colour was held to be a present force. Technical journals tell us that Indigo was "formerly" considered to be a fully developed colour of the spectrum. I am amused by this word "formerly" and its sly implications. Why, then, did we lose it? Did someone steal it from us? Did it leave the planet of its own accord? Is it divine or natural punishment that we are denied its beauty? Are other members of the spectrum also likely to desert?

The truth is, we had it, and now it has gone. I know some of the rare places in which traces of the fugitive Indigo may still be found, but I have no way of knowing if the thing I promise to deliver to you is a pale vestige of the glorious original. Perhaps what I unfurl for you here is a faded banner, a tattered remnant. But having followed my instructions and having seen the fugitive Indigo with your own eyes, you will then see faint traces of it everywhere. Your visual world will be transformed.

The sight of Indigo is an unexpected gift and side effect of mastering the art of Invisibility.

To practicalities. First you must change your diet. You need high levels of iron and calcium in your bloodstream to apprehend the colour Indigo, because of the presence of these elements in colour radiation. Perception of colour is a complex neurophysiological process and diet can influence the dynamic relationship between the observer and the thing observed. In addition to the vision-boosting vitamin A, I recommend a daily dose of 1.5 milligrams iron and 2 milligrams calcium. These are high doses, and the iron in particular will often lead to constipation. You will need to monitor your diet accordingly to be sure to purge yourself.

Bathe your eyes twice daily in a solution of witch hazel (*Hamamelis virginiana*) and borax. These you will find available at any pharmacy.

This regime should be strictly applied for one month before moving on to the next step, but you can use the intervening period to do two things: to develop the art of seeing and to build yourself a blacklight box.

The first exercise is known as palming. Simply close your eyes and place the open palms of your hands in front of them, palms lightly brushing your eyelids. Only a sea of blackness should be available to you, whether in your imagination or in reality. Hold this position for five minutes. When you open your eyes again, do not be alarmed that things seem slightly out of focus for a few moments. Indeed, you should not try to focus on anything at all for the initial few moments.

Practice this exercise frequently. After having been plunged into utter darkness, your eyes, upon opening, will see refreshed. This has something to do with the electrical impulse of the palms of the hands upon fatigued organs (the palms of the hands emitting vital force, hence their celebrated use in healing processes). Further, while in darkness, your eyesight shifts in its benighted search to the violet end of the spectrum and the area in which we need to be looking.

Having become familiar with the practice of palming, take a walk in the fields and do likewise. Better still, go to the woods and begin again. Even better, find a quiet stretch of woods at dusk and repeat the exercise. The results will surprise you.

While training your eyesight with vitamins and exercises, you can begin to construct the blacklight box. Most people will be able to clear out a closet or a cupboard under the stairs. If not, you must employ a carpenter or set about making one for yourself. In any event, the blacklight box would normally need to be roughly wardrobe size, with enough room for a chair and head clearance.

Your first task will be to make the box impenetrable to white light, sealing any cracks with black masking tape. Your next job will be to install an ultraviolet electrical light and a switch. This must be fixed exactly overhead of your seated position, and you will need a trailing cord so you don't shift your body posture when switching the light on or off.

After a month of adjusting your diet, of palming, and of constructing your blacklight box, you are now ready to pass on to the next stage in the process.

EIGHTEEN

AFTER SPENDING ALMOST FIFTEEN MINUTES IN THE "SMOKE CUPboard" under the stairs, Jack began to feel foolish and self-conscious. Certainly nothing had happened, and as his hand reached up for the trailing cord to switch on the UV light, the doorbell rang. The UV light grazed his eyes. He blinked. Groping for the sliding door, he heard Louise in conversation with someone.

Jack recognized Alfredo's voice, muffled, then coming closer, chiming a greeting. He and Louise paused in the hallway for a few moments, mere inches from where Jack stood under the stairs, separated from him only by the width of the sliding wood panel. Jack gathered that Alfredo had called to deliver his valuation of the house. He heard Alfredo ask where Jack was, and Louise saying she didn't know. Their voices retreated as Louise led Alfredo into the living room, where Billy was playing unattended.

Jack sat on the chair again. He wasn't hiding from Alfredo exactly; he just didn't want to draw out the man's visit. He would wait until the estate agent had gone before emerging from the smoke cupboard. As he sat, his reflected face gazed back from the mirror. A light misting had condensed over the surface of the glass.

Jack got up and wiped it clear with his sleeve. Then he heard Alfredo's voice raised, followed by Louise's wind-chime laughter. The two came out into the hall again. Jack could hear their voices quite clearly.

There was a mysterious silence before Alfredo suddenly started to say astonishing things. Louise was indescribably beautiful. Louise was a goddess. All night Alfredo had lain awake thinking of her, tormented, tortured by thoughts of her, until at 6 A.M. and unable to stand it he'd dragged himself out of bed and had to leave his family home to walk on the Monte Mario.

Jack, listening to this, instinctively jammed his fingers in his own mouth and bit hard.

It was misery, Alfredo reported. He couldn't be happy until he'd come back here to see her; just to lay eyes on her; just to spend a few moments in her presence.

"My goodness," said Louise.

Then a rustling sound, as of clothes meshing; followed by a thud against the wooden panel, strong enough to make a structural shudder pass through the smoke cupboard, and to make the cord from the UV light swing slightly. Jack heard a gasp, a snort, a slight panting.

Stop stop stop, Alfredo; You think I'm a fool, Louise; No I don't; Yes you do, well maybe I am; Look, I enjoyed the kiss, Alfredo, I really did, it's just that this is the wrong time for many reasons, it has nothing to do with you; I should go back to work or maybe home, today has been a disaster; Don't take it to heart, please don't, it's just—; No, you're right, I should go, please forget I came here today; I'm sorry; I'm sorry too.

Footsteps skittered. The door was opened, changing the pressure in the house, and there was a yawn of traffic from the street before the door closed again. Then a cry from Billy in the living room.

Jack heard Louise groan and run to him, whereupon he very quietly opened the sliding door and slipped out into the hallway.

"Where did you go?" Louise asked Jack a few moments later. "You just disappeared."

"I stepped outside for a stroll. You look flushed."

Louise ran a hand through her hair. "Billy's acting up. You want coffee?" Jack said no but she didn't seem to hear, and poured it anyway.

"Did I just see someone leaving the house?"

"You might have. It was the estate agent."

"You mean Alfredo?"

"Yup. Alfredo. Bringing the valuation."

"Personal touch, eh?"

"You know, this house is actually worth more than the apartment on Lake Shore Drive?"

"Who would have thought it? Alfredo have anything else to say?"

"He was in kind of a hurry. Why are you looking at me like that?"

"Like what?"

"Jack, how long were you thinking of staying in Rome? I mean, our business is done, isn't it?"

Jack gave up teasing her. He had given some thought to the matter of leaving Rome. Natalie had been contacted, the house was on the market. They couldn't hang around until the house was sold. But he had no intention of leaving just yet. His lonely business in Catford offered little to draw him back to England, but he reminded himself that he should phone Mrs. Price.

And anyway, Rome was beginning to work on him. Antique dust had embedded itself under his fingernails. The din of epochs was beginning to subside into a background roar. The patina of history was peeling back to reveal a bright and iridescent new Rome beneath. And then there was Natalie.

"You missing Chicago, Louise?"

"No; but I just thought I'd ask what your plans are. I thought it would be nice to stay a couple more days, and then I'll want to take Billy home."

. . .

They knew they should make the most of the confectionery of Rome. So they gorged on the Vatican, Bernini statues, and the Fountain of Trevi. Jack carried Billy on his shoulders for much of the day, playing Dad again. Jack and Louise were like a married couple, out with their son and not holding hands.

Indeed, they spent three happy days together before Louise decided she was ready for home. During this time Jack made no attempt to contact Natalie, and Natalie didn't call Jack. Neither did Alfredo or Louise trouble each other. And something was happening with Billy.

As the boy became more familiar with Jack, so he became drawn to him. Billy would leave his mother's side, tottering toward Jack, clasping him at the knee. If carried, he would lay his head on Jack's shoulder. He let Jack dry him with a big towel after bath time. He would open his arms for Jack, spontaneously, his eyes huge and shining. Sometimes in these moments Jack would look at Louise, returning the half-smile but detecting anxiety, too. Because bricks were snapping into place in an unstoppable construction, an architecture more sacred and precarious than all the monuments of Rome, and more ambitious than all the skyscrapers of Chicago.

"Come to Chicago," Louise said, half joking, prying Billy out of Jack's arms. "Remember, you have family there now."

"Maybe I will."

. . .

Jack placed his call to England, finally managing to speak to Mrs. Price, and she was not at all pleased. Not good enough, she lectured him, that he'd not been in contact since he'd left for Chicago; and she'd deliberately disconnected the answering machine so that he would be forced to speak to her directly. Cases were going unanswered, she pointed out, and there was a complication in the Birtles matter. Furthermore, her direct deposit had not been honored by the bank, and since, she assumed, he wasn't paying her she was giving him a week's notice.

"Slow down, Mrs. Price! There's plenty of money in the number three account!"

"And as you well know I don't have access to that account."

"But you can write a check for yourself. Go ahead, I trust you. Simply scribble my signature on the check."

"I've never done such a thing in my life and I won't start now."

"They won't know any difference, Mrs. Price! I'm anxious to pay you!"

"Absolutely not."

"All right. I'll arrange a bank transfer this very day. I promise. Tell me what happened over Birtles."

"The brute lied in court, claiming that you never served the papers on him. He says he can prove he wasn't even in town that day."

Jack's heart sank.

"You did serve him properly, didn't you?" asked Mrs. Price, amending her tone.

"Mrs. Price!"

"Excuse me for asking. But Birtles raised such a hue and cry; and the court wanted you to appear. Well, I explained you were in foreign parts, and so of course the judge proceeded on the basis of your affidavit. The judge told Birtles that in his experience process servers had nothing to gain by lying, and granted the injunction anyway."

126

Jack assured Mrs. Price he would return just as soon as he was able; he placated her; he cajoled her; he pleaded that his business would cease to function without her. He promised more regular contact before putting down the phone. He felt dreadful about the Birtles case, not because he'd lied to the courts or cheated Birtles, but because he'd let Mrs. Price down.

. . .

But still Jack wasn't done with Rome. There was nothing to pull him back to England when the Eternal City was a yawning sky-vaulted cornucopia stuffed with churches and palaces, which on closer inspection proved to be hinged caskets containing treasures, secrets, artifacts, all of which when cracked open released crowds of ghosts. Why would he want to go back to England when there was no one there for him?

And then there was Natalie. With her wolf gaze and her balle-rina's legs. She stopped by the afternoon before Louise was sched-uled to go home. Louise was in the hallway when Natalie let herself in through the door. The surprise of seeing each other made the two women freeze.

It was Louise who spoke first. "I see you have a key," she said, unable to unfix her gaze from Natalie's tight-fitting leather trousers and the massive buckle at her midriff.

"That's right. I told Jack about it. In fact, I came to return it. Here."

"Maybe you should keep it."

"No. There are too many of them floating around as it is. I'd pre-fer not to have it. Do you like black-and-white films?"

"As a matter of fact I do. You said you knew Nick. Were you and he lovers?"

"Yes. Billy looks like him, don't you think?"

Louise was unable to prevent her neck and ears from flushing with anger. "Have you said anything about Nick being Billy's father to Jack?"

127

"No," Natalie lied. "What concern is it of his? Or mine?"

"I'd prefer it if you'd keep it that way. Jack doesn't need to know."

"I understand. Jack told me you were sizing him up as a stand-in father."

"He told you that?!!" Louise was appalled.

"I see I'm speaking out of turn. Now we both have something we'd better not tell him. Here, take the key. I have to go. About the black-and-white films: I thought you looked the type."

. . .

Jack rented a car and drove Louise and Billy to the airport. Before passing through the departure area, Louise turned and grabbed his lapel. "Can I say something? It might sound a little weird. Keep away from Natalie."

"Why?"

"She's a bad liar, for one thing."

"Is this sisterly advice you're giving me?"

"It's just advice. You might think you want her. But you don't."

Then she kissed him fully on the lips. The kiss was thrilling and disconcerting, and unexpectedly long. Then she went through the gate, and only Billy looked back to see Jack waving.

. . .

Immediately upon returning from the airport, Jack called Natalie.

NINETEEN

"THE YOUNG ITALIAN ARTIST ANNAMARIA ACCURSO SLIT HER wrists at midnight on February fifteenth. The American, Nicholas Chadbourne, vanished from his apartment the same evening."

"You have a mind that purrs," said Natalie. "And it never stops."

"I looked into it," said Jack.

Bright sunlight was bleeding through the gap in the heavy blue velvet curtains. It was their second day in bed together. Natalie lay on her stomach. Sheets tangled her thigh, winding her damp waist like ivy or honeysuckle. Her head was buried in the pillows, her hair spilling across the sheets. They were drenched. It was like the aftermath of an atrocity. The room hung heavy with the smoke of fuck and sweat run cold, cloying like mayflower in its scent, opalescent where the light struck. They were doped on each other.

Jack lay propped on his elbows, tracking a shining bead of perspiration along Natalie's flank. Her skin flamed in the light, tanned, smooth, and lustrous, and on her shoulder was the small tattoo he'd always known he'd find there: the spectrum—not a rainbow, but a

129

lightning bolt surrounded by six tiny stars. There were only six colors.

In the middle of the night he'd bitten that tattoo. Natalie, hoisting herself up on her knees, pressing her head into the pillows and grasping the iron bedstead with her arms spread, inviting him to take her from behind. Already sore from lovemaking, squeezing inside her, pushing hard against her aggressively offered buttocks until she breathed his name and bit the pillow; nipping the tattoo between his teeth, almost as if he could strip it from her shoulder. She triggered dark appetites. For a moment he lost all sense of himself before releasing her from his wolf bite.

"The point is," Jack said, "that these two people had one thing in common."

"Amaze me," Natalie said sleepily.

"My father. Tim Chambers."

"Wrong."

"Wrong? Why wrong?"

"You asked what they'd got in common. It wasn't your father; at least not just your father. What's the significance of the date?"

"February fifteenth? What's that?"

"Lupercalia." Natalie drew herself up. Sex had relaxed her features and her beatific face had a dark radiance. "The feast of Lupercalia."

Jack blinked, waiting for an explanation. Instead she laid her elegant hands on his shoulders. Locking her fingers in his hair, she pulled herself to him. Her tongue probed his mouth, carefully at first, then recklessly as she craned herself onto his lap. Her mouth tasted of sleep and last night's wine, and rainwater slightly saline, and berries and litchis and citrus, but through it all the odor of her sex overwhelmed him. He could taste it even on her kiss. Something mineral in it daunted and excited him. She bit his lip, holding the flesh of it between her teeth without puncturing the skin; she slid her silky tongue across the hard palate to the soft. She dropped her hands to his cock, squeezing it, stretching it, pumping him double-handed. He was sure he had nothing left. He'd already flensed himself inside her, left a layer of skin behind, but this voracious woman was ready for more.

"I can't go again!" he laughed.

"Oh yes you can."

The room was blueing over. A kind of mist; an odor; a presence; blue shadow; violet hue; Indigo rising.

"Fuck me again."

. . .

"Again. That's it. Again. Speak to me, Jack, don't close me out."

"I can't. I go beyond. Words. Beyond words."

"Stay with me. Again. That's so good."

"Why do you love it so much?"

"You have to ask me that? It's not just the . . . though that would be enough. It's the—the—*the insight.*"

How shall we speak of the wolf? Through your dreams? Where to begin? You come to me so untutored, Jack, outwardly a man of the world but I see you and know you come to me clean. I lick the fine downy lanugo covering your naked body, sniff the waxy *vernix caseosa* of your skin; I don't even have to show you the nipple, for you come at me mouthing air, hungry for the lupine milk.

Perhaps you didn't believe me when I told you I choose only one man every two years. Now when you see my ardor you might believe it. Even though I am not new to men, I come to you reanimated, clean, hungry. And though naive, you are a good lover, considerate, attentive to my pleasures. How can

131

you be your father's son? He was not unselfish like you. He was found wanting.

Are you aware of the presence of the wolf, in this the city of the wolf? Can't you hear her low growl in the night? Hear her panting low and hard? Scent her breath, smelling of ewe milk and corpse flesh and earthworm and acorns and berries; or her fur, reeking of the wet summer night and the muddied meanders of the Tiber? Don't you see her shadow at the window?

No. It's not possible for you to see her. Yet. Because she is the Indigo shadow, and in that you are but a neophyte.

But you'll come to know. Who can live, like men, in caves or holes or in the hollows of trees, comfortable on the prairie, in the forest, or on the mountain, other than the wolf? Who selects her mate for life, and therefore must betray herself, subject to infidelity, venereal affliction? Why so close and yet sworn enemies?

So glad that American woman went. Didn't like her. Too human. Too controlled. Too alpha female. In the way. Held you back. Kept you from me. Though I knew you'd come. Her scent still on you. Let me lick you clean. Let me drench you in the heat and appetite of my love, denude and devour you, suck every drop of your come, leave you with nothing to burn but sleep, so that I can pad, in my Indigo fur, like a shadow, through your dreams.

"What day is it?" Jack groaned.

Natalie, wearing a brocade dressing gown formerly owned by old man Chambers, opened the curtains and flung up a window. She carried a tray of strong black espresso with toast and Marmite spread. "You slept for ages. If you're going to keep coming at me like that you're going to have to keep your strength up," she twinkled. "But all I could find was Marmite."

"I was dreaming. I dreamed you were a wolf. You're not, are you?"

"A wolf? Not unless I don't know about it. In my dark half. You were dreaming about wolves because I was telling you about Lupercalia. Before you dropped off to sleep. Did you dream the color indigo?"

"No. It was in there somewhere, but I didn't see it."

"I did. Something's happening while I'm with you. For the second time in a week, I've dreamed the color indigo. What is it about you, Jack?"

"You see it in your sleep?"

"Yes. Very clear."

"Describe it."

She paused, her eyes drawn upward, looking for inspiration. "I can't."

"Try."

"It's futile. It's always running, like water, or at least like molten metal. But then when I wake up the memory of its precise nature has gone."

Jack remembered some of what Natalie had told him about Lupercalia before he'd drifted off to sleep: the ancient Roman festival staged at the cave sanctuary where the she-wolf suckled the abandoned Romulus and Remus. Naked young men smeared with blood, cleansed with goat's milk, were equipped with strips of goat's hide; whereupon they would run through the city lashing women with the hide to ward off infertility. Tim Chambers, Natalie had suggested, made a bid to revive the custom, and found plenty of willing volunteers.

Jack munched thoughtfully on his toast. "Did you ever take part in the old man's Lupercalian games?"

Natalie looked disgusted. "Look, once and for all. I let him *fuck* me; I didn't allow him to *fuck me up*."

133

"What do you know about Accurso and Chadbourne?"

"Oh, they were deep, deep in it."

"Meaning?"

"Meaning I was only on the periphery of these events. I saw some strange things going on, but I avoided getting drawn in. You know, your father cast a long shadow and he—" She stopped what she was saying.

"Natalie! Why are you looking at me like that?"

"The light. The way it settles on your shoulders. Blue. Violet. God, Jack, I hope I'm not going to fall in love with you. I would hate for that to happen." She tossed a towel at him. "Go and get showered. This place smells like a cave."

TWENTY

A VOICE, TELLING JACK TO GET OUT OF ROME, CUT AND RUN, GO
home. Things felt wrong, out of joint. When Natalie finally insisted on getting back to her work, Jack was left cooling his heels. His task was completed. Apart from Natalie there was nothing to keep him in Rome. The longer he stayed away from England, the more he neglected his small business. Clients would stop coming; the lawyers would steer jobs elsewhere.

There were several good reasons why he should leave. This thing with Natalie was voiding out. He felt that her "fear" of falling for him was a device, a prepared escape route, *oh let me not fly too near the sun.* He perceived that her way of handling men was not unlike the way men often treat women. She used them up and retreated to her own business, easily extricating herself. In bed, she even came like a man, with a sudden, fierce, barking climax. Drained, he returned to her again and again, but he always felt oddly tainted; chiefly by the fact that his father had been there in advance of him, and if in a moment of passion he ever forgot the fact, there was always the sexfoil tattoo to remind him, like a proprietary brand.

That sense of his father's long, creeping shadow perturbed

135

him. He felt manipulated. As if his father had enticed him to Rome, knowing he would be drawn to Natalie, predicting, even engineering, his response. There was only one thing he could do to beat it for sure, and that was to leave. You can't sprinkle salt on a shadow. Despite all this, leaving Natalie wasn't easy.

One night, five days after Louise's departure, Jack woke beside Natalie with a strange sensation that someone was standing at the foot of the bed, peering at them. When he gathered his wits and sat bolt upright, there was no one there in the darkness. That time he simply went back to sleep. On another occasion, he thought he heard someone moving about the house on the floor above.

His suspicions began to intensify when he returned to the house one afternoon to hear opera music playing, as on the day when he and Louise had first arrived in Rome. A deep contralto resonated from the floor above, down the stairs, and along the empty hall, moving through the house like an aerial spirit. A scratchy recording of Kathleen Ferrier in *Orfeo ed Euridice*. It was one of his father's—and Natalie's, though he'd left her only half an hour before—favorites. Maybe it was a message. A wicked memorandum. He switched off the music and made a brief search of the house. Nothing.

He telephoned Louise in Chicago. "Louise, you saw the old man dead, didn't you?" He was afraid things might turn out as in a bad movie, in which the ghost is alive all along.

She was relieved to hear from him. "He was as dead as they get, Jack. I was there, remember? I called the doctor. I closed the coffin lid when they put him into the flame. It was no trick. Man, you sound so unhappy. What's keeping you in Rome?"

"Oh, I don't know. Another few days and I'll go back to London."

"Then you can come and see us again. Billy keeps asking for you."

"Really?"

"Sure."

"You're not just saying that?"

"No, I'm not just saying that. You come here whenever you want. We've got coffee and blueberry muffins waiting for you here."

"You know what, Louise? I love you."

"And I love you too, Jack. Remember that."

After he put the phone down, he felt strange. He'd told Louise he loved her, but he'd managed to say it quickly enough so that the sentiment had no real heft. And she'd managed to lob it straight back that way.

He made a second, more thorough, search. There were rooms at the top of the house he hadn't been inside since his first day. One of them was locked, and he couldn't recall having turned a key in any of them. He had to go downstairs again to fetch the jailer-size set of keys.

When he got the door open, he saw that someone had been camping out. Though the wallpaper was unrolling itself from the wall in musty coils, above the smell of damp plaster and ancient paper was a human smell. Someone who didn't wash. There was a stained mattress on the floor with a couple of scattered blankets. But next to the bed was a stove identical to the one in Natalie's studio, plus an aluminum saucepan and a tin cup containing coffee dregs. Jack touched the stove. It was still slightly warm.

The catch on the window was broken and the sash was loose. Someone could come and go via the rusting fire escape bolted to the wall beneath the window. Alternatively, he or she might have a key both to the front door of the house and the bedroom if the old man was as free with his place as Natalie claimed. Maybe the person just picked certain times to come and go.

Jack went out and found a hardware store. He changed the locks himself. He used a hammer to nail shut any loose windows. He decided not to tell Natalie about changing the locks.

. . .

"How are the experiments coming along?" said Natalie.

"What?" Jack forked spaghetti into his mouth. They were eating at The Poisoner again. "Experiments?"

"You're such a bad liar, Jack. Hopeless. I thought an ex-cop would do better. If you want to lie you've got to keep your feet still, avoid swallowing hard, and prevent your eyelashes from fluttering. You leak information from every pore."

"Don't miss a trick, do you?"

"Surprising, though, isn't it? The results. I mean, once you start with those little exercises. And then the blacklight box. It's as though you somehow peeled a layer of misty film from your eyes."

Jack planted his feet, put down his fork, and stilled his eyelashes. "I haven't got a clue what you're talking about."

"That palming. I still can't figure out how that works. Then after a session in the blacklight box, the world is like a summer garden after a shower of rain. And you notice small things about other people. Like the slightly bloodshot eyes of someone who has been a regular visitor to the blacklight box. Don't worry; that passes quite quickly."

Jack sighed. "I gave it a go. So what?"

"This is how it starts."

Before he had time to answer, there was a brief power outage. All the diners cheered spontaneously. In the dark, Natalie's face seemed illuminated by an ethereal blaze, backlit, woad-like. The way she smelled when stretched out on the bed came back to him. The taste of her displaced The Poisoner's best efforts. He sniffed his fingers for residual fuck. He could *smell* the color of her; *see* the odor of she-wolf like an aura around her.

A new element was coming into their lovemaking. Natalie took him to the wall of experience. She maddened him with appetite. In the dark, she would spit on her fingers and stroke the stringy saliva under the glans of his cock; he imagined he could see this Indigo potion bubbling in the blackness, and he would have to have her, again and again, and at all hours.

His dreams were chaotic and full of salamanders and wolves and confused images of her, and he would awaken, nursing an ache. One night he woke and had to rouse her. Sleepily pulling her to him, she gasped as he pushed inside her. Then she came with a soft, lupine howl of pleasure. Afterward, while he recovered his breath, she flicked her head from side to side, as if looking for something in the dark.

"What is it?"

"Shhh! Be still," she whispered. "No, stay inside me. Listen. Something has come into the room."

He listened. All he could hear was his heart hammering, but the tang of their sex had never been so absolute. He could taste it. It was like a burning vapor; a fused odor; something was coalescing. The darkness around him was congealing, emulsifying, like a shell. He thought he heard a faint hissing.

"See it?" she whispered. "Can you see it? Can you taste it?"

"What is it?"

"Indigo."

He rolled off her and peered hard into the darkness. A needle of blue-violet shadow, a fine vertical line, floated between him and the window like a mystical sword. After a moment, he realized that what he was looking at was the light before dawn bleeding between the floor-to-ceiling blue velvet curtains of the room. He pointed this out to her.

She shook her head sadly. "You missed it, Jack. You had a chance there and you missed it."

"Missed what?"

"Don't worry, it will come again for us. I know it. It's happening for us, Jack."

The following day, she laughed off the matter. But now he stared at her in the darkness of The Poisoner and wondered if the odor he could sniff on his fingers was residual Indigo.

He recalled her question. "How what starts?" he asked as the lights flickered on again.

"Seeing. Properly. For the first time. Just be careful you don't want to see too much."

. . .

Seeing too much. That was why Jack quit the force, seeing too much.

As he'd told Louise, it wasn't that he'd seen things of heartbreaking sadness or unendurable ugliness, though he'd had his share through seven years in the drug squad. But it wasn't all that. It was the habit of *looking* that wore him out.

He was amazed that the police offered no training in the art of looking, in the skills of observation; and astonished at how little some of his colleagues could actually see. Men who couldn't tell that glass lying outside a window indicated a means of egress rather than ingress; oafs who couldn't spot a forged signature; policemen who could be halfway through an interview without recognizing the special college in which the interviewee had studied the rolling of masterfully thin cigarettes.

But he had the bobby eye from day one. Though armed against the danger of first impressions, he always *knew.* He could tell within a second if he was talking to someone who had served time. He could spot *scrotes* and scumbags at twenty paces.

But he couldn't switch it off, this bobby eye. There were times when he didn't want to know if someone was lying. Just as sewage workers carry home a smell on their coats, he began to see rot and lies everywhere, and he remembered a line from Matthew in the

140

New Testament that went: "And if thine eye offend thee, pluck it out." So he'd done the next best thing, hoping that if he got a job where he didn't have to look for lies, he might stop seeing them.

But right now there was no danger of him seeing too much. He couldn't even see to the end of his feelings about Natalie. Or Louise. Or his father, come to that. He claimed to despise his father; yet here he was not only executing the will but embroiled in the old man's blasted step-by-step manual of weirdness. The *looking* had been triggered all over again. In the pages of the manuscript, and through its exercises, he knew he was hunting for something. For what? Approval, yes; and insight, true; and the lost and missing substance; and genesis and revelation. All of that.

But what couldn't be denied was the positive effect of these exercises. He had followed the instructions with diligence, hoping to prove very quickly that the old man's mind was unsound. He'd even tried hard to deny to himself the results he experienced. Though not spectacular, these were undeniable. The palming and the other small acts of visual training, the dusk observation, the eye gymnastics: The first thing he noticed was, simply, a greater lucidity, as if he'd taken an eye bath or the world itself had been rinsed. Marginal but unmistakable. Then a minor expansion at the periphery of his vision, so that he had greater perception of movement at ninety degrees right or left.

In the blacklight box, Jack found an optician's eye chart. As suggested in the manuscript, he'd tested himself before the exercises. When he came to test himself again, his sight had improved moderately in each eye. He wondered seriously for the first time whether his old man had been on to something.

. . .

As he sat mulling over his predicament and coiling his spaghetti in The Poisoner, his visual field seemed to hum with merriment. The deep blue of Natalie's blouse was moist, fluid. The starched white

141

shirts of the waiters flickered with energy. Light strummed the fretwork of the red-and-white-checked tablecloth. It was possible to be plagued by doubts about everything he was doing in Rome at that moment, and yet still to be happy.

"What do you want to do now?" Natalie asked him, finishing her dessert and scowling at a waiter.

"Let's go and make some Indigo," Jack said.

TWENTY-ONE

Having grappled with the principles of Colour and Light, you must now study the properties of the Cloud. There are adepts who claim that this third step should more properly be described as the principle of Breath. No matter. If you have followed my instructions faithfully this far, you will understand that as the optical world peels back, layer by layer, in a shocking striptease, words too are falling away.

Language is nothing more than a modest covering we give the world. Practitioners of the literary arts are tiresome and obsessive prudes given to fussily shifting fig leaves back and forth across acres of flesh. Poets, writers, wordsmiths: equivocators, all of them.

Breath, though, does have its significance in the formation of the kind of Cloud I am talking about. It has been observed since the time of Aristotle, who wrote of the phenomenon in his essay "On Dreams," that a menstruating woman merely by staring at a mirror for a fixed period can produce on the surface of that mirror a light film or mist. Aristotle considered that menstruation affected the eyes, and that the eyes in turn set up a movement in the air that affected the mirror. While science has demonstrated that menstruating women can indeed produce a mysterious coating on a reflective surface, it is not through the process of the eye acting upon the object that this happens.

Aristotle, however, was not entirely off-beam in his surmise. The eyes do indeed emit a minimal vapour easily measured by sophisticated technical equipment, and this vapour plays its part in the complicated psychological relationship seen in the practice of hypnotism, or mesmerism. And while this vapour is emboldened and altered in women during the onset of menstruation, its production and enhancement is not restricted to women. Further than that, with a little training, this substance can be summoned at will.

Though not lightly. It is more valuable than gold; rarer than radium; and more dangerous to the hearts of men than either.

You have become familiar with the conditions of the blacklight box, having spent enough time inside the box, in and out of ultraviolet light. You have surprised yourself with the subtle texture of reflections from the mirror in conditions of absolute darkness; you have seen the hazy aura or energy colour emanate from your fingertips, and then eventually from your entire body, and you have seen this too reflected in the mirror. You have followed my instructions precisely, switching instantly to ultraviolet light, and have thereby caught, in the mirror, the strange and deeply unnerving afterimage of yourself in the moment your eyes adjust from the thorough darkness to the UV condition.

Moreover, you have understood that this afterimage is not merely reflected light but is also a substance capable of leaving a smear or mist on your mirror. This substance is what I referred to earlier as Cloud.

This Cloud is formed in a manner not unlike the formation of clouds in the sky. That is to say, rain clouds and the like are formed by the constant movement of air currents, in which cool and warm air masses come into proximity, combining to produce vapour. You, in the exercise of your blacklight box activities, are producing minute currents and vibrations, extending as visible auras and setting up tremors in the air immediately around your body. In your blacklight box, you are influencing your immediate environment, creating almost a microclimate, and producing the substance I call Cloud in very tiny quantities.

You have also replaced your ordinary workaday mirror with one sil-vered instead with arsenic, antimony, and mercury. I recommended that you actually produce this yourself rather than leave the matter to some local craftsman; though I suspect in your eagerness for shortcuts you will not have heeded my advice or my detailed directions regarding quantities and the sequence of events. That is your own affair. Regard this as my last warning on the matter of straying from my precise in-structions.

I prefer the word 'Cloud' to 'Breath' simply because I would hate for you to make the mistake of thinking I was talking about something as banal as condensation appearing on a mirror. In order for you to under-stand the difference, all you need to do is to shoot a pencil-thin beam of UV light through the substance collected on the mirror.

You will be astonished at what you see. You will cry out. Whereas mere condensation dulls the angled beam of UV light, the properties of Cloud come back at you like hissing serpents, glittering with colour of electrical intensity. As the colours vibrate and refuse to stay still before your very eyes, you will try to count them. You are convinced there are seven, if only they would be still for a moment. For a new colour has made itself available to you. I do not have to tell you the name of this colour.

But back to the substance I have described as Cloud. Switch off your UV light. You are now ready to collect this substance. You are going to need lots of it.

TWENTY-TWO

Natalie introduced Jack to what she called hidden Rome, propelling him through private courtyards, along dark alleys stinking of piss, behind buildings famous and obscure, under monuments, beneath arches, over crumbling Trajan masonry, through gaps in walls. She knew Rome like she knew her lover's body. She had touched her tongue to every spot. "You said you wanted to look. But are you prepared to let a little magic into your life?"

Many of Rome's most spectacular secrets were underground. Hundreds of pre-Christian houses and temples lay, broken but still breathing, beneath the medieval and Renaissance palaces and indeed under modest residences and civic buildings. She showed him a cat from a temple of Isis that formed a cornice; ancient sundials lodged in foundations; salamanders and serpents pillaged to decorate the facades of Christian churches; arches, pillars, dressed-marble bearing Latin inscriptions, all supporting the structures of modern-day Rome. Acres and acres of city struggling to remember itself.

Rome was a mythical creature of mixed elements, a chimera,

only understanding its true nature in the dark, when sleeping, when allowed to dream; and that rich dreaming exuded from under the pavement level of the city like a narcotic gas.

Jack asked if they could visit the site of the Lupercalia, the location of the cave on the Palatine where Romulus and Remus were suckled by a she-wolf. Natalie obliged by taking him to the place, but told him his father had explained the site was bogus.

"I expect he had an alternative," Jack said cynically.

"More than that. He had a system for proving the original location. Come on!"

She took him to a sundial in a silent, sun-warmed square near the Church of Saint Sabina. It was almost three in the afternoon and the sun cast a strong, healthy shadow. A small boy sat on a white brick, a soccer ball at his feet, watching them intently. "We have to wait for the hour."

"Why?"

"Wait and see."

The gnomon from the sundial was missing. Natalie scouted around until she found a discarded popsicle stick and rammed it into the hole on the sundial. Then she lit a cigarette, refusing to answer any questions for the next ten or twelve minutes, smoking in silence. The boy grew bored, took his ball, and left. When the hour came around, she told Jack to follow the shadow from the stick. The shadow deflected at the edge of the sundial, chased up the adjacent wall, and pointed to a small circular hole smashed in the wall. "You have to look through that hole."

Jack suspected a joke. He stepped up to the hole: Through it he could see a marble-faced block, obviously pillaged from a ceremonial monument. Chased in the marble was a Latin inscription, but through the narrow chink in the wall Jack could only make out the letters TVM. He turned back and shrugged at Natalie.

"What you're looking at is a clue," she said. "But I'm not going to help you."

Jack squinted again through the hole. TVM. It meant nothing to him. He tried to think what the three initials might represent. "Wait here," he told Natalie.

"I'm not going anywhere."

Jack paced the length of the wall. He had to cover thirty yards before he could go behind it to check out the marble-faced stone. It was clearly of Imperial age, and had some kind of triumphal origin. But it had no context. It was cemented into a crude brick wall built probably fifteen hundred years later. The inscription was broken, too. Only a section of it remained. He could make out that the letters TVM belonged to the word PROPAGATVM, in a phrase that read PROPAGATVM. INSIGNIBVS. VIRTVTI, then the rest was lost. There were numerals and other bits of broken phrases, but nothing signified.

He returned to Natalie. She sat on the plinth under the sundial, smiling, sibyl-like. The sun was full on her. "I don't speak no Latin," he said.

"You're on the wrong track. Start again."

Irritated by the game, Jack looked again at the sundial and at the hole in the wall. Then he noticed other holes in the wall, all at the same level, spaced at equal intervals. He squinted through a second hole. This time he could make out the letters NVS.

"You've got it," Natalie cheered. Through the third hole he glimpsed the numerals XII. He moved back to the hole to the left of the first, spying the letters POR. "Put them all together."

"PORTVMNVS XII."

"Exactly."

"Oh, exactly! Excuse me, what the *fuck* are you talking about?"

"Think. Use your brain. Nature gave you one in good order."

"You're beginning to sound like that old bastard."

"So, in Roman letters the V sounds like a U. Portumnus."

"I'm no wiser."

"Portumnus was the Roman divinity of the river gate. Are you ready to go to his temple?"

"If we must."

They walked down to the Boario Forum. Natalie linked her arm through his, and for the first time he thought she looked truly happy in his company. Her skin was clearer, the pupils of her eyes were dilated; the perfume of confidence streamed from her, and a luminosity clung raggedly to her clothes, like blue fur.

If it wasn't love, it was a close neighbor. But Natalie's ways were strange, and even though he felt she was dangerous, he was coming to trust her. The previous night, they had drunk a barrel of wine and smoked a bushel of hash, and he was barely conscious when she had said, "Do you trust me?"

"Yes."

"Get naked."

"No, not that," he'd protested when she produced the Stratton headgear.

"Hush!" She had kissed him. "I want to take you to the very edge. Trust me."

She told him to close his eyes while she buckled on the headgear. She placed cushions behind his head and gently laid him down, instructing him not to open his eyes until he was relaxed. She subdued the light by tying a violet scarf over the lamp shade and by lighting candles; she took a swig of red wine and squirted it between his lips; she sucked on a joint and breathed it back into his mouth. "Without moving your head, you can open your eyes."

When he did so he felt as if he were floating. Blue-violet light rippled like a sea below him. Soft white flames smeared the periphery of his vision. Her face came at him from above, upside down. He heard her disembodied voice say, "Close your eyes if it gets too much." Then he felt a warm, moist nuzzling and lapping at his cock. He convulsed and the lights were sent spinning out of focus. He reached for her but grabbed at air. Then there was a shocking fur odor under his nose. If he closed his eyes he almost slipped from consciousness.

He heard her padding around him on all fours, felt her snow-cold nose nuzzle his ribs. The fur odor came at him again, like a lick of flame. He opened his eyes to see her inverted jaws, teeth gleaming in the blue light, closing in on his face as a packet of fiery smoke exploded in his mouth. Other smells winged in on the hashish smoke: smells of timber, snow, berries, lamb, carrion. He opened his eyes again, trying to rein in the hallucination, but he was frightened by her eye, up close to his, yellow-gray, deliquescing. Then he fell back as she mounted him, and when he ejaculated the room became a cave and the shaded blue light became the moon, and he howled.

All that had happened the previous night. He'd awakened in bed, with the headgear removed. They said nothing about it. Now here she was leading him through Rome, and he speculated on what other Roman citizens did here of an evening in the privacy of their small homes. They arrived at a well-known monument, a circle of Corinthian columns enclosing a cylindrical cell of yellowing marble. "But this is the Temple of Vesta!" Jack protested.

"It was misnamed because it has the same shape as the Temple of Vesta in the Forum. Scholars know that this belongs to the god of the river gate. Portumnus."

"What's the significance of XII?"

"You have to find the twelfth pillar."

"In a circle? Where do we start counting?"

"How about the one nearest the river?"

150

Counting obediently, Jack found the twelfth pocked column, which was marred by a diagonal line cleanly scooped out of the fluted stone. Perfectly aligned with the stripe, but on the thirteenth column, was a decisive arrow. It pointed back up the hill at the tower of the Chiesa di Santa Maria in Cosmedìn. "You need to sight the tower exactly along the arrow to know where to go."

It did indeed point to the western arch of the bell tower, but Jack wasn't buying it. "You're saying that some ancient Romans placed all these clues to the location of the cave of the Lupercalia?"

"Don't be an imbecile. It was done *much* later. These clues were placed here by a group of Renaissance artists who'd stumbled on the secret. They wanted to keep it to themselves. That's why they went to so much trouble."

"Renaissance? How do you know?"

"You date the walls and edifices in which the primary clues are lodged. Like the first stone you saw. Do you want to go to Santa Maria or not?"

"How long does this go on for?"

"We've only just begun."

. . .

Two hours later, Jack stood on the Ponte Fabricio, watching the twilight descending over the fast-flowing Tiber. He was waiting for Natalie, who'd spotted someone across the street and was locked in conversation. The river was swollen and rushing swiftly under the bridge, churning as it had done on the day he'd seen—or thought he'd seen—a corpse in the water. He looked back. Natalie was on the other side of the road in a pool of neon-blue light, talking to a young man on a Vespa scooter, laughing about something, her hand resting lightly on his arm. Jack felt the brief stiletto-jab of jealousy. He took the steps down to the bank of the river and stood on the edge, inhaling its primal odors.

Natalie's trail—or, more properly, his father's trail—had led him to the Basilica di San Clemente: according to his father, the authentic site of the Lupercalia, the wolf's lair. The references, the signs, the clues were so extensive it had taken half a day to follow them. Natalie refused to shortcut, and neither would she say whether she thought the thing was valid or bogus—preferring instead to let Jack make up his own mind.

What couldn't be denied was that some people had gone to a great deal of trouble to lay a trail. Unless of course they had invented a trail out of preexisting signs, markers, and tracks, overlaying it with one or two of their own. But why would they do that?

The Church of San Clemente was a twelfth-century basilica built on top of a fourth-century temple, which in turn had been built into the first floor of an ancient palazzo. This had itself been constructed over several layers of ancient Roman buildings. Layer upon layer upon layer. Steps led down from the sacristy to the fourth-century basilica, where a confusion of supporting walls bore faded and obscure frescoes illustrating the miracles of Saint Clement's life. Further stone steps led down to the dimly lit remains of an ancient vault deep below the pavements of the modern city. There was a temple to the cult of Mithras.

They had been alone in the crypt. There was an anteroom with stone benches, a sanctuary with an altar depicting Mithras slaying a bull, and an initiation chamber. A hole above the altar had been filled in. "This is it," she'd breathed. "These chambers were scooped out of a natural cave. Tim said this place was the source of the myth."

Jack had looked around him, his breath congealing on the ancient, poorly illumined stone. She'd beckoned him into the initiation chamber.

"How good is your mythology?" she'd asked him. "Romulus

and Remus were the offspring of the rape of Rhea Silvia by Mars. Rhea was a virgin goddess, in other words, a lunar goddess. She was surprised, raped, in the grotto by Mars, a solar god. Here's the magic I promised you: It's the story of an eclipse. The hole in this cave roof sighted the eclipse and trained its shadow across the altar.

"The twinship of Romulus and Remus," she'd continued, "represents the balancing of two traditions. But Romulus, the solar aspect, triumphed over Remus, the lunar aspect. Mithras, also a god of light, is Romulus's martial incarnation, which is why he was adopted by Roman soldiers in their campaigns and taken as far as Britain. This cave is where it happened. The eclipse. The birth of Romulus and Remus. The she-wolf only appears during a total eclipse. This is the cave of the Lupercalia."

Jack had looked around the chamber—for what? Shadows of an ancient eclipse? "It requires a leap of imagination," he'd objected.

"Everything worthwhile does, Jack," she'd said fiercely. "Everything does."

Now, some hours later, as he stood on the banks of the Tiber waiting for Natalie, it was not lost on him that he was implicated in a fresh goose chase of his father's stewardship; the first of these had brought him to Rome; the second had him chasing around crumbling antiquities looking for the grotto of the she-wolf and finding mythologies in the bending of light. It was maddening, because once you were on the trail you couldn't let go until it proved itself decisively fake. And the things Natalie had shown him were set out in mathematical order. No "sign" was ambiguous. At no point could he argue that this arrow or that word or that pointer was simply a scratch or a bullet mark or a mere grab iron in the stone.

Jack had another thing on his mind as he stared into the black water, something that kept returning to him with a nagging insistence. It was the Birtles affair. Irrationally, in the midst of all he had seen that day, a worm gnawed at him, a worm wriggling out of his own dishonesty.

A "touch" of the court papers to the servee was all that was required under British law. If the servee saw the server coming and chose to make a run for it, he was not "served." Birtles seemed to have a nose for Jack or any other court officials, and Jack had spent three dedicated weeks trying to serve Birtles with the papers for an injunction that would restrain him from terrorizing his former wife. But he couldn't get near him. He'd waited outside Birtles's house dawn and dusk; he'd loitered in Birtles's favorite pub, the Haunch of Venison; he'd followed him through a busy marketplace. All without success. Birtles always saw him coming and gave him the slip. On one occasion, he'd even jumped out of the window at the Haunch of Venison, to the applause and entertainment of his boozing cronies. Jack called him the Vanishing Man.

Then Jack had simply thought, *To hell with it. What difference does it make?* The act of serving required no witnesses. If he ever did get near Birtles, the man was the sort to deny it. So he filed the papers with an affidavit saying that Birtles had been served. It was his word against Birtles's, and the court would always believe the process server. It was the sort of thing you could get away with once or twice, and scum like Birtles deserved no better. The papers went forward, and Jack had flown to Chicago to see about his father's will.

That should have been an end to the matter. But it kept coming back. Jack couldn't escape the feeling that he'd violated a profound principle, some elemental code. He'd allowed a small but brightly burning light inside himself to be snuffed out, some precept that divided him from people like Birtles. He wondered whether it was too late to return to England to put things right.

He shook his head, looking for an answer in the inky water just inches from his feet. A new breeze picked up off the river, bringing with it silt and animal odors, mud and carrion. Jack looked back and thought he saw a shadow flit under the Fabricio. He checked his watch. He looked again at the churning waters.

He was about to turn around and go back up the moss-carpeted steps to find Natalie when he felt a wind at his collar and a weighty, thudding impact in the small of his back. There was blurred movement at the periphery of his vision, and an extraordinary envelope of light surrounding him as, failing to keep his balance, he toppled headlong into the foaming Tiber.

TWENTY-THREE

LOUISE WAS HAVING DIFFICULTY WITH BILLY'S SLEEPING. HE WAS waking in the night, wailing, refusing to go back to sleep. And when he finally did sleep, the slightest noise would wake him. The sound of a siren in the Chicago night, the click of a closing door, the rattle of ice in Louise's vodka glass in the next room. Which is how Louise happened to be awake at 4 A.M. when the telephone rang. She was surprised to get a call from Rome.

"It's Natalie Shearer. We met briefly when you were in Rome with Jack Chambers."

"Sure, Natalie. What can I do for you?"

"I wondered if you'd heard from Jack recently."

"Not in a while. In fact, I called him in Rome a couple of times but I never got an answer."

"He kind of went missing over a week ago."

"Missing?"

"Yeah. He ran out on me one night. That's his business, but there are a lot of things to clear up. Like the house. Selling it. He said it all comes to me. I just don't know what to do about it."

156

"You haven't heard *anything* from Jack?"

"Don't rub it in, Louise. Haven't you ever had a man drop you like a hot brick?"

Louise heard Billy turn over in his cot and begin to cry. "Sure. But . . . Natalie, it's four in the morning here. Can I call you back?"

"Four in the morning? Why didn't you say so? Sorry. Do you want to take my number?"

Louise did so. Her first concern was to deal with Billy. Sleep training required her to return to him at timed intervals, to reassure him, but not to comfort him as a reward for screaming. She was certain he was having nightmares. She just couldn't think what material could be scraped together from his daily experiences to produce them. By day, he was a happy, confident, and advanced little kid cushioned by maternal love. But in the dark he generated demons.

Tim Chambers had told Louise that all civilization and progress was achieved by deflection of gratification. That through training, the human mind could withstand pain, conjure rare pleasures, and see the invisible. But that it all started with training in infancy for eating, sleeping, and defecating.

Louise knew that as a father he'd never been called upon to face a one-year-old in the dark, the child quivering with terror, eyes like liquid pools of need, mouth open, arms outstretched. And if he had, she conceded, he would have been heartless enough to study some Martian timetables and to close the door on the wailing child. She broke the rules, picked up Billy, and took him to her own bed.

Within moments, he was asleep in her arms, and she was thinking about Jack. The last time she'd spoken to him was the day he called her for reassurance that the old man was dead. She understood Jack thinking like that; it was the kind of stunt of which Tim Chambers was entirely capable. But she knew it was no trick this time. She'd been there. She'd called her own doctor. She'd laid him out herself. Washed him and laid him out, as they did in the old days. She'd forced herself to do this because she hadn't been able to shed a tear over him. A service offered in lieu of weeping.

Unlike Jack, Louise had never felt an obsessive need to find favor with Tim Chambers. In the intermittent periods when she, as a child, had spent any time with her father, she'd found him strict and intolerant, though he'd never done any unkind thing to her. He'd always provided her mother with enough money to make them comfortable, though Dory, like Jack's mother, had wanted nothing else to do with him.

Neither as a child nor as a woman had Louise ever felt any great warmth toward the man. She respected him, it was impossible not to; she occasionally admired him, as many people did. She just never *loved* him, either as a girl or as a woman. For many years she had thought that there was something wrong with her for failing to love her father fully.

But as Louise matured she realized that she'd never once seen her father bare what might be described as an open emotion. The coldness she felt was an infected chill passed on by him.

There was only one time when she saw him visibly moved. She was eleven years old and felt wonderfully adult when he persuaded Dory to let him take Louise to a classical concert at the Civic Opera House in Chicago. It was time, he said, for Louise to educate her finer feelings, to which only the condition of music could attend. Attired in evening dress himself, he not only took her to the concert but first he took her to Lord & Taylor and had her fitted in an evening gown and in sensational gloves reaching up to her elbows. He carried the bags from Lord & Taylor containing the discarded clothes in which her mother had dressed her for the evening.

She found a thrill that night in being escorted to the concert by her father. She intuited that he had brought her to the brink of life itself. She felt that her life would be transformed from that moment on.

Louise barely recalled anything of that evening beyond the entrance to the Opera House opposite the sleek twin towers of the Chicago Mercantile Exchange; that and the foyer full of concertgoers parading themselves before the commencement of the charitable event. She breathed something about the building, its scale and proportions, before they went in.

"Built by a shark," he had said to her. "Just remember that most American culture is underwritten by dirty money. Unfortunately, most of these people are here to be seen, not to listen to the music. But we won't let that spoil our evening, will we, Louise?"

Louise hadn't been about to let *anything* spoil her evening, not the least his obscure and un-American remarks. The concert itself passed in the unreal time of dreaming. Occasionally, Tim Chambers leaned across to whisper things she didn't understand. "The contralto, which you are hearing now, is superior to the female soprano. Why? Because, unlike the soprano, it does not live at the extremity of the range; its resonance is much deeper; and its shadows are therefore richer."

She nodded and compressed her lips and squinted slightly to savor the preferred riches of the contralto. She knew absolutely that the hidden and adult facts of life were being disclosed to her early, and that she must make a semblance of understanding lest greater treasures should be withheld. Then at some point during a contralto performance in Bach's *Saint Matthew Passion,* she looked up and saw her father's eyes were glittering wet. The track of a hot tear ran down his cheek.

"Why are you crying?" she whispered, horrified.

He turned and said, "Grief for sin, Louise." Then he turned back to the concert.

So maybe it had been exactly that, grief for sin, that had made her want to wash him and lay him out and prepare him for the undertaker when she was called to his deathbed that night. She'd had

159

no practice for this. After getting rid of the girl he'd been with, she'd just swung into action intuitively. She cleaned him and stripped the sheets. She'd sponged his body from head to toe. She'd closed his eyes and she'd folded his arms across his chest. It had been her way of saying good-bye. It was a tender act in place of love.

Love was something that came far more easily for Jack. She'd been anxious when he failed to contact her, but in one sense she'd let him go. She'd predicted this thing with Natalie would burn itself out quickly, and then maybe they could get on with the job of getting to know each other, sister and brother, late, but with enough time to build up the affection missing from other areas of her family life. She wanted a brother for herself. She wanted him for Billy, too.

Now that Natalie had reported him missing, she was baffled. It also disturbed her that Natalie had seemed more concerned about the house and the prospects of its sale than about the safety or whereabouts of Jack. Rome was a radiant city, but it cast a long shadow. Already she was regretting not staying with Jack. She felt he was naive. He was vulnerable. She had bad thoughts about Natalie Shearer.

Holding her sleeping son close to her, she fell asleep thinking about Rome, about Trajan arches silhouetted under a falling, thickening mauve light.

. . .

In the morning, Louise had other things to worry about. She was one of those women who can conduct two dozen part-time jobs simultaneously. For her, it was like spinning plates on sticks, and it was a matter of personal pride not to let anything crash. Thus she freelanced her organizational and administrative skills to various charitable and community organizations and to a number of campaign and political groups.

One involved working for the Chicago Architecture Foundation. The CAF had an office downtown and she had a meeting there at 10 A.M. She left Billy with his baby-sitter and drove across town, still thinking about Jack, and about her father. She recalled the time when Jack appeared from England all those years ago, and then just as suddenly went home.

"Why did Jack take off?" she'd asked her father.

"He didn't take off, my darling. I sent him away."

"Why? I didn't want him to go." She was just a kid; her views had never counted for anything.

"He disappointed us. English people can be so disappointing."

"But you're English!"

"How quick of you to remind me."

"But what did he do, Daddy?"

"Let's just say he didn't make the grade, and leave it at that."

But Louise, age eleven and no slouch, knew exactly what Jack had done to get himself sent home. He'd turned up one day wearing a pair of expensive Ray-Ban sunglasses, obviously without knowing how her father felt about people who wore sunglasses. Louise also knew who had given Jack those sunglasses. It had been Nick Chadbourne. Nick hadn't liked the fact that one particular girl, encouraged by Tim, had taken a shine to Jack. So Nick gifted the fancy sunglasses to Jack, knowing he would instantly lose favor with the old man. It had worked. Jack never knew how it happened. Nick Chadbourne was on the periphery of the crowd in those days, and the sunglasses were just one gift in a shower of gifts that Jack had been given. Jack had hardly noticed.

As she crossed the Chicago River, a lance of October sunlight bounced off her mirror and made her squint. She reached into the glove compartment for her own dark glasses and fumbled them on as she drove. But when she approached Roosevelt Road, she took them off again, flinging them aside, irritated. Because even though he was dead, and even though she'd never loved him, her father still had a way of controlling her.

. . .

"Look at that, Louise," her father had said, pointing at a towering church steeple. "Now tell me. What is architecture?"

Thirteen years old at the time, already experienced in how easy it was to give her father a disappointing answer and accustomed to avoiding the obvious, she paused and said, "Music in stone."

He'd frowned at that. "Don't try to be clever. Just tell me what you see."

"Use of space."

"More than that. It's not just the shape of the building. But the space *around* the building. What use is a church spire if it doesn't puncture the skyline? That's why they don't build spires like that in the cities anymore: no skyline. A building is as much about what you don't see as what you do see."

She squinted at him, not entirely understanding.

"One day," he said, "I'm going to take you to Rome. Then you really will understand about architecture."

That was one of the many promises he'd failed to fulfill. Nevertheless, he had succeeded in equipping her with a delight in architecture. It was why he loved Chicago. Though she never loved him, she always felt a curious tingle whenever she was with her father. There was unpredictability, a sense that the day could go in any direction.

He took her to look at 333 West Wacker Drive from across the river, a smooth curve of glass more than a hundred yards long breasting a bend of the Chicago River, and, inside, the spaceship Illinois Center, with its dazzling, dizzying mirrors and atriums and opaque glass.

She'd read something about the place. "What does postmodern mean?"

"Forget all that silly talk. Think how they managed to make light feel just like rain pattering on your face." It was always the quality of *light* he was after. "Light, Louise, light. A great building is one where technology and philosophy meet in a point of light. That is what we're after."

Many years later, he had secured her a position at the Chicago Architecture Foundation, a group that lobbied senators and local politicians to save valuable structures from demolition or destructive renovation. It had not escaped her that he had extended his obsession. He had successfully instilled in her a passion and a knowledge that would ensure her dedication to the cause of resisting the corporate vandalism that had already deprived Chicago of some of its architectural glories.

He had gotten his own way again.

TWENTY-FOUR

WHILE LOUISE SAT IN HER MEETING AT THE CAF FRETTING about Jack and worrying that the Greenslade Corporation was about to bulldoze an art deco palace, her cell phone rang and gave her a third reason for disquiet. It was the realtor charged with selling the apartment on Lake Shore Drive. An anxious tone in the woman's voice made Louise excuse herself from the meeting to take the call.

"It makes a poor impression," the realtor was saying. "I had a buyer lined up. When I took him by there yesterday he decided to keep looking."

"You're certain someone has been living there?"

"It was like the *Marie Celeste*, sweetie. A half-finished meal was on the table with a glass of wine. And one of the beds was unmade. After my buyer had gone I checked around for any signs of a forced entry. Nothing. It's someone with a key. You haven't been there yourself?"

"Not for a couple of weeks. And if I'd made dinner there, I'd re-member."

"Maybe you should have the locks changed."

"I'll deal with it."

"We lost our buyer over this, sweetie."

Louise cut the conversation short and returned to her meeting.

. . .

Later that morning, she drove over to the apartment to take a look for herself. The half-finished meal remained on the table as described, along with an untouched glass of Chardonnay. The bottle stood beside the glass and a fork had bayoneted a greasy twist of noodles. A dirty sauté pan lay on the counter in the kitchen.

In one of the spare bedrooms, the duvet cover had been cast aside. There was still an indentation in the pillow. Picking up the pillow, Louise pressed it to her face, inhaling. Whatever clue she had hoped to scent in the pillow just wasn't there. She tossed it back, straightened the duvet cover, and returned to the kitchen to clear away the debris of the unfinished meal. Otherwise, the immaculate order of the apartment remained undisturbed. Even a forensic team would have failed to find further information.

Since Jack had cleared out all her father's personal effects, the apartment had a chill about it. Tim Chambers's presence still lingered, in the way a strange odor will persist even when masked by antiseptic or floral sprays. Otherwise, the place was clinically dead, and sterile. The paintings on the walls had a collapsed air, like work hanging in a gallery during the dismantling of an exhibition. Louise stood before the Chadbourne pictures, the sequence entitled *Invisibility*, and decided to salvage one of them. There were plenty of paintings in the otherwise cleared junk room with which to replace it. She chose a daubed offering of the same dimensions and hung it in place of the painting she'd chosen.

Before leaving, she left a note on the kitchen counter. It said simply, "Why don't you call me?" Then she let herself out.

. . .

In the afternoon, Louise placed a call to Rome. Alfredo was astonished and delighted to hear from her. He looked forward to her next visit, he cooed. He'd already decided which restaurant he was going to take her to.

"Might be a while before I get back to Rome, Alfredo."

"Then I wait." He thought she'd called to ask about progress with the sale of the house in Rome, since Jack hadn't called. Things were progressing, but slowly. Only one viewer.

"I'm not concerned with that. It's about Jack. He went missing in Rome."

"Missing?"

"Well, you remember Natalie? The night we went out together?"

Alfredo used an expression that meant you were expecting wine but you got vinegar. "The unforgettable Natalie."

"That's right, the unforgettable Natalie. She said he disappeared. Just like that. Would you do me a favor? Find out if he's still living at the house? Find out anything you can?"

"I'll stop by on my way home from work this evening."

"Alfredo, you are a sweet, sweet man."

"You know," Alfredo said, "you Americans are all charm."

. . .

After speaking with Alfredo, Louise picked up Billy from the day-care center. Mrs. Lincoln, the woman in charge, beamed on handing him over and said, "He slept the entire time!" Louise, herself exhausted by nights of sleep training, resisted a disgraceful impulse to slap her. But at the handoff, Billy woke up and gave her a thousand-watt smile.

Back home, while Billy emptied a pot of spices onto the rug, Louise switched on her computer and drafted a plan for trying to save the art deco palace on North Michigan Avenue from demolition.

· · ·

Her father had once asked, "What will you study at university, Louise? Architecture or philosophy?"

Even then she'd had a crystalline intuition of how important it was to resist this man or else risk being absorbed by him entirely. Louise had replied, instantly and decisively, "Social sciences."

There was no further discussion, but she learned that day how effortlessly a father's blank expression can cross a galaxy of space.

When she tumbled out of the University of Wisconsin with a degree during a major recession, when everyone was downsizing, Tim secured her a temporary job with the Historical Buildings Institute out east; and even though she took other work in between, that first connection almost inexorably led to her picking up work with the Chicago Architecture Foundation. There, her enthusiasm and ability, plus her extraordinary skill at working a room full of people, counted for everything. Tim Chambers had eventually gotten his way, and here she was, looking after Chicago's best buildings.

Chambers knew better than to gloat, but he did advise her usefully. "You're going to the Tailtwisters luncheon. The senator always drinks too much at these charity events, and he's a pushover for a good pair of legs."

"Dad, please."

"Plus he's a Packers fan and likes Steinbeck."

"Dad, I don't work that way." But she brushed up on the Packers' statistics, polished off a book of essays on *The Grapes of Wrath*, and wore a feverishly short cocktail dress. Just one lunch—at which the senator and his three businessmen cronies scrambled to stand next to her—and a turn-of-the-century Burnham skyscraper got a miraculous reprieve and restoration. Louise found it corruptingly simple to manipulate people. It gave her an insight into how her father operated.

When Louise had finished drafting her plans, she got up from the computer and went to the window of her apartment, looking across the city. Dusk was pouring in fast, purple shadows and sable pools fattening, pinprick lights going on everywhere. Darkness in this city tended to spread like fire, licking first at the corners of buildings, forming links between shadows before accomplishing surprising leaps, until it was finally out of hand, running everywhere horizontally and vertically, and it would rage until morning.

Louise gazed out into the swirling, slow-falling twilight. Held at bay by the neon and the sodium vapor and the albedo glare of city lights, the sky crumpled and rolled some shade between blue and violet. She thought about Jack. She wondered if he was all right. She hoped he hadn't joined the hunt for the fugitive Indigo.

TWENTY-FIVE

I intend to show you how to convert Cloud into Smoke. The intuitive amongst you will already have guessed that this property of Smoke is what you will eventually hide behind in order to make yourself appear invisible. The conversion of Cloud into Smoke is a tedious process but not a difficult one. The accumulation of the fine mist evinced on the mirror in your blacklight box will continue, but you need to develop some faculties of perception in order to make this conversion. This process involves, again, exercising your eyes.

It is extraordinary just how many people, especially the young, are terrified of the light. I have a notion that they are really afraid of seeing, as if contemplation of what actually lies before their eyes—too much reality—is too awful a prospect. Witness the craze over the latter half of this century for wearing black sunglasses. It is inconceivable to me how these black goggles—once the emblem of the blind or the mark of the diseased man—have become a fashion accessory considered chic and sexy. (This weird habit developed after a false alert emerged in medical circles. The scare concerned exposure to UV radiation in ordinary sunlight, though when the medical alert proved false it had already been exploited by vendors of opaque glass and cheap spectacle

169

frames. So prevalent is the craze that I regularly see young men and women, in Rome or in Chicago, wearing outlandish dark glasses not only on the beach but indoors or at dusk.)

It hardly needs stating, but this vapid penchant for black goggles is, contrary to the advantage it was once supposed to afford, decidedly harmful to the human eye. The more frequently goggles are worn, the weaker vision becomes, and the more the eyes in turn begin to need genuine protection from the light.

The chromatic brilliance of our day-to-day experience is Nature's greatest gift. Anyone wanting to dull that gift, opting instead for a grey or sepia demiworld, is barbarous and beneath contempt. Why would any-one want to muddy the organ of light? I cannot abide giddiness and will not tolerate such a person in my company for a single second.

Strong light is not harmful. Neither is bright sunlight, so long as we do not spend the day staring directly into it. On the other hand, we can retrain the eye to enjoy the rewards of bright sunshine by the practical technique of Sunning.

First, to develop confidence, close your eyes, relax, employ the breathing exercises I have described elsewhere, and turn yourself toward the sun. Feel the sun on your eyelids, but avoid internal staring. you will notice that you are flooded not with the impression of black-ness, as with palming, but with redness. This is because the light is be-ing filtered by the blood behind your eyelids. In order to avoid exposing any particular part of the retina, you should swing your head gently but decisively to left and right. Move your head from side to side a few inches and keep this up. In this way, the closed eyelids may be sunned for five minutes at a time. Repeat the process several times a day.

You will soon be able to take the sunlight directly upon the eye. Cov-ering one eye with the palm of the hand, you should open the other eye, continuing to swing the head as before but letting the open eye travel to and fro across the face of the sun three times. Then cover the exposed eye and repeat with the other. Leave each eye exposed for one minute only.

Now, pick up a bone spatula, pull down the lower eyelid, and insert the spatula under the eyeball to effectively scrape the humor or fluid from around the eyeball. (This technique is described by Sir Isaac Newton in his research on optics and light, though he was extreme in its application.) You need to press down hard, with the spatula, on the cheekbone below the eye to effect a good scrape.

Your vision will suffer from afterimages, which you will try to blink away. Don't. If these are very uncomfortable, then palming the eye will make them disappear. But for the moment, tolerate them if you can. Newton described these afterimages as concentric circles, though I tend to see them as fuzzy parabolas. When these afterimages have disappeared naturally, you will be astonished at how refreshed your eyes feel. You will be even more astounded at how fresh is your field of vision. The world has benefited from a good rinse in sunlight.

(Exposing the eye to a long series of photoflashes will also produce spectacular results. Those advanced in the techniques of Sunning sometimes use the flash effect of the industrial welding torch to short-circuit or speed up the effects. I do not recommend this unless you have actually spent considerable time developing your exposure to light; otherwise, you are more likely to experience the unpleasant sensation of grittiness in the eye produced by the brilliant arc of the torch.)

After a few weeks of practicing this exercise, you will notice the results transferred to your experiments in the blacklight box. The phenomenon of vision is produced by radiant energy. What you have been doing is developing your capacity for receiving, interpreting, and discriminating among the forms of that radiant energy.

Consequently, you will notice an increase in the density of the property of Cloud, and in the mist forming on your mirror. Repeat the Sunning experiments, substituting the UV light for the direct sunshine, and you will experience a mucus-like thickening of the afterimage; and as that afterimage recedes you will notice that it takes a spiral form and begins, very slowly, while commingling with the property of Cloud, to spin.

The speed of this spin is extraordinarily slow; but it is quite unmistakable. While your afterimage thins, the condition of Cloud will perforce thicken. Congratulations. You have begun, for the very first time, to form out of optical and mental power the necessary condition of Smoke.

TWENTY-SIX

IN THE MIDDLE OF THE NIGHT, THE PHONE RANG AGAIN. LOUISE WAS dozing, groggy, having only manged to get Billy back to sleep half an hour earlier. This time the call wasn't from Rome; or Louise suspected it wasn't, supposing that people tend not to make nuisance calls at such long distance. No one spoke, there was no breathing, but Louise knew someone was on the other end of the line. "You can talk to me," she said after a whkile. "You can always talk to me."

No answer came, but Louise hung on anyway. After a while, she said, "I'm still here," but soon the line went dead. She replaced the receiver and went back to sleep.

Some hours later, the telephone hauled her out of sleep again. This time the answering machine kicked in before she reached for the phone, and she heard Alfredo calling from Rome.

"Louise! You were screening. I didn't call at a bad time? It's late afternoon here."

She blinked at her watch. Her mouth felt sticky. "No. It's not a bad time. Thanks for calling—did you find out something?"

"I drop by your father's house yesterday evening, as I promise. You know how it is to find somewhere for park, so I park in the next street and walk. When I get to the house the door is already open. Opera music playing *very* loud, Louise. I go inside and I smell cooking from the kitchen, and I think, ah, Louise's brother must be back. But then I hear voices coming from the kitchen. Arguing.

"From the recess in the hallway I can see through to the kitchen. Well, hello, it is our friend Natalie. She is arguing very strong with two young men, like hippies, Louise, dirty hippies or something like that. You know the kind? But I can't hear what they say because the music is so loud. Puccini frightening your ears. Now Natalie throws a pan full of sauce at one of them, hot sauce I think, it hits him and spills on his arm. He wants to kill Natalie, but the other one pulls him back. Some more words, then the boys leave.

"And here is the amazing thing. They walk right by me without seeing me. Sure, I stand in the recess, in the shadow a little, and they come full-face toward me but they don't see me, and then they are gone. Natalie is banging pots in the kitchen, shouting, and—Louise, she is a foul-mouthed woman, completely foul—then she comes out of the kitchen, exactly the same, directly toward me, fails to see me, then I hear her go bang bang bang up the stairs. But she stops halfway. Are you still there?"

"I'm still here," said Louise.

"Slowly, very slowly, she retraces her steps, descending, then back along the corridor to look at me a second time. 'What the fuck are you doing here?' she says to me. Well, I respond in formal Italian, because, excuse me, if I'm going to scream with someone I prefer to do it in my own tongue. So I say, 'I might ask you the same question.' 'This is my house,' she says. 'No, it's not, and I'm trying to sell it dah dah dah.' Well, half an hour of this and finally she leaves, but before she does I ask about Jack."

"Did she tell you anything?" Louise tried to cut through Alfredo's excited account.

"Natalie shuts up when I ask about Jack. She goes quiet. Looking at me, very strange. 'Why you ask me about Jack?' she says.

'Well, you're his lover, *si*?' 'Fuck you,' she says. 'And fuck you,' I say. Then she smiles, very nasty, and she says, 'Jack has gone over.' 'Over? Over where?' Then, 'Are you going to get out of my house?' 'Madam, it's not your house and I'm getting the *carabinieri* to take a look at this little pot of stew.' Well, that's it, Louise, more filth, more shouting, a mouth like a Sicilian whore, that one, then she pushes past me and leaps on her scooter, rrrrm rrrm, and I'm standing on the doorstep in a cloud of Vespa smoke. What can I say?"

Louise sighed into the receiver. "What can you say, indeed?"

"What a bitch, huh?"

"Quite."

"But you know Louise, I need to speak to Jack, to ask him what he wants me to do. I mean, all these people shouldn't be in this house. Do I involve the police?"

"I don't know what to say to you, Alfredo. You should do what you normally do in these circumstances. But we still don't have any idea about Jack."

"That's right, we don't." There followed an international silence, until Alfredo perked up and said, "So tell me, next time you're in Rome, where do you want to go?"

. . .

"What do I care if he's gone missing in Rome? What the hell does he have to do with me? What the hell does he even have to do with you? You concentrate on lookin' after your own," Dory said, jabbing a finger at Billy.

Dory cut a couple of wedges of her mother's-own apple pie and offered it on plates, along with all of this advice, first to Louise and then to Billy. Louise accepted her plate but couldn't help wincing, just slightly. It was the strangest looking apple pie, collapsed into a pool of stewed fruit, the pastry ballooned on one side and burned on the other. Billy tried a piece and blew it halfway across the room with a rasping of his little tongue.

"He already ate something in the car on the way here," Louise lied. "He's not hungry."

"Maybe he just doesn't like my pies." Dory leaned forward slightly, a dangerous gleam in her eye.

"Nah. He's just not hungry." She bit into her own slice of pie, and its tartness made her eyelids flutter.

Dory leaned back. "You are *such* a bad liar, Louise. Such a bad liar."

"Really?" Louise lay down her plate. "Okay. I'll come clean, Mom. Your pies are disgusting. In fact, all your cooking is sensationally bad. For about the last twenty-five years I've been meaning to ask you: How come your cooking is so spectacularly awful?"

Dory scratched her head, hardly offended. "Wasn't always this bad. But your father was such a picky eater. Then when things got real rotten I used to think about poisoning him. Not that I ever would have. I just used to *think* poison into the cooking, you know? Think it in. Every single mealtime. Even long after he'd gone I couldn't boil an egg without thinking angry thoughts about him. Maybe that's what happens."

"Mom, you must have loved him once. There must have been qualities in him that drew you to him."

"Oh, there were. I just forget what they are."

"You took a honeymoon in Rome. Can you remember that?"

Dory looked at Billy molding his pie into a sticky ball. "He sleeping nights any better?"

"No. He sleeps on and off through the day because he's so exhausted. It's as if he fights it. As if he's afraid to go to sleep at night."

"Looks more like that guy than you." Louise had dragged Billy's father up to Madison a couple of times.

Louise searched Billy's face, looking for buried features. "Yep. he does. You know, one day you're going to have to tell me what that man did to you."

176

Dory sighed. "It's more what he *might* have done. I kind of saw what was ahead, and I got you out and I got me out, and if it hadn't been for the courts and his monthly checks he'd never have seen you again.

"If your father had ever raised his fist to beat me, it would be easier to tell you. But he was never violent. I sensed he had a lot of violence in him, but he didn't work that way. Do you know he wouldn't let me choose a single piece of clothing for myself? That's how controlling he was. One day I met him in downtown Chicago. Beautiful sunny day. I'd bought a really cool, expensive new pair of sunglasses, and as we were crossing the bridge he grabbed them off my face and tossed 'em in the Chicago River. We'd been married six months, and the only bells I could hear by then, honey, weren't coming from the church. He would do things just to get me pissed off at him. And then he would play with me.

"This stuff went on for too long. There were lots of things he tried to get me to do, and I just don't want to talk about it. One time there was this guy from the crowd we used to drink with at the old Rendez-Vous. He had the hots for me and your father wanted me to bring him home and get it on with him in the bedroom while he watched from inside the closet. That's how he was. It was part of some big plan.

"But what really made me run was when I caught him starting in on you. He liked to manipulate and control everyone around him. Manipulate and control. He studied it, for Chrissakes. When your behavior started to change, I couldn't figure out why. You were about the same age as Billy is now, just starting to talk. I got back from someplace a little early, at that apartment we used to have over on Dearborn Street. He was playing with you all nice, with a ball and cookies and stuff. I was sneaking up to give you both a hug from behind, you know, then I stopped because there was something weird about what he was doing. You reached out for this

177

bright blue ball with your right hand, and he slapped your hand, very hard. You wailed. Then he put your left hand on the ball, and give you a hug and a cookie. Then he said, "Take the ball, Louise!" You reached out again with your right, and he slapped you and repeated this thing again. I watched with my mouth open. The motherfucker was trying to train you to be left-handed! He was experimenting on you, Louise! Like some barbaric thing people used to do to get left-handed kids to use their right hands; but he was reversing it. On you. For curiosity.

"Did he jump when I came up behind him. He denied it, of course. Tried to tell me I was crazy. But I was on to him and lots of things fell into place. Funny things going on with our friends, his art circle, all kooky stuff. I knew I had to get you out, and I started legal proceedings. He was evil when he found out. I'm only telling you half of it, Louise, because half is enough."

"I'm a big girl, Mom. I can take it."

"But I can't."

There was a silence in which Louise saw Dory's eyes swivel briefly toward the corners of their sockets. A stranger would have missed it, but not Louise. She knew Dory was an epileptic, a condition held in check by carbamazepine pills. She recognized all the tiny indicators, the flickers and the nuances behind the carbamazepine, gone almost the moment they arrived.

A new line had been drawn, and Louise knew not to try to cross it. Dory had already gone further than ever before in discussing Timothy Chambers. "I guess I was hoping for some clue," Louise said, "about what Jack might have gotten mixed up in."

"Can't help you there. Rome was where we spent our honeymoon, and I've managed to forget almost everything about it."

Louise reluctantly took another forkful of apple pie and shuddered. "Really, Mom, how do you make this taste so bad?"

TWENTY-SEVEN

TWO DAYS AFTER VISITING DORY IN MADISON, LOUISE WAS BACK in Chicago, driving down Jackson Street after a lunch date with a friend, when she passed the Chicago Board of Trade: a 1930s vertical thrust trailing a financial rocketburst the length of La Salle Street. A couple of pit traders still in their lightweight acid-lemon jackets were leaving the building in a hurry. She couldn't see those sporting colors, or even pass by the grand building, without triggering the memory of one of her father's sermons.

"Your mother told you about sex yet?" This was what Chambers had said to her one afternoon before ferrying her back to Madison. Louise was thirteen at the time.

"Sure," Louise insisted. In reality, she'd picked up a couple of clues from Dory, plus a few weird stories from her friends, and that limited information amounted to more than anything she wanted to hear from her father on the subject.

"Everything?"

"Everything." The important thing had been to remain cool and convey the impression that it would be too tedious to cover all this again.

179

"What kind of things?"

Louise waved a jaded thirteen-year-old hand through the air. "Cunnilingus. Horatio. Everything."

Chambers had smiled. "Seems like you've got all the mechanics covered. But what about the invisible?"

"Huh?"

"You mean your mother never told you about the invisible thing?"

"Huh?"

"Looks like I'm going to have to tell you about that. I'll swing the car around. We need to go to the Board of Trade."

Louise assumed her father meant that he'd forgotten something, and that they needed to visit the Board of Trade before he was going to spill the excruciatingly embarrassing jumping beans about invisible sex. They'd been inside the forty-five-story skyscraper together before, and she'd learned the gospel of art deco from the Holy Trinity of its three-story lobby. Also unveiled to her at that time was the bedlam of the trading floor, though she never understood how the bawling and screaming and ticket-tearing functioned as trade. On that particular day, however, Chambers took her directly to the observation gallery to gaze down on the activities of the futures traders.

Chambers was a patient explainer. He saw it as his duty to interpret the world for her. Nothing came unmediated by his particular vision, and nothing, he told her frequently, was what it seemed on the surface. "Do you remember how I explained cricket to you?"

She nodded. She remembered indeed. Louise figured she was the only teenage girl in the United States who understood the arcane laws of English cricket. She was also probably the only teenage girl, whether in the United States or the cricket-playing counties of

England, who understood that the game was not actually a sport but a rehearsal for life. Life pitched obstacles your way, sometimes fast and sometimes spinning and it was up to you to defend your honor, dignity, and integrity (the reason for three stumps in a wicket, Chambers had explained) with a straight bat. If you took your eye off one for a second, or played the other carelessly, you lost.

"What you see here is similar to cricket," he said, "minus the honesty, integrity, and dignity. Especially the dignity."

"But this isn't a game!" she protested.

"Oh yes it is. They look like wolves, don't they? But while it seems like chaos to you, it is actually tightly controlled. This is called the pit. The men are trading in futures. Let's say they're selling wheat. That means they are selling it now, even though the price might change in the future. If they stand in a certain place—look—that means the month the wheat has to be delivered. Between now and then there might be too much rain, or not enough rain. You don't know. By the time the delivery month comes around, the value of your wheat might have gone up or down.

"That man with the palm of his hand facing out is selling; palm-in is buying. What they're screaming to each other is the quantity and the price, *now*. Some of these men will take a risk. Some of them are scared by risks they've already taken, and are trying to offload the risk onto other people."

After outlining a few more conventions of the trading floor, he turned to Louise and said, "There you have it. Same with sex." Then he looked at his watch and said, "Come on. We have to get back to Madison."

The three-hour drive seemed longer than usual and was conducted mostly in silence. Louise knew from experience that if she didn't ask, nothing more would be said. But she was burning with

181

curiosity, and it was not until they swung off the freeway that she said, "I don't get it! How is it like sex?"

Chambers was startled by the outburst. His mind had obviously moved on a long way. "How is what like sex?"

"The pit! The trading floor!"

"Did I say that? Right. Did you see all those men and women kicking and screaming and signaling in the pit? Now imagine any group of people dining together or having a party or social occasion. Inside, they are shouting and screaming and signaling like those folks in the pit, but the rules are that they can't show it. They have to keep almost perfectly still. Deep down, all that ravening chaos is still going on, but it's now invisible. You have to look for it in tiny signs. Raised eyebrows. Half-smiles. Fluttered eyelashes. Tiny flickers. Underneath, they're all dancing in the pit, selling themselves, understand me? Inside every one of them, the pit is raging."

Not understanding at all, Louise looked back at her father with horror and fascination. Then he leaned across her to open the passenger door. "Off you go," he said. "Your mother gets difficult if you're late."

. . .

Something in these memories made Louise turn the car around and return to the apartment on Lake Shore Drive. This time there was no half-finished meal and no slept-in-bed; but she knew someone had been there because her note had been removed.

It was something she'd tried to avoid doing these past few months, but instead of driving home she gave in to an old compulsion and turned southwest, heading for the old Mexican neighborhood of Little Village and beyond. There, she cruised her car slowly for more than two hours, going as far beyond Little Village as the city limits, and returning to cruise around Douglas Park.

Nothing. She was hit by a sudden wave of exhaustion and hopelessness. Her search would have to continue, as usual.

Louise stopped the car near Douglas Park, locked the doors, and surrendered to a fit of weeping. By the time she was cried out, dusk was falling like violet soot. She felt uncomfortable spending any more time in that neighborhood, so she drove back to Hyde Park, picked up Billy, and went home.

Dory called her that evening. "You asked me if I could remember anything about Rome. I've been thinking about it. He used to get fixed on certain buildings and places, you know? The Pantheon, primarily. Because it had a hole in the roof, he used to go there all the time and look up at the changing sky. He said a person could disappear from the Pantheon. Make themselves invisible. I stopped listening after a while; as you do. He also talked about a building in Chicago in the same terms. It made me think of this Jack disappearing. Oh, forget it, it makes no sense."

"No, it doesn't, Mom."

"So that bum still hasn't turned up yet?"

"No, Mom."

"So, big deal. How's my grandson?"

TWENTY-EIGHT

MOOCHER'S ON GRAND AVENUE WAS ROONEY'S SECOND-FAVORITE hangout for the close study of nude girls. A lot of men might have found the South Side location of Moocher's a little intimidating. But then Rooney wasn't like a lot of men. For one thing, he projected his excess weight forward, like a bull, rather than rolling it downward in the manner of many Americans, and this offered an impression of aggressive confidence. Second, he was a genuine gourmet when it came to Chicago's "exotic" dance halls, and he knew, as every connoisseur or collector does, that the rare, the unusual, and the mysterious are not to be found by staying at home.

As a customer, he was discerning and demanding. Unlike most patrons of these exhibitions, he kept up a critical review, most of which was barked at the performers over a bottle of beer. If he thought he was getting good value for his money, he would express his satisfaction in his silence.

If not, Rooney was known to bellow, "This is not a life-drawing class! Do you see Degas before you? I'm laying out ten fucking dollars a beer for this?" In a quiet room with sometimes only two or three other customers, such a critique could be quite distracting for the performer, who would sometimes be stupid enough to try to take Rooney on in a verbal spat that could only produce one winner.

Rooney sorely lamented the degeneration of the stripper's art. He recalled performers who could whip up a tempest of lust and expectation in the slow, sinuous peeling away of extraordinary lingerie. All that had been replaced by a depressing near-nude starting point and full revelation two minutes into the performance. On the other hand, he detested the lap dance and G-string culture, and any coy routine in which lights dimmed and the stripper exited stage left before revealing herself.

"Lady's gotta show!" he would stand up and bawl. "Don't count for nothin' if the lady don't *show!*"

Moocher's, on the other hand, was never a disappointment. It was owned by a Sicilian, Gianfranco, who ran an orderly club, and Rooney never once felt obliged to heckle. Rooney was habitually made very welcome. He and Gianfranco, another connoisseur of the skin trade, would sit, backs turned on the shimmying efforts of whichever girl happened to be on stage, passing information about the girls they'd seen recently, like two crusty philatelists thrilling each other with descriptions of the watermarks on a rare Penny Black. Both men agreed they could happily burn out their retinas sunning their eyes on naked women.

Take the girl dancing at Moocher's at that precise moment. A Puerto Rican water goddess—now where had Gianfranco found her? That was talent. What feathery physique! What fluid bone structure! Heck, the face wasn't worth going to war for, she wasn't Helen of Troy, but she had anatomy that ran like a sparkling river.

Classical form, fair carriage, catwalk elegance, centerfold proportions: None of these things particularly interested Rooney. He came armed with his own system of classification, an irregular taxonomy for what made a great nude dancer, a system subdividing into the properties of tone, light, and heft.

Tone related to the condition of the skin, in that Rooney was a great believer in the principle that what was on the surface was all he wanted. He didn't buy the notion that the external was a visible sign of the inner condition, and he didn't give a damn whether the dancing girl had brains, personality, or a declared interest in world peace. Skin blemishes, slack flesh, or an unhealthy looking dermis therefore disappointed him; moles, birthmarks, prominent veins, or underarm hair, on the other hand, he regarded as exciting enhancements. Good tone suggested an almost invisible bloom, such as appears on the autumnal grape or plum. Take this girl: Her skin radiated a delicate glow, even under the colored crossbeams of Moocher's lazy staging, which in turn triggered the desirable property of light.

Light cascaded from the girl like phosphorescent spring water. It fizzed from her shoulders. It foamed down the hollow of her spine, sparkled over the hemispheres of her butt, and winked out in the cleft before flash-flooding the descending slope of the girl's thighs. The play between the light of her flanks and the dark of her cavities was as invigorating as ozone.

But these factors counted for little without proper heft. If a girl was too light on her feet, she failed to ground her erotic power; too heavy and she couldn't spark it; too nervy in her movements and she discharged it; too quick and she dropped it; too slow and—well, Rooney wished that some of these so-called exotic dancers would get other jobs. Proper heft was something a girl was born with.

"Look at that," Rooney muttered to himself or to anyone else who was listening as he attended to the girl on stage. "Fucking Chippendale couldn't carve a leg like that."

There was even a fourth quality he was after, though Rooney

felt less confident in talking about this. He thought of it as a kind of inner radiance or magnetism, but it confused him and he wasn't sure whether it more properly related to his sense of smell. That dancing girl had to *generate,* and the property she had to generate was mysterious. Perhaps it was merely pheromones, maybe it was plain simple odor, he didn't know. But a dancer couldn't fake it. She had to be enjoying herself. She had to want to be there, giving it out.

Sadly, the Puerto Rican performer on stage at Moocher's, after scoring spectacularly on three counts, was not giving it off. It was a pity, Rooney thought sadly, that some of these young girls lacked instinct. She was up there maybe thinking about what she was going to have for supper, or where she was going to get her car fixed.

Rooney took a slurp of beer. He had a notion that one day he would see and recognize instantly the perfect nude dancer. All four qualities would align like planets, and he would *know,* and in unnecessary confirmation of the event a G-string would be removed and there would be an intense burst of magnesium light followed by an array of colors—gold, silver, maybe even some color he'd never seen before—and he would be ready to make all his assets— and these were surprising and considerable—available to the extraordinary creature concerned in an honest offer of marriage, an offer she would be unable to resist, even to a fat fuck like him.

Yet before the girl on stage shimmied and pouted and stepped out of her G-string, he knew she wasn't it. And at the same time as she did so, Rooney sensed a shadow at his back, and lost interest in what was happening on stage enough to turn and raise an eyebrow at the familiar man standing behind him.

"Thought I'd find you here," said the man.

"Hey!" said Rooney. "Look what the cat dragged in. Sit down. Have a beer. Watch the girls."

TWENTY-NINE

Darkness is a most misunderstood concept. Already you have succeeded in producing what I have called Smoke out of thin air. This is
nothing compared with what is to come. But in order to put your Smoke
to effect, you need insight into the alchemical properties of darkness.

You have not been so stupid or so shortsighted as to try to shortcut
any of the practices divulged here. Because from this point on the game
becomes dangerous. Those who have passed this way before you have
left behind them a mantra, almost a chant, indicating the danger for any
of you who might risk setting foot off the path.

> *Darkness is the wolf.*
> *The wolf is Indigo.*
> *Indigo runs to Void.*

Consider my instructions to be a shining path, a pencil-beam of light
to carry you through the dark and safely over the abyss. Don't deviate an
inch to the right or to the left. Should anyone try to tempt you from this
path, they may have been sent.

By now you will be seeing, on almost a daily basis, an imprecise movement at the periphery of your vision. You will have entertained the sense of something stalking you, and you will have turned around many times only to see it dissolve before you are able to define its character.

Your nostrils will have been alerted during these times to an elusive scent, strikingly familiar and yet simultaneously new; you will almost not believe me when I tell you that it is indeed the scent of your own glands, the activity of which has been subtly altered by your adherence to the exercises. I concede that this scent does seem like an external presence. Your ears, too, will have turned to try to detect a disconcerting sound, of panting breath, maybe; of padding paws, perhaps; of a low growl, for instance. But it is still indefinable. Because we have no words, no suitable language for this new presence, you will forgive me if I refer to it as the Wolf.

Be assured that the Wolf is not about to leap. As I say, it is a figure of speech. At the moment, the Wolf cannot be seen, but from now on it is always present. Before you are able to see the Wolf, such as it is available to be seen, you must first be equipped to see the colour Indigo, for that is the Wolf's true colour; and before you can see the colour Indigo, you must know how to manipulate darkness.

Darkness, and its attendant properties of shade, shadow, silhouette, adumbration, and the like, are all the allies you need in your sorcery. Twilight, as you will see, is the crack between worlds. Similarly the grey light of dawn. The instruments of darkness, however, may be unfamiliar in your hands, and improperly understood.

Consider the shadow. Most people, if asked to draw a figure of a person or a house or some other object and then asked to draw its shadow, would dip their brush in india ink, or in black paint. Though they have seen a thousand thousand shadows in their lifetime, they have failed to use their eyes, and will fail in their visual representation of shadow. They do not easily see, as an artist does, that just as a hue is a colour tint plus white, a shade is a colour tint plus black. That is the meaning of the word 'shade'. Darkness is a universe away from true blackness. Be grateful that you have never experienced the latter.

Darkness admits a hundred discriminations. For this reason, it is possible to see in the dark. This is the next step in your optical training, to be able to get along quite happily in the dark.

In order to do so, you must foster the notion of Unconscious Vision. That is to say that the eye reacts, on an everyday basis, to a mass of data, much of which is filtered out before reaching the brain to avoid sensory overload. Nevertheless, the binary switch of registration has been tripped. That surplus information is available. In times of stress or danger, the nervous system will offer a reflex reaction before the source of stress or danger has been apprehended by the mind. I myself have pulled back my hand from a rock, only to see afterwards that I was about to place it on a live scorpion. The eye is capable of registering and processing information that the mind may or may not have need of a split second later.

Often, I have seen people, either in the busy high street or in the open countryside, deep in conversation, utterly abstracted. Yet they negotiate their way around traffic or across rough terrain. How? They have given themselves over to Unconscious Vision.

In the jungles of Borneo, I found myself with a small group of tribesmen and in a position of some danger. We were in a place where we should not have been, and we had to move very quickly to avoid being taken by other tribesmen hostile to my guides. It was dead of night. There was no moon. The paths were overgrown and ran alongside plunging chasms of more than three hundred feet. We had to run.

I was slowing my guides down by blundering into trees, and stumbling over roots and rocks strewn in my path. I was in fear of injuring myself, and eventually my fear threatened to paralyze me. The oldest man amongst my warrior-guides jerked me to my feet. He saved me by telling me not to look at the path in front of me, but to swing my eyes back and

190

forth, switching focus to anything but the path. At first I couldn't see what he meant, but he forced me to focus on the back of his tattooed hand in front of my face. He ran ahead and I followed, with him moving his hand to and fro in a curious waving motion. I got the idea, and we picked up speed. By shifting my vision across the darkness, I began to trust a new reflex. In this way, we escaped the attentions of the head-hunters, who were in full pursuit.

The point of this story is to tell you that before I discovered how to see in the dark, I had been *looking too hard*.

In order to develop the powers of Unconscious Vision, you must pro-ceed now with a final exercise, that of Trawling, which is the opposite of staring. Staring itself is the least productive of all visual activity, since it produces tension around the organ of sight and inevitable loss of focus. Trawling, on the other hand, increases the collection of visual data a thousandfold.

Most people, when regarding an object, will gaze fixedly until forced by strain to look away. Trawling requires you to break that object, that face, that figure into a number of discrete points, in much the same way as an image on a computer screen is divided into pixels. You should allow the eye to dart back and forth at random, never permitting it to settle. This shifting of the eye feels uncomfortable at first, but it soon becomes second nature. Test yourself by looking away from the object in question and calling to mind its features. You will astonish yourself with the amount of data you have absorbed by using this tech-nique.

To practice Trawling I recommend works of art—sculpture and paint-ings in a gallery—or architecture. All these are objects of concentrated focus, and as such they store massive amounts of information to yield up to the eye, much of which is hidden or buried deep in the form.

Be prepared for a flood of such information. It may take you by sur-prise.

Be prepared also to find, after some time spent on the faithful application of this exercise, surprising things in the darkness. Have not your eyes been made new, stripped of layers of scale, peeled, husked, rinsed in the dew of a glorious new world? Then you are ready to see a new colour. The elusive Indigo. It waits in the darkness. It was there all the time.

THIRTY

LOUISE PACED THE ARABESQUE FLOOR OF THE THOMSON CENTER, checking her watch again. If whoever was coming didn't show in the next five minutes, she was out of there. She wasn't even sure why she had agreed to this meeting; she didn't even know with *whom* she'd agreed to meet.

A call had come to her home that morning. The caller had a strangled Chicago accent she didn't recognize. "Miss Durrell, can you be at the Thomson this afternoon at four-thirty?"

"Why would I want to be?"

"I don't know why, Miss Durrell. I've just been instructed to ask you and I'm asking."

"So who are you?"

"I'm just me. Now I've asked you and that's that. If you don't go, well, that's up to you."

"Wait a minute. You mean I should go to the Thomson to meet someone?"

"I didn't mean you should go to look at all the glass."

"Okay, who? Who wants to meet?"

"Bye-bye."

And that was it. She had a pretty clear idea who was behind the call. She had, after all, left a note at the apartment on Lake Shore Drive. Maybe he'd even seen her cruising the Little Village neighborhood that day. Though she couldn't understand why he hadn't contacted her directly. Then again, very little he did made any kind of sense to her.

She crossed the floor again, and her heels clicked softly on the polished granite. A few passing state employees eyed her appreciatively. Compressing her lips, she ignored their half-smiles and turned on her heels. That's when she saw him.

He was sitting in a lounge area, his hands folded in his lap, regarding her steadily. She almost did a double take. He'd had a rather severe haircut since the last time they'd been together, but it was him, all right.

She bustled over to him, grabbed his hand. "What the hell are you doing in Chicago?"

"Meeting you," said Jack.

"I mean, you're missing in Rome! No one seems to know where you are?"

"You look surprised. Were you expecting someone else?"

Louise narrowed her eyes at him. "Actually, I was. But never mind that. Tell me what you're up to. And this had better be good. First of all, who was that guy on the phone?"

"His name is Rooney. Remember the publisher I went to see, about the old man's book?"

"Why couldn't you just call me yourself?"

Jack sighed. "I've been in Chicago a day or two. Rooney's a good guy. He even let me crash at his place a couple of nights. I've been sleeping on his sofa. You ought to see his place: He's got this huge bathroom, papered floor to ceiling with . . . well, maybe you don't need to see it. The thing is, Louise, I've been a bit paranoid lately. I had this idea that . . . I had to take you by surprise, to see how you reacted when you first saw me."

194

Louise shook her head. She didn't know what he was talking about. But as she looked back into his eyes she detected a brilliance, a flickering, as if his eyes were not settling on hers but darting minutely to and fro without appearing to shift, and then she knew what he'd been doing. She knew too, now, the source of his paranoia. And even though she knew the answer, she asked him, "Why did you want to meet me here, Jack?"

Jack looked up through the splendid atrium, to the disk like an eye at the very top. Darkness was pouring down outside, battered back by the electric lights of the offices. "Twilight. But I forgot about the electric illumination from within."

Jesus, thought Louise, *he's even starting to talk like father.* "You need to come here when the building is closed for holidays. I could get you in."

"You could?"

"Sure. I work for the Chicago Architecture Foundation. I can get in most anyplace. But it'll cost you."

"Cost what?"

"A full explanation. Come on. Let's go someplace where we can get a drink."

They went to Rock Bottom. The place was just beginning to fill up with office workers. They found a place by the bar and made a cocoon inside the boisterous rock and roll. Louise ordered two large glasses of Dalwhinnie. She could hardly believe what Jack had already told her. She leaned an elbow on the bar, searching his expressionless face in disbelief. He lightly placed the fingertips of both hands on the edge of the bar and gazed steadily ahead.

· · ·

After finishing his faithful report of events to Louise, it was almost as if, staring into the middle distance of the raucous bar, he couldn't quite believe it himself. He could play it over and over on the back of his retina, like a fantastic movie.

"My first thoughts had been that Natalie had pushed me into the river as a kind of joke. Some joke. I know I got swept under four different bridges. There was a hideous moment I thought I wouldn't get out, that I would die in the Tiber.

"I was half dead when I saw the Ponte Sant' Angelo coming up. When I looked up there were all these stone angels, wings at full pinion, looking down and doing nothing to help me. Two young lovers were out strolling by the river. They were hugging and kissing and laughing. I saw them in silhouette. I got lodged in the mud. My head was streaming with blood and I was caked in gray filth and green slime. The girl screamed.

"I can't remember any more. The young lovers must have come down and hauled me out. When I woke up in a Rome hospital a couple of days later, a nurse confirmed that a young couple had brought me there in their car. I'd been concussed and unconscious for two days. My throat was swollen from where they'd inserted a pipe to pump my stomach. Somewhere in the buffeting I'd broken two fingers and cracked a rib.

"The hospital didn't know who I was. My wallet went down with my coat in the Tiber. They couldn't identify me. They kept me there for another three days. I might have called Natalie, but at the time I still thought she'd been the one who'd pushed me into the river, and anyway I couldn't understand why she hadn't come after me, checked the hospitals, or whatever. So I hadn't called her. Instead I lay in my bed. Thinking.

"I thought about the old man. I thought about him a lot. How I've spent my life either chasing after him or running away from what I know of him. There I was in Rome, doing his bidding, pursuing his business, even sleeping with one of his women, and I had this appalling insight that the old man had set me up. That even though he was dead, he was still jerking my strings.

196

"I lay in the hospital bed, brooding. Three days passed before they discharged me. I'd decided to go back to England, to put my business back in order. But first I went to the bank to report the loss of my cards and to arrange credit. Then I went back to the house.

"It was the middle of the day. Bright autumn sunshine. The front door was ajar. Mahler belting out from the hi-fi. Contralto. Ferrier, someone like that. No one around on the ground floor, so I moved quietly upstairs, creeping past those bright-eyed mannequins. Even above the high-decibel music I could hear them fucking. Natalie, and one of the young Italian men I'd seen hanging around her studio when I first met her. One of her cat-boys. The bedroom door stood slightly open. She was naked on the bed, arched in crab position, legs open, her cunt offered up to him. The boy on his knees, taking her, but blindfolded and with his hands tied behind his back. One of her esoteric games; something she used to like to play with me.

"I watched for a while, through the crack at the hinge of the door. Then she suddenly darted a look in my direction. She hushed the boy, peering hard through the crack. She withdrew from him, so I hurried downstairs and hid in the blacklight room.

"I heard them coming, opening and closing doors. I unscrewed the UV bulb above my head; a good thing, because after a couple of minutes the door opened and a hand came in to flick the light a couple of times. Then a shout from Natalie took the hand and its owner away again. I heard feet thumping back up the stairs, and I used the opportunity to slip out of the front door unseen.

"I went down to the Gate of Saint Sebastian: didn't know what to do; nowhere else to go. Then it occurred to me that I had more right to be in the house than they did. Why was I the one doing the running? I went back with the intention of evicting them, but they'd already gone.

"I decided I wanted my pound of flesh before returning to London to rescue my business. I admit it, I wanted to hurt Natalie. Then I had the idea that if someone had been using the house unseen while I was there, then I might do the same.

"I opened up the attic, made a bed up there. After a couple of days, Natalie and her boy came back. They were rowdy lovers. I spied on them. On one occasion, Natalie put on the strange head-gear contraption, remember that? She wore it while her Italian boy was fucking her. Or she'd get him to wear it. Sometimes they were drugged out of their gourds on cocktails of hashish, speed, cocaine, acid, and other stuff.

"Once I heard them arguing fiercely. Natalie would to-and-fro from Italian to English. 'Stupid, jealous wop fuck-wit! If you hadn't got rid of that Englishman, this house would be ours now!'

"'*Strega! Prostituta!* I didn't do nothing, *niente,* to your English fuck!'

"I didn't understand all this: The house proceeds were hers anyway. But knowing how stoned they were made things easy for me. I started tripping the opera music at odd times while they were out of their heads. Always Kathleen Ferrier, *Orfeo ed Euridice,* in the middle of the night or while they were whipping up a storm in bed. Plus I kept leaving the door to the blacklight box open for them to see. One time I smashed a pair of sunglasses belonging to the boy.

"I did everything to try to make Natalie think the old man was still alive. When the kid replaced his sunglasses, I broke those too. I found her keys, went over to her studio, took a collection of paints, all at the blue and violet end of the spectrum, and left them in her fridge. I even returned her keys before she'd missed them.

"One night, while Natalie and her lover were sleeping off a chianti-and-dope binge, I went into their room. I put my nose *this* close to Natalie's sleeping face. In a way, I wanted her to wake up and see me grinning. But neither of them awakened. I was just stepping back from the bed and was moving into shadow when she opened her eyes and looked at me. I froze, and simply closed my eyes, An old burglar trick. I opened my eyes and she was asleep again. If she remembered anything the next day, she would have thought it a dream.

"And all the time I was there, lying in the darkness of the attic, I played over and over in my mind the moment I was pushed in the Tiber. I recall a swirl of lights. There were a few passersby, faces lit by the orange street lamps, ribbons of light in the dark, and there, on the bank, the one face of the figure who had pushed me into the water. I've replayed that image again and again. The face is fuzzy and out of focus; distorted, demonic. And sometimes, by a little resetting of the features, I can make it look like the face of my father."

Louise at the bar pulled him out of his reverie. "But you came through, Jack. You came through." She raised her glass. "Here's to the unknown lovers who pulled you out of the river."

"I've drunk to them before and I'll drink to them again." He drained his glass.

Louise yelled across the bar. "Another two shots here!" When the drinks came, Jack reached for the glass, but Louise closed her hand over his fist. "Were you in love with Natalie?"

"I'm not even sure I knew who Natalie was."

She gave him a quizzical look. Jack reached into his inside breast pocket and pulled out an envelope. "I was living in the attic like a wraith, and I didn't know where all this was leading. Then I found something, right there in the attic, where I'd been sleeping."

He opened the envelope and spread its contents on the bar in front of him. "In the attic was a shoe box containing these things and some other stuff. Personal documents, letters, insurance certificates, and the like, all belonging to Natalie Shearer. This one," he said, waving a folded card at Louise, "is a British-issued international driving licence."

"So?" said Louise.

"Look at that sad girl in the photograph," he said. "That doesn't look like Natalie Shearer to me."

THIRTY-ONE

Louise took Jack home. When they picked up Billy from Louise's baby-sitter, the boy shouted, "Unk Jack!" and threw himself into Jack's arms. Jack was astonished, as was Louise. "We talked about you a lot," Louise said by way of explanation. Billy hung on to Jack's neck for a long time.

"He looks older," Jack said stupidly.

"Well, he is older. By a few weeks." But Louise was more concerned with the fact that it was Jack who looked older. He looked tired. He sneezed a few times, like someone who just contracted a heavy cold. His eyes looked sore and wormed with blood, though his irises were clear and healthy, glittering with that almost imperceptible darting movement.

"Jack, I want to talk to you about that book."

"Book?"

"You know perfectly well which book. I know what you've been doing. You're doping on that book, Jack."

"It works."

"I know that. I told you that from the start."

"I thought it was all gibberish; a farrago. But it works. You start to see things."

"How far have you gone with it? I'd like to know."

Jack didn't get a chance to answer because the telephone rang. Louise dumped Billy on Jack and grabbed the receiver. Her voice modulated quickly from loud and breezy to low and circumspect. She turned her body away from Jack, and seemed to wait for a long time without speaking. But Jack heard her whispering, "Don't hang up this time. You can ask me for anything."

Whoever was on the end of the line didn't seem to want to speak. Occasionally, Louise made a murmur of encouragement, a caress of pity. After a while, she covered up the mouthpiece and hissed at Jack, "How much ready money do you have?"

Jack checked his wallet. "About a hundred fifty dollars."

She nodded, and murmured into the phone. "I could let you have a couple hundred right now. Sure. No. No, I won't do that. You've got to give me an address." She scribbled something down on a scrap of paper. "I'll be there in an hour. Don't let me down. I don't want to be wandering around the neighborhood on my own. I know. I know you won't put me in danger."

Louise replaced the handset. She was already struggling into her coat when she said, "Billy, will you be a very good boy and let Uncle Jack give you a bath and read to you and put you to bed? Mommy has to go out for a while but I'll be back soon."

Billy had no problem with that.

Jack did. "What was that call?"

"Got that hundred fifty dollars?"

Jack handed over the money. "What's it for?"

"I'll give it back to you first thing. Can you handle Billy?"

"Yes, but I mean—"

"I'm so glad you're here, Jack." She kissed him on his brow. Then she was out the door.

"Gone," Billy said to Jack. "Gone."

"When did you start speaking?" Jack said.

· · ·

It was almost three hours before Louise returned. She came back looking crumpled and exhausted. Jack had the lights turned down, Muddy Waters growling soft and low. Before saying anything to him, Louise looked in on Billy. "You got him to sleep. You do a better job than I do." Jack shrugged. Louise examined an empty bottle of Macallan on the table. "You finished off my best whiskey."

"And you should know I always carry a spare."

She nodded, finding a smile from somewhere as he unzipped his bag. He poured them both a stiff shot. Louise sighed a lot and they drank their whiskey in silence. He sensed that if he was patient, an explanation might emerge. "That," Louise said finally, "was the person I really expected to see in the Thomson Center today, instead of you. I would have taken you along with me, but it's difficult. In fact, this is the first time we've spoken in a year. Tomorrow, however, I'm going to take you to meet this person."

Without warning, Louise bent forward and began weeping. Her brow contorted, her lips twisted, and her tears made hot, angry gashes over her cheeks. "Hey!" said Jack, moving to comfort her. "Hey! What's happening here? I'm the sad one, remember?"

She looked up at him and bit her hand. "Would it be terrible," she said, "if we went to bed and you held me, just held me, just for tonight? A brother and a sister? Would that be so terrible?"

"No," Jack soothed, kissing her tear-stained hand, "that would not be so terrible."

THIRTY-TWO

Rain lashed the Windy City the next morning, bouncing high off the sidewalk as Jack helped Louise strap Billy into his car seat. Every passerby had a wind-stung look. That cold-day-in-Chicago face he'd noted before. He wondered how long he needed to stay in town before developing that look. Louise had that look this morning, but there was more. She looked as if she'd spent the evening fighting off demons.

She drove steadily through the pelting rain, the hypnotic swish of her windshield wipers beating back small talk along with the water. Jack hadn't asked where they were going or with whom he was about to meet, though he had his suspicions. He turned his face in the direction of the boiling lake, above which clouds gathered, poisonous and bruise-colored.

Louise came down off the expressway, driving through and beyond the neighborhood of Little Village. She parked alongside a wall painted over by a garish acid-inspired mural. A generation of graffiti artists had lain their signs over the mural in black and silver spray paint, like the script of a lost civilization. The wind and the rain were doing their best to chisel it all off again, urgent to get back to bare brick.

Jack held an umbrella as Louise unstrapped Billy from the car seat. She carried the child to a three-story building. Leprous pink paint was flaking from the stone. Outside the entrance, knotted garbage bags were piled high. Louise touched a buzzer; the intercom crackled and Louise stated her name. The lock shot back and they went in.

"There's no elevator," Louise said.

There was no light either. The dark stairwell smelled of urine and damp concrete. One of the doors to a downstairs apartment had been split open and repaired with galvanized metal sheeting. Jack looked for numbers or nameplates but saw none.

Louise tapped softly at a door on the top floor. Another lock tumbled, and as the door opened Jack glimpsed a man already retreating back into the room. "He's not very sociable," Louise whispered. Jack closed the door behind him, studying the massive barrel of the lock. The door was also armed with four heavy bolts.

The room carried a sharp, chemical tang. Jack saw a reflex hand go up as Louise flicked at her hair. How many times had he seen that gesture? Not just in Louise but in all women. The brief self-monitoring, the instinctive checking. She was dressed today in a no-nonsense pantsuit. Little makeup. Smart and efficient. Jack wondered who this guy was, living in this rat hole, that she still cared about how she looked.

The man retreated into a corner of the room, his bare arms folded, squinting back at them through wire-rimmed glasses. He had a jaundiced look. Though his hair was long, it was shaved high above his ears. The man seemed vaguely familiar, but Jack couldn't place him.

Jack's eyes swept the walls of the room, clouds of color, all at the blue and violet end of the spectrum, and overpainted with swirling slogans. Almost every square inch of the wall was overwritten. Some of the writing was indecipherable without close inspection; other slogans were a foot tall:

205

This is the lair of the Wolf

Billy gazed around wild-eyed. Louise, failing to hit a casual note, said, "I guess I'd better introduce you guys."

"Guess you'd better," said the man.

The man was trying to study Jack, but was unable to sustain eye contact. His own eyes oscillated weirdly, flicking frequently to an upper corner of the room, as if checking something out there. He bore the six-color spectrum tattoo on his skinny forearm:

Never seen but always present

Jack guessed his identity long before Louise said, "Jack, this is Nick, Billy's father; Nick, this my brother, Jack. Is it all right if we sit down?"

"Yeh."

Nicholas Chadbourne. The vanishing artist. Another absconding father in a world full of them. Chadbourne failed to offer an American handshake, and neither was Jack in a mood to make it easy for him. Jack had seen all this before many times, and right now he was too busy scanning the exploded sofa behind him for syringes.

"You brought me a cop," Chadbourne sniffed. "He's checking for needles."

Jack turned a cushion over. "Wouldn't like a little baby to sit on a *sharp*, would we?"

"I already checked it out before you got here. So you are a cop."

"Not any more. You're very perceptive."

Chadbourne choked back a laugh, somewhere between a snigger and a bronchial wheeze. "Perceptive. You could say that. I see a lot of things other people don't. Take you, for example. You fuckin' hate junkies, but twenty bucks says you've got a quart bottle in your pocket right now. You don't have to answer. I know. There's an alphabet on your face, dude." Chadbourne traced lines across his own cheeks and under his eyes. "Here. And here. And here. You're drowning in booze."

There is Indigo There is no Indigo

"You can see right through me, huh?"

"I know you, dude. I know who you are."

Jack stared back. Again Chadbourne looked somehow familiar, but Jack dismissed the thought. Meanwhile, Louise, not liking the way things were going, said, "I spoke to Nick last night, Jack. Nick's been having a hard time lately. He was grateful for your money."

Chadbourne softened, and swung toward Billy. He chucked the boy's cheek. Billy stared back in astonishment. "How's my little boy?"

"He's doing great, Nick. Walking and talking; well, talking sometimes. He's a bit overwhelmed right now. Nick, you promised me you'd tell Jack about Natalie Shearer."

Chadbourne's eyes went dead. "Sure. You can sit down," he told Jack. "You won't spike your ass. Can I hold him?"

"Sure," Louise said. "If he starts kicking I'll take him back."

Billy went to his father, gazing up at the jaundiced face with brilliant blue eyes. He seemed content. Chadbourne glanced at Jack and wheezed another laugh. "Look at your cop brother. He's jealous of me. Real nice."

Jack couldn't deny it. He felt a thrill of concern for Billy's proximity to his junkie father. But he said, "What about Natalie Shearer?"

Chadbourne gave him a full smile. His gray teeth were in shocking condition. He lit a cigarette, clinking the cap of his Zippo lighter decisively. "Natalie was one of those dangerously suggestible people, you know? Always in an excitable state. A good-looking girl—all of Chambers's girls were good-looking—and she was totally fixed on the old man. I think he went around looking for girls with a father thing because he found them so easy to manipulate.

"That was his thing, Tim Chambers. Manipulating people, for amusement, for entertainment. Like social experiments. We were all younger then. We all looked up to him."

Jack couldn't keep his eyes from straying to the writing on the walls. In addition to the slogans, there were vertical lists:

Chroma
Brilliance
Tint
Hue
Shade
Black Light
White Death

"The thing was to be in his inner circle. He had tons of young people hanging around him, all serious-minded young artists. If you were one of his favorites, it opened up all kinds of doors. Anything was possible: exhibitions, contacts, exposure, the circuit, travel. He had huge influence.

"But you had to be in the inner circle. Outside of that could be fun, but you might be picked up one week and dropped the next. People would find themselves out in the cold and they didn't know why; others were smart enough to stay plugged in. I was clever and *in*. Natalie was too, and so was AnnaMaria."

"She was the girl who killed herself in Rome?" Jack asked.

Chadbourne stubbed out his cigarette with a kind of venom. "She and I were a thing. Scratch that. She and I were in love. But the old man got in the way of that.

"He took delight in setting up relationships between people and then busting 'em up. He once told me he was astonished at how easy it was. And you know what? I didn't even realize that while he was telling me this, he was doing the very same thing to me. That was his technique. You never saw it coming. And I was younger then. I didn't know anything."

Color

Light

Cloud

Smoke

Darkness

Indigo

Void

"So he broke up you and AnnaMaria?"

Chadbourne shook his head. "This was before. I was with Natalie Shearer at that time. Natalie had been together with the old man, but he introduced us and encouraged us to spend more time together. Took us to Rome. Gave me cash to lavish on her. Natalie didn't know it but he was passing her on. Then he introduced Anna-Maria Accurso into the equation. Italian beauty. A scene-stealer. AnnaMaria and I were hot for each other, anyone could see that. Except that the old man had chosen AnnaMaria for himself, so he took me back to Chicago with him, leaving AnnaMaria and Natalie in Rome. He controlled all the purse-strings, remember.

"That's when he introduced me to Louise. I didn't realize it at the time, but I was being expertly steered away from AnnaMaria, since Natalie could no longer be depended on to do the job. It was a

209

good choice. Louise was getting over some unhappy times, and we clicked."

Jack looked to Louise. She refused to meet his gaze, intent instead upon Chadbourne's account.

"With me taken care of, the old man went back to Rome and AnnaMaria. We were left alone in Chicago, and we had some good times, didn't we, babe? Only soon the old man needed me to unload dear old AnnaMaria. By now, Louise was pregnant and had decided she didn't want to spend her life with me anyway."

"Dad told me things about Nick," Louise interjected, for Jack's benefit. "Things that I now know aren't true."

Chadbourne snorted. "That's how he operated. Just a tiny piece of misinformation at the right time. Iago had nothing on this boy. I've seen him set lovers and couples and old friends at each other's throats, and then step in with a piece of wisdom that made everyone feel childish and ignorant. It guaranteed loyalty. We somehow abdicated all responsibility to him."

"But why?" Jack wanted to know.

"You don't see this until afterward. You just see this generous, sophisticated man of the world helping you out of your own assholeness. It's like you, cop brother Jack. You know what he's like. Everyone has told you. You've seen it for yourself. Yet you're still playing the devil's game."

"What are you talking about?"

"The book, dude. You're doing the book."

Jack shot a look at Louise. She shrugged and said, "I didn't tell him anything."

"She didn't have to tell me. It's on you, like I see the booze on you. It's in the gleam of your eye. It's in the way you take in the room. You're carrying Smoke and Shadow, man." He peered hard at Jack. "How far you gone? Done the Indigo rumba yet? You will. You can't help yourself. That was Natalie for you. She went all the way.

Right into the void. She went through the book, man, and clean across to the other side. The seven-star Indigo rumba."

Jack pulled a photograph from his pocket. It was a photo of himself and the woman he'd originally thought of as Natalie Shearer, taken at the Trevi Fountain. "Is that Natalie?"

Chadbourne shook his head. "Nope. This was another one of the crowd, hanging around. Sarah Buchanan, another of your old man's girls." Not until Jack showed him the driver's license taken from the attic did he say, "Yep. That's Natalie. Old picture, but that's her."

Jack got to his feet. He'd heard enough and he wanted to leave. "What are you gonna do with this information?" Chadbourne asked.

"Maybe I'll kill somebody."

"Good idea. You gotta go too?" he asked Louise.

"I do, Nick. Remember what I said, and keep away from the Lake Shore house. It has to be sold. If you need anything, you call me, okay?"

"I try not to," Chadbourne said sadly, handing Billy back with infinite tenderness. "I really try not to."

Louise placed a finger on his cheek, and Jack thought he ought not to be watching. "I give you what I can, Nick."

Jack took Billy from Louise's arms and went out, leaving them to have a moment. Outside, it was still raining, so he waited on the ground floor in the dark, piss-smelling stairwell. After a few minutes, she emerged, buttoning her coat as she came down the stairs, her lips tightly compressed.

They climbed into the car. Before Louise turned the key Jack placed a hand on her wrist. "How long has he been doing this to you?"

"It never stops."

"It must."

"Please. I want to get out of here."

THIRTY-THREE

The tattoo is of interest in this regard. As the skin is punctured, the flow of blood to the damaged skin will, some time after the tattooist has left his impression, scab over. After the scab has dried, it is tempting to pick at it, and this will spoil the impression underneath; but if this can be resisted until the scab dries, flakes, and floats away naturally, a bright and brilliant tattoo will be revealed.

The visual world in which we live, with all its interest, is no more than such a scab. The true nature of the world waits, underneath, to be revealed, and the primary colour of this hidden world is Indigo.

I know of only two accessible places where this peeling back of the universe can be experienced quite naturally. In each case, a quite different oculus blinks back to admit the Indigo light, at a precise time of the year and when certain conditions are aligned.

These two places are to be found in the ancient Pantheon of Rome and in the Thomson Center of Chicago. Rome is the apotheosis of classicism; Chicago the zenith of modernism. Return to Rome time and time again and you will find it almost unchanged but for a few bricks—the Colosseum still intact, the Forum still dominant, the baroque fountains springing eternal. Visit Chicago after a single decade and it seems like a different metropolis: Can this really be the same city? Rome burrowing deeper and deeper into an illuminating history. Chicago soaring faster and faster to the dark future.

Buildings delineate the dreams of a city's people. Rome and Chicago stand like bookends at the starting point and at the state of the art in the dreaming power of architecture. Buildings, thinks the vulgar man, exist to accommodate the functions of those who use them; but the great architects are those who know that buildings have a secret mission—to delight and to instruct.

Go to the Pantheon in Rome and survey the oculus in the centre of the roof. Is this invisible keystone designed to admit light or to let darkness out? Is it a channel for prayer and an invocation to journey upward or does it invite the eye of heaven to look down? Go there on the eve of the Lupercalia. If you have followed my instructions to the letter, if you wait until the onset of dusk, then you will see through the oculus the eye of heaven blink back at you. You will see for yourself the elusive colour Indigo. You will scent the wolf. The world will seem a larger place. You will want to die for wonder.

Go to the glass miracle of the Thomson Center on the same night, at the same time. Where the Pantheon deals in shadow, the Thomson trades in light and transparency, and the round disk on top is an inverted oculus. In no other building in the world will light operate as an architectural element as effective as steel or stone. The building is buttressed by light. Go when I have told you. The atrium will flood with Indigo light.

The size of the wolf will dismay you. The nature of the universe will be expanded. You will be maddened with awe.

I have instructed you in the collection of Smoke. You have seen, in the spinning of this substance, how to transport it from one place to another on your retina. I have taught you the art of trawling, so that darkness has become a dimension rather than a mere absence of light. And I have told you the precise moment when, in the exercise of these seeing arts, the colour Indigo will briefly make itself available to you.

213

This is the alchemical triangulate, the confluence of optical elements. Smoke; Darkness; Indigo; each forming a vertex of the triangle through which you must pass. In each case, you represent the median; and the eye within the triangle is the oculus of the Pantheon and the disk of the Thomson.

At the precise moment indicated, the elements snap together. Your task is to fold the triangle inwards, until it becomes a single vertical beam, an obelisk of Indigo light. You step into the beam. You have achieved Invisibility.

Now everything you see is Indigo light. All other colours of the spectrum have vanished. The wash of Indigo light is dazzling. You can even taste the colour. Though you tremble, though the intensity and anxiety of your condition threaten to fracture your mind, you must test out the possibilities of your condition; though quickly, because the state is but temporary.

You see someone nearby. You whisper strange words in that person's ear and you terrify him, because he cannot see you. You openly steal from another and the act goes unremarked. The possibilities occur to you. You are attracted to a woman moving among the visitors, you sniff her from head to toe and her sexual cassolette inflames you; you go as close as you dare, under her skirt; but you are careful not to touch. Beware. You are like an electrically charged photon beam, and your supernatural energy will trigger orgasm, shock, even epileptic seizure. You are invisible. You are dangerous.

But no sooner have you glimpsed this holy terror than the eye will blink shut. You have peeled back the scab of the glorious hidden universe for a few seconds only. You have tasted the miraculous. Then you will wander the globe, as I have done, trying to recapture that unearthly experience. You can never be satisfied again. Not until you have found the way to wedge open the oculus, the blinking eye, the passage into Indigo light, forever.

THIRTY-FOUR

"CHICAGO IS A STRANGE CITY," DORY GROWLED. "PEOPLE HERE disappear all the time. Sometimes they turn up again; sometimes they don't." Louise had invited her down from Madison expressly to meet Jack. Dory had refused, so Louise left Jack and Billy for the day, drove up to Madison, and dragged her back under protest. On their return, Jack had looked out of the apartment to see a complaining overweight woman get out of the car. Jack saw instantly where Louise had gotten her habit of clamping her lips.

When she'd bustled into the apartment to find Jack carrying Billy, she'd compressed her lips even tighter and relieved Jack of the child without a word. Then she'd apologized and tried to hand him back; but Jack said, no, go ahead, Billy wants some of his grandmother right now. Maybe she was mollified to find that Jack didn't especially resemble Tim Chambers, and, finding a living, breathing human being more difficult to resent than her notion of a Chambers clone, Dory softened visibly. It was apparent, at least to Louise, that Dory felt ashamed of herself.

They'd had dinner together and now they were drinking wine. Dory was talking about her native city. A Chicagoan to the bone, she

215

had what she herself described as hog-butcher's biceps, and eyes the same vitreous blue-gray as Lake Michigan. Her remarks about people disappearing followed their comments regarding the real Natalie Shearer going missing in Rome and Nicholas Chadbourne's reemergence in Chicago. "Before they raised the streets a level, there used to be signs here and there showin' where a team of horses dropped through the mud; and one time there was just a hat and a sign sayin', 'Man Lost here.'"

Jack laughed. "You're making it up!"

"I'm not. I wonder if all these missing people are going to show up one day in Lincoln Park. They've got to go someplace."

"Anyway," Louise said, "at least Nick turned up again."

"Now if *he* dropped through the mud that'd be a good thing." Dory looked at Jack. "Never did have any time for that son of a bitch."

Jack concurred silently, but Louise objected. "That's Billy's father you're talking about."

"Billy's in bed and he can't hear me; and when he grows old enough you'll do him no good if you try to hide it from him that his old man was a junkie. Am I right, Jack?"

Jack thought for a moment. "I suppose you are right."

"Damn right I'm right, and if he asks me I'll tell him. Been enough lying around here." Jack looked to Louise, to see if he'd missed something. Dory spotted his sidelong glance and said, "I'm talking about your old man, honey. Jack, you know something, when he came from England, that no good piece of shit—I'm sorry, and no I ain't—didn't even tell me he was married back in England? Didn't tell me he had a little boy named Jack."

"I thought you didn't like to talk about him," Louise remarked.

"I don't. And I don't want you thinking I do. Jack, you've gotten awful thoughtful. Tell me about your mommy. I'd like to hear about her. Seeing as how it was kept from me and all."

Dory had drained her glass, so Jack reached to fill it up again. "She was weak, Dory. Easy meat for someone like him."

"Easy meat, huh? Guess that's what I was before I turned."

"All I know is one day he just took off to the U.S. and didn't come back. She never got over it. There was never another man to replace him. She was a pillar of respectability—conservative, dull, narrow—and I think it was all a reaction against him. Then I had to go and break her heart when I finished college by going to New York to visit him."

"She'd know what he was up to. How he would work to win you over." She jerked a thumb at Louise. "Just like he worked on this one. Mothers know."

"He never worked on me, Mom, and he never won me over."

"So you say. But you kept in touch with him, against my wishes."

"He was still my father," Louise said. "And anyway I spent more time with you over the years, and I never loved him like I love you. So what's the point of all this bitterness?"

"The *point,* darlin'," Dory was almost shouting now, "the point is that he ruined people's *lives.*"

"Yeh, well, he only ruined the lives of those people who let him ruin them."

If Jack took that last comment to heart he said nothing. He stared morosely at the floor and sipped his wine. No one seemed to have anything left to say.

Dory got out of her chair. "I'm beat. I'm gonna hit the sack." She gathered up the quilt she'd brought with her from Madison. There was something sad and weary in the way she folded it under her arm.

"Let me see the quilt, Dory," Jack almost shouted. "Louise told me all about this." She released it and Jack examined it minutely, cooing over the workmanship. Then he blurted, "Dory, there must have been *something* about him. Something in the man that made you fall in love with him in the first place!"

Dory looked annoyed with Jack. She peered hard at him, but he held her gaze for an uncomfortable time. Then she took back the quilt and pointed to the abstract square. To Jack the square looked confused: a tight, angry scrawl of blue cross-hatchings on a violet field. Or maybe the erratic recordings of an electroencephalograph.

"See that?" Dory said. "That's the field of fear and wonder, Jack. Fear and wonder. That's why I fell in love with your father. He could light up the world. He could make the world a bigger place. I thought he was going to fill that square for me, fill it with wonder. Now I don't know if anyone can do that for anyone." She looked at Louise, who was watching this exchange. "I'm gong to get to my bed."

Dory surprised Jack by kissing him goodnight. Then she kissed Louise, and took her quilt with her.

. . .

Dory sat up in bed, spectacles nipping the tip of her nose, working on her quilt. She was busy with her abstract square, her Indigo square. She was unpicking it, because you could never get the Indigo square quite right. Lifting the thread to her teeth, she bit.

She could hear Louise and Jack talking in the next room while she worked. She'd arrived in Chicago hoping to take an instant dislike to Jack, but had softened too visibly and too promptly for her own liking. All of Louise's life, Dory had played the game of peering hard at her daughter, examining the bud of her lips, the retroussé turn of her nose, the structure of her cheekbones, the tuck of her chin, searching always for signs of herself and willing away all genetic resemblance to Tim Chambers. She'd spent the evening similarly scrutinizing Jack whenever his eyes were averted.

But Chambers had been there. Though Jack wasn't instantly recognizable as his father's son, Dory knew the stamp. It was in the way he focused his eyes on random objects in his field of vision; the way he paused too long and turned his head before answering a question; the way in which you thought he wasn't paying attention but never missed a thing. But these traits had been filtered, blended, moderated. They lacked the father's acid edge. They engendered sympathy where once they'd inspired fear.

She unpicked some of the confusion of blue thread from the abstract square and started in on it again, stitching with the same thread. Problem was that she only had a fuzzy idea of the effect she was after. The effect she wanted to render had never been available to her during full consciousness. It was a blur, almost a pattern but unresolved, a visual shock manifested to her during the onset of the seizures, before the drugs had stopped all that.

The epileptic seizures, though embarrassing, dangerous, and sometimes painful, were not universally unpleasant. The pre-seizure moment, the instant before the terrible falling away of consciousness, had always been bathed in this indescribable light. Blue on violet, that's how it had seemed. And somewhere inside the seizure was a roar of pleasure, a promise of revelation, as if the universe itself might split open and admit an incident of angelic ferocity. A message. A meaning. For behind the messy reticulation of lines stamped on the retina before her seizures there was, Dory knew, some indeterminate design: perhaps a trilobite figure; some fractal; maybe a letter or a glyph in a heavenly alphabet, the letter that precedes the start of the first word that signals the radiant flowering of all creation. But she could never get it right. She sewed and sewed and unpicked the thread and sewed again, knowing she would recognize it when she saw it again, but sensing with dismay that its realization would always be denied. It was maddening.

Exhausted, she put down her needlework and leaned back

against the headboard of her bed, listening to the tender murmuring of Jack and Louise's voices from the next room. She thought again about Jack, about how like his father he was, and how unlike. It was a relief to her that she didn't have to hate him. Not evil, no, she thought. *That* comes from somewhere else.

. . .

"Dad scared people," Louise said some time later. "You do realize that."

"He certainly scared me," Jack said.

"When Nick came over from Rome he didn't want to go back. He was afraid to be with Dad. And yet he couldn't tear himself away. I think they were all like that. Mom's nasty when it comes to Nick. He's a wreck now, but he was a different person when I met him. A talented young artist. Full of ideas. Of course I didn't know we'd been set up by Dad. How could I?

"But Nick had a morbid streak, too, and an obsession with these seeing exercises. I told him to get away from it. Then Dad called him, said he needed him back in Rome. Sure. Needed him to deal with AnnaMaria. I told Nick to refuse to go, but it was impossible. Even though he was afraid of him. He diminished in my eyes when I saw how much in awe he was of Dad. I let him go, and I knew it was over for us. A couple of weeks later I found out I was pregnant with Billy."

"Did you tell Nick at the time? Maybe that would have brought him back."

"I didn't want him. It may sound brutal, but it's the truth. Billy was six months old when I next saw Nick and by then he had a very serious habit. There was something willful about it, like, you know, 'I'm going to drug myself to death so let's get it over with.' I know something awful happened in Rome, but he never told me what it was.

"He asked me for money. I went to meet him and I showed him Billy. He cried, and he swore he would never ask me for dope money, and that's when he vanished. But from time to time I'd get phone calls with no voice on the other end of the line, and I always sensed it was him. Occasionally, he'd spend an evening at the apartment on Lake Shore Drive if he knew Dad was away. So I'd leave money there. All contact between him and Dad had stopped. I think Dad guessed Nick was Billy's father, though I never told him."

"Do you let Billy see much of Nick?"

She sighed. "I don't know if it's better to let Billy grow up with a complex about never having seen his father, or whether to let him grow up with a complex about knowing his father is an addict who ran out on us. What are you thinking, Jack?"

"I'm thinking about your mother. She's been staring at me all evening."

THIRTY-FIVE

Jack gave Rooney a call and arranged to meet him for a drink after work. Jack still hadn't resolved the matter of publishing the Manual of Light and wanted to do so quickly. They met at the Tip Top Tap, a place Jack requested (to Rooney's chagrin) because he liked the great jazz. Rooney wasted no time explaining his idea of publishing the manuscript with a tiny print run, contrary to the spirit of the will. "Listen, Jack, no one, and I mean no one, is going to give a flying fuck in a fairy's ass about a vanity-published catalog of exercises in twitching your fucking eyelids."

"So you did read it!"

"I spent three and a half minutes skimming it, which was more than it fucking deserves, and what I read made me want to shit a brick."

"Maybe we'll put those words of praise on the dust jacket."

"And should some goofball stick his fat fuckin' nose in, well, you've got enough copies you can toss 'em at him like bananas and say the rest are in storage. But that won't happen 'cause no one gives a shit."

"I do."

"Well, you're a fuckin' tight-assed Brit and now shut your trap 'cause here comes our gal!"

Rooney settled into his characteristic trance as the band started playing and the girl shimmied on stage. The floor show projected colored lights across the dancer's body, another reason why Rooney didn't fully sanction the Tip Top Tap. Jack tried hard to enjoy the show as much as Rooney; but he always felt self-conscious in these dives. It seemed that the girls could detect his innate shyness, because some of them would fix him with glassy eye contact, and despite his best efforts, he would always look away first. The girl on stage wore only a cowboy hat and spent too much time looking back at the audience from between her legs.

"How does she keep the hat on?" Jack asked Rooney.

It wasn't until at least five minutes later, after the girl had finished her performance, that Rooney turned to Jack, quizzical and bent out of shape. "What'd you say?"

"It doesn't matter."

"Well?"

Jack knew by now that Rooney wanted him to rate the girl on a scale of one to fifteen, each point subdivided into tenths. "She's got no sense of irony and she can't dance."

Rooney looked Jack up and down, shuddered, and ordered more beers. While they were coming, Jack told him about the encounter with Nicholas Chadbourne. "Sure," Rooney said, "there's a lot of drugs in Chicago. What else is new?" A slender topless waitress delivered two bottles of beer to their table. "It's a neighborhood thing. Each neighborhood's got its dope specialty, like with ethnic food, so if you go to the South Side . . . Hey! You're getting the idea, buddy!"

Rooney had suddenly realized that Jack wasn't listening. He was staring hard at the retreating back of the waitress.

"Too skinny," Rooney said. "You've got untutored tastes, pal. I know her anyways. Girl's from up Pilsen way. Used to be a dancer here but they stopped her on account she lost a lot of weight and got kind of unhealthy looking."

"She's got a tattoo," Jack said. "On her shoulder." Rooney narrowed his eyes. "Can you get her over here?"

Rooney beckoned a burly floor manager. "It'll cost you. Got a twenty?" He asked the floor manager to send the waitress back to the table. When she returned, Rooney laid the cash flat on the table, though he rested a fat finger on it. "I'm sorry, honey, we forgot your tip. Why don't ya sit down a while?"

The woman looked relieved to be asked. It meant she could take the weight off her feet and she'd get a commission on the glass of "champagne" that another waitress delivered, unordered, within seconds. Orange juice and fizzy water, and at fifteen dollars per shot it bought you ten minutes.

The woman crossed her legs and pretended to sip her drink. She wore sheer black nylons, ankle-breaking polished stilettos, tight-fitting black satin shorts, and nothing else besides but a choker. Her blond hair was cut in a neat bob but her black roots were exposed. She was Chicago-wind stung, and her teeth seemed a little too large for her mouth. Her poppy-red lipstick smeared on the glass she sipped. Her small breasts had a disappointed, downward turn and Jack also noted, despite the subdued lighting in the club, the prominent veins around the fold of her elbow and a cluster of needle punctures like a rash. She vexed herself with a half-smile.

"Cindy? It is Cindy, isn't it?" Rooney said,

"Terri."

"Yeh. Knew it was something like that. How ya doin', Terri?"

"Doin' good." She looked nervously at Jack.

"This here is Jack. He's kind of a student of the noble art of the tattooist, and he couldn't help noticing that whistler on your back."

224

Terri involuntarily touched her shoulder. "Yeh?"

"Did you know a guy called Tim Chambers?" Jack asked.

Rooney slapped his hand down on the table. "Jack, you sound like a fuckin' cop! What do you think, Terri? Doesn't my buddy here come across like a fuckin' cop?"

"Sort of." She shuffled uneasily. "He's got a funny accent."

"That ain't funny, that's British. What is it? That tattoo. I mean, it's a bolt of light, right? Colors of the spectrum. Real pretty. Unusual."

Jack gave it another try. "Tim Chambers was a guy in his sixties, big mane of white hair and—"

"What my buddy is saying is this guy was a john who liked to get his ladies tattooed. Who knows?" Rooney drummed his fingers on the twenty-dollar bill. "Maybe it helped him get it up. Take your tip, honey."

The half-smile went from her face. She took the money, folded it, and stuffed it into a tiny pocket in her shorts. "Naw, he was a much younger guy. Head shaved at the sides and long on top. Got the same tattoo himself and he paid me extra to have one. That's all he wanted. Junkies can't get it up. So what? I wanted a tattoo anyways."

"Chadbourne?" said Jack. "Was his name Nick Chadbourne?"

"Hell, I don't know. Just some stoner from Little Village or up that way. Speedballer. Strange dude. He had a hole in his head."

"Yeh," Jack said. "He is pretty blown away."

"No, I don't mean that. I mean he's got a hole in his head. Right here." She tapped the side of her head just above her ear. "He parted his hair and showed me. You guys gonna buy me another drink?"

. . .

The following morning, Jack made an international call to his office. He felt it was urgent. He caught Mrs. Price just as she was about

225

to leave. Jack drew a deep breath and said, "Mrs. Price, I want to talk to you about that Birtles case."

"Yes?"

"There was a mistake, Mrs. Price. That is, I made a mistake. I want you to apologize to the court and say that I was in error, and that Mr. Birtles was telling the truth. He was not correctly served."

"Well, I suspected that. So just to ensure justice was done I made a copy of the papers and I went to that ghastly place where he spends his time drinking. The Haunch of Venison. I had a large gin and I waited until the lout came in. Of course, he wasn't looking for an old lady, so I served him correctly with the papers. There. So you can forget all about that."

"Mrs. Price," Jack said. "Have I ever told you I love you, Mrs. Price?"

"Never mind all that, when are you coming back?"

. . .

"He got to you, didn't he?" said Louise that evening.

"What?"

"That crack Nicholas made about your drinking. It really got to you." Louise and Jack were on their way to see a movie. Dory was only too happy to baby-sit Billy.

Louise was driving. "I saw how it got to you."

"I have nothing but contempt for someone like that," Jack said. "He tried to make me feel like him, like I was one of *them*."

"You're not."

"There's a difference between an addict and an alcoholic?"

"There's a difference between *you* and *him*."

"Another thing made me hate him. He's had something that I want so badly, but that I know I can never have."

They both stared dead ahead at the road. After a moment she took one hand from the wheel and stroked his shoulder. "I know," she said. "I know."

The movie was not a great success. Jack developed a migraine halfway through the film. He saw flickering, iridescent beads behind the images on the screen, as if the celluloid in the projection-booth machinery was about to melt or ignite at any moment. He excused himself and went to the men's room. Instead of returning to his seat, he sat in the empty lobby, sipping coffee, wiping blisters of perspiration from his forehead. Louise came out to look for him.

"Go back in. I don't want to spoil it for you."

"Nah. The movie's a dog. Let's go to a bar."

So they found a bar, and after a couple of beers he felt better. They sat on stools facing each other, knees touching. Heads propped by a hand, and elbows polishing the bar, they were almost mirror images. They talked about childhood. The bartender or anyone observing them would have thought they were lovers.

THIRTY-SIX

J ACK TOLD THE DRIVER OF THE YELLOW CAB TO WAIT. A STINGING
wind lashed the desolate street and he had to rest his finger on the
intercom button for a long time. It seemed like Chadbourne wasn't
going to let him in, but Jack persisted. Eventually, the buzzer vibrated and Jack climbed the dank stairway. Still, he had to hammer
on the door of the third-floor apartment.

There was an acrid, burning smell in the room; recently fired
dope. Plus another, lupine odor. "Dough-ray-me?" Chadbourne
said.

"When you've told me what I need to know."

"No dough, no know. Show the dough-ray-me." Chadbourne
was speedballing. The pupils of his eyes were shrunk to tiny obsid-
ian beads and his eyes were bulging, spinning with nystagmus. Nuances and inflections flew in and out of his speech like a flock of
crazed birds. Spaces between vowels were crowded with meaning.
Chadbourne prowled, clawing his own torso.

Jack flashed his roll of bills. "You don't get it until I get the
story." Jack sat on the sofa, relaxed, comfortable, showing he wasn't
going to be deflected.

"Hex-cop wants the story? Naturally Natalie. Herstory. The up-

228

perstory, how high can you go? Ho. Shout for needles when you sid-down, Jack. Watch out, washout. Heh heh don't sit on the wolf."

"Yeh. The wolf."

Chadbourne sniggered, jabbed a nicotine-colored finger. "Of him you know *uno*, nothing; *due*, everything; *tre*, go! *Auribus teneo lupum*, that's the rip trip. The hoary story of the hoary wolf, the hor-rorwolf, the whorewolf."

"You never got to see the Indigo, did you, Nick? Never got there. Bottled out, didn't you? You're scared of the wolf."

"Fuck you, Jack. I got the holy whole hole. The hell-holy oculus. I'm on the sacred inside."

"Sure. Let me see that hole in your head. The one you show the girls."

Chadbourne looked distracted, as if trying to remember. "Na-talie, gone over. Pure *lupus*. Pure Indigo. She's doing the Indigo rumba in San Callisto."

"San Callisto? What's that?"

"*Ospedale*, dude. Up against the white wall. But you can't see her. No one can."

"What is this San Callisto?" Jack tried again.

"There were four, me and AnnaMaria, and naturally Natalie, and one more. Then the oculus. Tell me something, dude, are you fucking your sister?"

"Tell me about Natalie."

"I hold the wolf by the ears now, don't I? By the years. Hole the wolf by the ears."

Chadbourne couldn't stay focused, and Jack wanted to do something violent to the man. Suddenly losing patience, he got up to leave, but Chadbourne flew at him, grabbing his arm. "The dough-ray-me! You promised the dough-ray me!"

Jack put his mouth very close to Chadbourne's ear, and in do-ing so saw what could have been a puncture in the junkie's skull.

"Know something?" Jack whispered. "I took a real hard look at Billy, and he doesn't look a bit like you. No hole in the head. No junkie eyes. No virus kiss. I don't even think he's yours."

"The dough?" Chadbourne shouted back at him.

"Tell me something, *dude*. Do you breathe on your little boy? Tell him poison stories? Do you wipe the spittle off his tiny face after you've kissed him?"

"The dough!" Chadbourne screamed, chasing Jack down the evil-smelling stairs. "The dough!"

The yellow cab was still waiting. Chadbourne scuttled just behind Jack, bellowing in his ear. "The dough!" Finally, Jack turned on him, pushing a wad of bills into his hand. "Here! Get yourself a hot dose. Go on. Take a few more dollars. Remember, I want you to have a really hot dose. One for your little boy."

Chadbourne closed his fist on the dollar bills, mouthing obscenities. Jack shoved him away from the car and climbed in. "Let's go," he told the driver.

"I'm already gone," the driver said.

Jack looked back. Chadbourne was a diminishing shadow, his mouth still working, his words snatched away by the wind.

. . .

"Got a lot of secrets, don't you?" Dory worked away on her quilt. She held the embroidery very close to her eye, stitching carefully and with extraordinary focus. Jack had returned from his fruitless visit to Chadbourne to find Louise out with a friend and Dory baby-sitting. Dory had generously prepared supper for him, and Jack wished she hadn't. "That casserole okay?"

"It's fine."

"Secrets can pull you down. Why not just spill the beans?"

"It's a national characteristic. We hide behind formality. Freeze you out with good manners."

"Where did you go tonight?"

"Had a few beers with a friend named Rooney. We went to a club and watched women dancing naked."

"Sounds sort of goofy."

"I've had better nights out."

"Louise is really into you, Jack. It's a shame. You and her being related and everything." Dory had the advantage of closely eyeing her needlework during this exchange. It meant that Jack could stare hard back at her. But he knew she was studying him at the periphery of her vision.

"Yes. It's a pity."

"Me, I wouldn't let a thing like that bother me. But then I'm, heck, what's the word?" She laid down her needlework and squinted at him.

"Unorthodox?"

"If I wanna smoke a pipe I'll smoke a pipe."

"But you don't smoke a pipe, Dory."

"That's only because I *don't wanna* smoke a pipe." Jack forced down another forkful of Dory's gray casserole, still studying her. What was this—mother's permission to go and commit incest with her daughter? "I had enough of secrets when I was with that bastard. I never knew what he was planning. What he was thinking. Why he was thinking what he was thinking. In fact, if he told you something it was probably just to manipulate you one way or the other. I figure secrets is the opposite of connectedness. So if you want to get connected with someone, you've got to spill your secrets."

Jack tried to think what secrets might be keeping him disconnected from Louise. "But I don't have any secrets. Not big ones, anyway."

Dory put the end of a thread between her teeth and bit it clean. "Honey, you're a walking talking secret."

Later, Louise returned from her night out, flushed from a few bears. Dory reheated her casserole and put it in front of Louise, who took a single mouthful before pushing the dish away in disgust. "Mom, this is shit."

"I know that," said Dory.

. . .

The next morning, Jack called the Italian agency in San Giovanni. He even got to speak with Gina, the young woman who'd helped him before. Yes, she said, she remembered him.

"You say you want to know about the catacombs of San Callisto?" she asked him.

"No, not the catacombs. Any other place in or around Rome that bears the name of San Callisto."

Within the hour, Gina got back to him with a short list. "Thank you, Gina," he said before putting down the receiver.

Dory caught him staring hard at his list. "More secrets?" she growled.

That evening, Louise got a call from the Chicago police department. Did she know a Nicholas Chadbourne? Yes, she did. How was she related? She was the mother of his child. Were they still together? No, they were not. Had she seen him recently? Yes, only a few days ago.

She had to go. Would Jack come with her? Would Dory stay with Billy? Louise would explain later.

She drove Jack to the morgue, where a young policeman awaited them. The policeman had a fresh bruise under his eye. His eye was still weeping and he nursed it with a handkerchief. As Louise went in to identify the body, Jack made some comment about the bruise.

"I was playing with my kid," said the policeman. "I was looking through a kaleidoscope and she banged the other end, just before I came on duty."

Jack went in behind Louise. A conspicuously bald mortician opened a sliding drawer. The glaring overhead light reflected from the mortician's head.

"The landlord found him in the stairwell of his apartment," the policeman said. "He'd been there several hours. We took a look inside his apartment and we found your phone number. That's about all we had to go on. He was obviously a chronic user. You can cover him up, Geoff."

The mortician put a finger above Chadbourne's ear. "There's an unusual wound right here. It's not recent, but would you know anything about it?"

Louise shook her head, no.

"Let's go," Jack said, steering her out. At least Chadbourne wouldn't bleed money from Louise any more. The junkie had taken Jack's advice and given himself a really hot dose.

THIRTY-SEVEN

It is at the introduction of the oculus, the void, that most students of the art of seeing lose their nerve. Having come so far, having traveled in good faith and with such high expectation, to be diverted by superstitious or scrupulous objections betrays a weakness of resolve.

Others, having bathed in the glorious light of Indigo for a few seconds, must go on. For them, it is not enough to wait for the calendar year to turn again before the next opportunity, nor is it enough to be confined to this or that geographical or architectural location. The wolf within howls for the condition of Indigo to return.

Those who have faithfully followed the programme will have seen wondrous things, and, impatient to complete the process, are unlikely to be deflected by nicety. The door has been opened, and must now be wedged ajar. I can do nothing about the fact that the infinite is not available to the meek or the timid personality.

I've done it; others have followed; you can too.

The introduction of the oculus itself is a little painful but absolutely safe if my instructions are carried out to the letter. This is hardly a new or modern operation, and has been performed, according to fossil evidence, at least since neolithic times. It is still practised today in many

234

Third World countries as an alternative to poorly administered modern medicine. Traditionally, the object of such surgery in dealing with fractures, convulsions, swellings of blood or fluid was to let pressure *out,* and although we are concerned with a bleeding of a different kind, we are also interested in the notion of letting certain forces of light *in.*

The aim is to produce an oculus that is as small and neat and efficient as is humanly possible. I myself, after a few days of itchy discomfort and self-consciousness, have hardly experienced a day's nuisance since the brief operation, and the rapid growth of human hair means that self-consciousness can easily be avoided. Tattooing or body piercing can sometimes be more painful. Of the small disk removed: I have kept it, drilled a hole in it, and wear it around my neck as a kind of talisman. You might want to do the same.

The operation itself requires the light grazing of a specific artery in the right temporal lobe of the brain, an artery that if otherwise damaged may induce epilepsy and further complication. But you need have no fear of that. If all my previous instructions have been followed to the letter and this operation is conducted with ordinary care, then the glories of the palace of Indigo will be thrown open to you. You will no longer be confined by time or place, calendar or geography. Permanent access to Invisibility will be yours and the magnificent effulgence of Indigo light will flood your days; I guarantee it.

Do you know your Dante? Study the *Divina Commedia. Purgatorio,* Canto VIII, lines 19 to 21:

> *Learn to see, reader: this time the truth*
> *Is veiled in a thinner mist, and now*
> *The meaning should be clear even to you.*

For myself, I have lived with access to the splendours of Indigo for many years. It is only now that I feel ready to complete the transition. I cross into Indigo now for the very last time, having made provision in this manuscript to enable those who would follow me. Will I see you on the other side? That's clearly for you to decide. Now it is only you who can truly say, *Auribus teneo lupum,* I hold the wolf by the ears.

The precise process of the operation should, with the utmost care, be conducted as follows:

THIRTY-EIGHT

AFTER DECLARING HER INVISIBILITY IN THE SUNROOM OF THE psychiatric ward, the real Natalie Shearer simply returned to her wicker chair to gaze out of the south-facing window. She remained impervious to any further questions.

"What do you mean when you say you're in Indigo?" Jack tried.

Natalie stroked her thighs with her fingers and ignored him. She seemed not even to hear him. Louise shivered. Jack looked at Louise and indicated the door. As they were leaving, Natalie turned and said, "Please tell Tim I waited."

They sat in a tasteful lounge, numb from the encounter. It hadn't been difficult to find the real Natalie Shearer. Jack had been able to ascertain the presence at the Ospedale San Callisto of a young English woman, and when he said he was returning to Rome, Louise had insisted on coming back with him. Dory had agreed to stay at Louise's apartment in Chicago to look after Billy.

"Poor girl," Louise said as they waited. "But she's scary. What did she mean when she said we were drenched in Indigo?"

237

Jack shrugged, but he knew.

The Italian doctor returned in his squeaky shoes, ready to escort them outside. He carried a file with him.

"We don't know how she came to be here," Jack said as they walked back down the corridor.

The doctor checked his clipboard and sniffed hard. "She was transferred from a private hospital."

"Could we find out who was paying before?" Louise wanted to know.

"It's possible." Sniff.

"Was it the trepanning that caused this?" Jack asked.

"We think so. The amateur trepanner came in at an angle and managed to touch both the temporal and occipital lobes. Quite an achievement. The skull can bear this, but as you can imagine, the area beneath is sensitive and the amateur trepanner managed to puncture both gray and white matter. We don't know what damage was caused here, but she was in terrible pain, and it's quite possible these delusions and her current state were triggered by the trauma of the intense pain. We don't know, you see, whether she had a previous history of psychosis."

"Is she ever violent."

"Not really. She's a nice girl. She just thinks she's invisible. She and her wolf. The money you mentioned will buy her more extensive treatment, better drugs, and superior care." He shrugged at her prospects.

Jack offered a hand to shake. The doctor regarded it for a moment as if uncertain whether it might communicate a virus; then he accepted it limply before passing on to Louise. He escorted them back to the reception area, along the interminable corridor, his shoes squeaking again like an unheard little voice on the marble floor.

"By the way," he asked. "You wouldn't know the identity of the amateur trepanner?"

"No," said Jack.

"Nor you?" he asked Louise.

"No."

Jack and Louise left the building in silence. It was not until they were passing under the row of dark cypress trees, between their poisonous, clawlike roots, that Jack whispered, "Amateur trepanner."

"You'd think," Louise said, "that he'd get some different shoes."

. . .

"He did die, didn't he, Louise?" Jack said. "He didn't fool everyone? Somehow?" Jack had taken Louise to the shrine of Mithras beneath the multiple levels of the Church of San Clemente. He wanted her to see what Natalie—or the fake Natalie—had shown him on their last day together.

"We've been through this before," she said sternly. "He was as dead as they get. I supervised the whole thing. Even the cremation. I saw his body go into the fire."

"It's just that Natalie back there in the hospital seems to be waiting for him."

"She's got a long wait."

"I don't know. I've spent too much time reading that book of his. I keep thinking: What if he found a way of becoming invisible, or of stepping out of his body?"

"Keep reading it and you'll end up where we just came from." Louise surveyed the Mithraic altar, and the carving of Mithras slaying the bull. "I'll tell you something about the cremation. He'd always said that when he died he wanted me to arrange a detail he'd witnessed in Hindu rites. At the funeral ritual, they place a brass dish of flour by the entrance to the temple. The migrating spirit is supposed to leave a sign, in the flour, of its means of departing this earth. I inspected it afterwards, skeptically, of course. There was a triangle bisected by a single vertical line in the middle of the flour. What do you think that means?"

. . .

Alfredo was thrilled to receive, at his office, a visit from Louise and Jack, though he did remonstrate with Louise for not warning him in advance of their arrival in Rome. He sent out for pastries, had his secretary make fresh coffee, and introduced them both to his colleagues as his "friends from America," Jack's British credentials notwithstanding. Louise admired the picture on Alfredo's desk of his wife and three children. Alfredo flushed with pride and chose to miss any irony.

"There has been an offer," he said, finally getting down to business, "on the house."

"Yes," Jack said, "and you're going to tell us it's a very low offer."

"Correct! *Very* low. How do you know this?"

"And this low offer was made by an English woman."

"The offer came by mail. I never actually met the woman." He took out a file. "Here. Sarah Buchanan. Sounds English." He took off his spectacles, the better to see Louise. "Louise? What's going on?"

They told Alfredo that Sarah Buchanan was almost certainly the woman impersonating Natalie Shearer; and that the real Natalie Shearer was in the psychiatric Ospedale San Callisto, though "invisible" and with little prospect of improvement; and that Sarah Buchanan's low offer came close to getting her both the house and the money that should be directed to Natalie Shearer.

Alfredo reported in turn that "people" had been staying at the house on an almost daily basis. Before leaving Rome on the last occasion, Jack had told him to do nothing. Now Alfredo wanted to bring in the *polizia statale*. He stalked the office, puce in the face, ready to lay siege to the house with rifles and a small cannon. Jack told him to wait.

Instead, Louise and Jack drove over to the place together. The door was unlocked, as usual, but there was no trace of anyone inside. The house was quiet yet in some disarray, the occupants having given up any efforts to disguise their presence. A tower of unwashed plates threatened to topple in the sink; empty wine bottles cluttered the kitchen; dirty clothes lay discarded across chairs.

Together, Jack and Louise cleaned up. They dumped clothes, bottles, magazines, and books in black plastic garbage bags and made seven bags of trash. "I don't believe it!" Jack cried. "They wiped out all of that wine! They're actually down to the last bottle."

"Open it," Louise suggested.

But Jack returned it to the rack. "You know, Louise, it would be better if you weren't here."

"What if she doesn't come."

"Why don't I call you a cab to take you to the hotel?" Jack suggested. "I'd like to do this alone." Their eyes met. "Really. It's kind of personal."

. . .

As Jack lay in wait at the house, Louise didn't make her way back to the hotel. Instead, she strolled the *centro storico*, wandering cobbled streets where oily motorcycle repair shops shared a wall with expensive fashion boutiques, and where chic girls laughed with boys in grubby overalls. Louise, too, couldn't get enough of Rome; especially after Dory had told her that Rome was where she was "made."

"Made? What do you mean, *made?*" Louise had asked.

"Hell, what do you think I mean? You were conceived in Rome, that's what I mean."

Dory had been talking about Rome on the night they all learned about Nick Chadburne's death. For the first time in her life, Dory spoke openly and intimately on the subject of Tim Chambers.

"I'll tell you why I was so opposed to Jack," Dory had blurted

241

out. "It was something your father said, years ago. It was when I was planning to leave him, and he told me I didn't have the strength. I told him I was taking you, hell or high water, and he said it would make no difference. He bragged that he would get you to marry his English son if he wanted. Louise, that was the first time I'd ever heard anything about him having a son in England."

"Is that why you didn't want me to go to Rome with Jack?"

"That and another reason." Dory paused. "Oh, I've been lecturing Jack about keeping secrets and there are many things I've never told you."

"When I first got together with Chambers I was dazzled. Blinded. But there was something I managed to keep from him, at least until he found out in Rome after we were married. My medical condition, the epilepsy, it's of the psychomotor type. I told you how I used to get not so much a convulsion, but an *aura,* a dizziness, strange sensations, odors, colors, lights. The most common manifestation was the occasional, well, involuntary orgasm, I guess you'd call it. Don't look at me like that—it's not as much fun as it sounds. These attacks could come out of the blue, wham, no warning, no matter where you were, no matter who you were talking to. It was pretty damned hard to disguise, too. I still have to take the carbamazepine pills to deal with it.

"He found out in Rome. We were in the Pantheon, looking up at that hole in the roof, and wham. There was no disguising it any more. Your father was amazed—why wouldn't he be? I sobbed and sobbed—I thought he'd leave me. But he was fascinated.

"I told him I could see strange colors, and he always wanted me to describe, describe, describe. But you know, when it happened there was this light and color and a taste in my mouth, things I had no words for. I think it was just to keep him quiet that I told him: *Indigo! It's Indigo!*

242

"It became an obsession. He researched all the medical details. I have a deformed artery in the right temporal pole of my brain, and it had ruptured, triggering this thing. The carbamazepine pills take good care of the problem, but your father was obsessed with how to *induce* this condition. Not that I'd want to wish it on anyone. Because every time it happened, I was *scared*."

"Oh, Mom," Louise said. "Why did you keep quiet about this for so long?"

"Honey," said Dory, wanting to close the subject, "did you ever come in the middle of a round of canasta?"

. . .

Louise walked the cobbled streets, reflecting on Dory's disclosure. In the Piazza Navona she sat, huddled into her coat, near the Fountain of the Moor. Powdery dusk spilled into the square like a fine mauve spice, and the piazza filled with lovers drifting between the fountains. The white marble inside the illuminated fountain pools discharged an extraordinary hue, streaming to infiltrate the dusk; and the spires of Saint Agnes in Agony punctured the sky to admit more of the contraband mauve powder.

Meanwhile, the Bernini figures dribbled water from their wreathed horns, commingling with an irregular background murmur, insistent, remorseless, and inarguable. The murmur said: Here is Indigo here is Indigo here is Indigo.

THIRTY-NINE

WHEN SARAH BUCHANAN DREW UP OUTSIDE THE HOUSE JUST before midnight that evening, she didn't have to quiet the engine of her Vespa for either her or her passenger to hear the music. Opera at high decibel. Contralto. That Ferrier thing again. *Orfeo*. She doused her lights, climbed off the scooter, and glanced at her Italian boy. He dragged on the roach of a joint and tossed it into the yard. Buchanan gazed down at the glowing end of the thing as if it might spark an explosion.

The door stood open. The two of them mounted the stone steps to see, in the hallway, a dozen candles aflame and quivering in the draft. Moving cautiously through the house, they found dozens more candles burning; in the living room, the kitchen, and on each step of the stairs. The boy flicked a light switch. It was dead. He tried another. Dead.

"Somebody has taken the lightbulbs," he said. "Chambers?"

Sarah pressed a finger to her lips and checked out the blacklight box under the stairs. The UV light came on, bleeding into the rest of the house. In the flickering, thin UV light, the boy examined the living room, backing into the mannequin there. The mannequin's head toppled from its shoulders and bounced along the floor, losing its

dark glasses and beret. The boy carefully, almost superstitiously, replaced it before rejoining the search. Sarah was already halfway up
the stairs, and he followed.

She flicked a light switch in one of the bedrooms, but it seemed
that someone had removed every lightbulb in the house. "Go back
down and turn off that fucking music," she hissed before disappearing into the bedroom.

The boy dithered at the top of the stairs, as if sensing something
wrong. There was a sudden noise like the flap of a coattail before a
sudden, heavy impact in the small of his back forced him clattering
down the stairs. He landed heavily, cracking his head on the tiles.
He sprawled on the floor, whimpering. By the time Sarah came back
to the top of the stairs, he'd dragged himself to his feet. He held his
arm stiff at his side and nursed his head, still whimpering. He muttered something in Italian.

"*Vattene!*" she hissed. "Get out of here! Useless!"

He protested.

"*Vattene! Vattene!*"

The boy hobbled out the door. Moments later, the Vespa outside
wheezed to life and accelerated, departing in a diminishing whine.

"He's gone," she announced to the house. "I've gotten rid of
him. That's what you wanted, wasn't it?"

She sat stubbornly on the stairs. "You can show yourself," she
said more gently.

Silence prevailed. The house creaked. There was a sigh from
over her shoulder. One of the candles at the top of the stairs sput-
tered. She spun around to look at it. Her eyes were wide, catch-light
darting from point to point. Then she peered hard at the mannequin
standing at the top of the stairs, the mannequin in the gas mask. It
came alive.

Jack pulled off the mask and stepped out of the coat, dropping
both to the floor.

Sarah tossed her hair. "There was really no need to throw him down the stairs. You could have killed him."

"He pushed me in the river. He could have killed me."

"How can you think that had anything to do with me? And that boy swore to me he'd done nothing to harm you."

"He was jealous. You were fucking him at the same time you were playing around with me."

"That's not true!" She got up and took a step toward him. Her hands were trembling and her face was set in a twisted geometry of fear. "You walked out on me! The only reason I went with that boy was to try to forget about you, Jack! I was hurting!"

For a shocking moment, for an atomic flicker of time, he felt himself turning back to her. There was a sound in his ears, maybe the sighing of blood, and a vapor pouring into the room; and there was that deliquescing of the light, and she was clothed in a new color of limitless radiance. He could have gone with it. But he stopped it. "Hey! I was just about to call you Natalie! *Natalie!*"

He hurried down the stairs to get away from her, but she followed, imploring him over his shoulder. "Talk to me! Where did you go? What did you co?"

"You know, you sound almost plausible?"

"Listen to me! We were right there, Jack. It *was* there. You and me. Indigo dust, pouring out of the sky. All around us. You just couldn't see it! You were looking so hard you couldn't see it!" She pressed her hands to his face and twisted his head so that he had to look her in the eye. "Listen, listen, listen. There was Indigo everywhere. I love you, Jack: That's the biggest seeing trick of all. I didn't know that was going to happen. I was coming undone. For the first time, I understood what it meant, this Indigo thing. I could see it everywhere."

"There is no Indigo, *Sarah*. You told me that yourself!"

"Believe any awful thing about me you want, but you have to believe this: It was there, Jack. It was there, even if now it's gone. You're lying to yourself if you say it wasn't there."

He couldn't bring himself to look at her. His own eye wasn't strong enough to withstand the Indigo flame in Sarah's searching gaze.

. . .

Later, they sat drinking the last bottle of Tim Chambers's wine. Jack told her about the visit to the real Natalie Shearer in the psychiatric hospital and about the demise of Nicholas Chadbourne in Chicago. Buchanan knew them all: Shearer, Chadbourne, Anna-Maria Accurso. She said she was sorry for Chadbourne. She'd always nursed a soft spot for him.

"We were the inner circle," she said. "Though we could never become too attached to each other. Your father prevented that. AnnaMaria was Italian, a high-society girl. She always had it easy. Natalie was already unstable. Nick Chadbourne was the talent. But after all that, he just lost it."

"Are you going to tell me what happened?"

She stood up and drained her glass. "Come on."

Sarah led Jack out to the blacklight box under the stairs, flipping on the UV light. Moving aside the central chair, she rolled back the rug beneath to expose a trapdoor. Opened up, it revealed a short flight of wooden steps descending into shadow. Jack peered into the dark.

"It's all right," she said wearily. "There's nothing down here."

This was not entirely true. There was another UV light, an old sofa and an armchair, and a battered mahogany sideboard. The walls were decorated in swirling abstract colors, overpainted with slogans. Jack saw instantly that Chadbourne had tried to duplicate the cellar in his Chicago apartment. A window at one end had the glass painted over from outside. Jack figured the window opened at street level. "Is this how people came and went when I first stayed here?"

She nodded.

"How come I didn't see the window outside?"

"It's painted to look exactly like the brickwork. You have to get up close to tell the difference."

"What happened here?"

Sarah Buchanan examined the painted walls of the cellar, hugging herself as if what she saw there made her feel cold. Dampness in the walls had blistered the paint. It flaked liked diseased skin. "We'd been building up to the anniversary of the Lupercalia for a year. You have to understand the state of mind of those involved. There were cocktails of drugs, all supplied by your father, even though he never used them himself. His word for psychedelic drugs was 'entheodelics.' From *theos*, meaning God. He said some inferior people needed to invite God inside themselves. Not him, of course; he had enough *theos* inside him to kill a horse. Whatever; if you mix psychedelics with that book of his you're asking for big trouble."

"The Manual?"

"The Manual of Light. Like I say, we'd been working with it for a year. This was the day Indigo was going to brighten the world for all of us. The day of the wolf. All that. And not just for us: A new color was going to come back into the universe and we were to be the ones to let it in. You've followed that book; you know remarkable things *can* happen. There was just one last step.

"Except I didn't believe it. Out of the four of us, mine was the only skeptical voice. The others were gung ho. I couldn't voice my skepticism because the old man used to preach, and I mean preach, that if any one of us doubted it would all go wrong. You know: Skepticism unsteadies the aim.

"He'd arranged for us to meet him, down here, on the eve of the

Lupercalia, on the stroke of midnight. He was going to perform the final act. But there was a hiccup. He called by telephone, said he was delayed, and gave us the code word 'Mithras.' This was the signal, agreed beforehand, that we would have to go ahead on our own. I think he'd planned it that way all along.

"In my memory, it all happens in a blue light. All the instruments are laid out on that sideboard: razor, local anesthetic, sterile bath, diagrammatic chart, trephine. I'd never seen a trephine before. A small, circular blade to cut the disk in the skull; a pin in the center to stop it from slipping. Works like a geometric compass.

"So there we are, all ready to call the thing off—hey, let's get drunk instead, is my idea—but it's Nick Chadbourne urging us to go ahead. He's in no mood to wait another year for the Lupercalia to come around. He sits in the chair and says, 'So, who's going to do it?'

"Natalie is completely stoned. She's been eating acid like vitamins; she's had so much Indigo she already can't tell the shadow from the light. AnnaMaria is tipping back cognac, slurring somewhere between Italian and English. So I volunteer."

Sarah angled a finger behind her ear. "You have to come in at a tangent, like this; at least, according to your old man, you just put a graze on the artery. I shave Nick's hair and apply the local anesthetic while the other two watch me with bleary, bulging eyes. It's all surprisingly easy. It must be hurting him like hell but Nick says all he feels is a chafing. I don't know what drugs he's taken. He's wincing and clenching his teeth, but the fact is I don't cut a complete disk. The bone flakes or something but I know I haven't penetrated. I haven't completed the oculus. I chicken out. I put a Band-aid over the incision and I step back. Nick gets out of the chair looking pale and shaky. 'Okay,' he goes. 'Who's next?'

"That's when I faint.

"When I come to they're gathered around me giggling. It's all a

249

big joke: Nick is the one who's been trepanned, but I'm the one who faints. Natalie is ready to take her turn and they want me to perform a second trepanning. But by now I just don't have the stomach for it.

"Natalie is in the chair. Nick says he feels shaky. I refuse to do another one and that just leaves AnnaMaria. She slams down her bottle of cognac and rolls up her sleeves. I can't stand it so I go out of the cellar. When I come back, AnnaMaria has removed a perfect disk, a plug of bone like an aspirin tablet, same shape as your old man used to wear around his neck, but Natalie has blacked out. I bend over to look at the incision. She's bleeding. Bits of gray matter and white stuff seeping from the wound. Then Natalie comes to and as she does she starts screaming.

"And she doesn't stop screaming. We try to pacify her with painkillers but she's in agony. It's hideous. She's convulsing, shuddering. Someone has the sense to call an ambulance. They carry her away, still screaming, into the Lupercalian night.

"And I can still hear her screaming, Jack. Every day of my life I hear her scream. Can we get out of here, please?"

· · ·

The house was silent now. They sat on the floor in the living room, smoking cigarettes, contemplating figures in the carpet. Occasionally, a candle flickered in an undetectable draft. Sarah Buchanan shook her head, more than once, in answer to questions posed by Jack.

"Your father managed to avoid any trace of blame. Though he did pay for Natalie's hospitalization. The rest of us scattered.

"All we knew about Natalie was that four weeks after the event she was still screaming. AnnaMaria was so consumed with guilt she spent all day and every day in her Catholic church, buried under rosaries and crucifixes. Nick went back to Chicago. I stopped taking drugs and went to live in Trastevere, where you found me. Buried myself in art. I had no contact with any of them. Then one day I read

that AnnaMaria had committed suicide. No one knew why this successful, well-heeled, beautiful young woman had done this thing.
But the date of her death was the anniversary of Lupercalia, and I of
course understood it perfectly."

"How did you get into the scam with the house?"

"I had an exhibition. Your father turned up. I wanted nothing to
do with him. He told me he'd made provision for Natalie, was going to sell the house and leave the money for her for when she was
back to normal. I don't think he realized there wasn't going to be
any back to normal for Natalie.

"Once, while your father was away in Chicago, I started squat-
ting in this house when I was stuck for a place. I found Natalie's
things here and it occurred to me that she might as well have disappeared off the face of the earth. Then someone in the art world told
me Tim Chambers was dead. I thought I could pull it off."

"But you were wrong."

"Sure was. What are you going to do about it."

"I don't know." He looked at her. For the first time since he'd
met her, that peculiar deliquescing in her eyes had stopped. Now he
saw only a profound loneliness. The sadness of the stray timber
wolf lurking in shadows cast by the campfire, seeking human
warmth, held back by fear of dogs. "Sarah, you're a lost girl, you
know that?"

"You say that, but in the end I was the only one who knew your
father was right."

"Right about what?"

"About Indigo."

"It's an impressive body count. One psychotic, one suicide, and
one dead junkie, and you think he was right?"

"That's because they took him literally. When he abandoned us
that night, he wanted to see if we were so stupid as to go through
with the physical thing, the trepanning. Can't you see it, Jack? The

251

Indigo? It represents what you hope to find. Love. Revelation. Inspiration. The moment that pours into your life and makes it bigger than it was before. The thing is, the moment you *stop* looking for Indigo, your soul is dying.

"You may never see Indigo. You may only fool yourself into thinking you've seen it. But you can never allow yourself *not* to believe in the possibility. The potential for transformation. The scientist says it doesn't exist. The artist says it does. Those are not the only alternatives."

"Oh, yes. Natalie, AnnaMaria, and Nicholas found a third alternative."

"I'd stopped believing in it, Jack. Until you came along. That dream I had about your father. He told me, in the dream, that I would only see it if I could lead you to it."

"Please."

"We were on our way. You know it."

"Don't."

"I love you, Jack."

He looked hard at her. It was no good. He would always think it was just some trick she'd learned from a book. You can't get pushed into the same river twice.

"You're not going to let us get it back, are you? Don't let your father do this to you, Jack."

"What do you mean?"

"Tell me something. Do you think it's possible that the old man might still be alive."

Jack shook his head.

"Maybe he was right. Maybe he is in Indigo, watching us all, manipulating us, laughing."

"There is no Indigo," Jack said.

"You're wrong, my love. You are *so* wrong."

FORTY

JACK RETURNED ALONE TO THE OSPEDALE SAN CALLISTO, ANXIOUS to make administrative arrangements for the funding of Natalie's care. In the cold marble reception area under the brilliant floor-to-ceiling window, he waited to see the doctor whom he and Louise had met on their original visit.

Eventually, the same doctor appeared with his clipboard, his shoes still squeaking along the interminable marble hall. The doctor shook hands solemnly. "I've come to discuss the financial arrangements" Jack said, "for Natalie's care."

The doctor looked confused, and spoke in rapid Italian to the lady behind the reception desk. She answered in staccato phrases. He turned to Jack. "But Natalie Shearer is no longer here."

Jack was astonished. "But she must be!"

"I assure you, she is not!"

"But she can't just have left!"

The doctor quizzed the receptionist. "She was picked up by someone."

"Picked up? By whom?"

"This lady just told me she was not here personally at the time, but she knows Natalie was collected by a man. I believe it was the same person who was paying for her to stay here."

"Paying for her?"

"Indeed."

Jack was thrown by this development. He was at a loss. "But aren't there papers or something? People can't just check out of an asylum like it's a hotel!"

"Asylum? Excuse me, you don't seem to understand some things. This is a private hospital and Natalie was a voluntary patient. She was not ordered by a doctor or a court of law to be here. She is, *was*, free to go at any time. And in any event, when her payments were stopped . . ."

"Who stopped her payments?"

He gave Jack a timeless Roman shrug.

"And you don't know where she's gone? Perhaps to another hospital?"

"We were not told this."

"Isn't there any paperwork?" Jack demanded.

"We have her case notes, of course. And that's all."

"But can you at least tell me who was previously responsible for paying her hospital bills?"

The doctor became irritated with Jack's manner. "Look, this is information that you are not entitled to see. Are you actually related to Natalie?"

"No."

"Then—"

"But I came here prepared to pay for her care!"

"What can I say? You want me to take your money for nothing at all? You want to make a donation? I can arrange that. But as for Natalie, she is not here any longer. Please. I am very busy. What can I say? Please." The doctor stood drenched in the sunlight flooding through the high window, holding his clipboard aloft in appeal. "Please," he said again.

FORTY-ONE

Two days later, Jack and Louise strolled the cobbled narrow streets of the *centro storico*, between the shadows of medieval buildings and locked churches, arm in arm. Late October had slipped quietly into November and there was a crispness to the air, a chill streaming off the Tiber. Even the scent of the river mud had turned. It was like an installment of winter. This was to be their last afternoon and evening in Rome. Tomorrow they would fly out.

Jack had been unequivocal in telling Sarah Buchanan she should make herself invisible or leave Rome altogether, and as far as he knew that is what she'd done, but not before she'd delivered him a note:

> *Mithras expected nothing less than self-sacrifice from his followers. Did you know that? I'm going to disappear for a while. But after you've had time to shake the scales from your eyes to see to the bottom of this, I'll find you again. Yours in Indigo, Sarah*

"What's that?" Louise asked, seeing him with the note.

"Just a note from Alfredo," he said, stuffing the letter in his pocket, "saying he intends to change the locks."

255

Alfredo did indeed change the locks on the house and had the hidden cellar window boarded. Jack transferred to him executive power to sell the house for the best possible price. The question remained about what to do with the proceeds, since they could no longer be directed to the care of the real Natalie Shearer at the Ospedale San Callisto. Meanwhile, Alfredo wanted Louise to spend her last evening in Rome with him; he was crestfallen, but gracious at least, that she preferred to spend it with Jack.

Lights began to flicker on in the shop fronts and the trattorias as the two headed for the Pantheon. "You let her get away with it too easily, Jack," Louise said.

But Jack argued that when it came down to it, she hadn't actually done anything to hurt anyone, except let people call her Natalie for a while; even while they made love to her, he thought, but didn't add.

He didn't want the matter dragged out. As far as he was concerned, it was finished. He'd even dealt with the problem of publishing the Manual of Light. It was Rooney in Chicago who'd come up with a solution. Jack had been going to tell him he didn't want to publish the thing at all, that the risk of another pliable idiot reading it and drilling a hole in his own skull would always be on his conscience, and that he was prepared to forgo his executor's fee. He called Rooney, informing him that the publishing plan was off.

"The hell with that," Rooney said. "I got a better idea."

Rooney knew of an exporter for what he called "erotic books." He knew of a state law that discriminated between "erotic books" and blatant pornography: For every page of photographic material, a page of printed text had to follow. Erotic books escaped a tax burden; pornography did not. "It's perfect," Rooney crowed over the phone. "We publish it as a magazine series, a page of beaver, a page of text from the Manual of Light. These things sell by the hundred thousand. Page of beaver, page of text. Beaver-text-beaver-text. What do you say?"

"I don't know about this," Jack tried.

"What the hell's the matter with you? You get to execute your old man's dying wishes."

"I don't care about his dying wishes. I'm more concerned with the idea of people reading dangerous material, Rooney."

"You're missing the point, asshole! Nobody who buys a beaver magazine reads the printed pages! You could just as well print the thing in invisible ink! This is the only surefire way in the world to publish extensively *and* guarantee no idiot will ever read it."

Jack thought about it. He held his hand over the receiver while he put the idea to Louise, who told him she wanted no part of it, but that he should do whatever he had to do.

"So?" Rooney said. "Do we go?"

"Well, yes. I suppose."

"Hoo-fuckin'-ray," said Rooney. "I'll get on it."

. . .

When Jack and Louise got up to the Pantheon, the light was dying outside. Before they went in, Jack said, "He went back for Natalie, didn't he? It had to be him."

"We've been through this," Louise said sharply. "We've been over it and over it."

"There's another thing. Do you think, Louise, that he planned it? That he organized it so we'd meet? That he engineered this whole thing, knowing we would have impossible feelings for each other?"

He was on hazardous ground. "Which feelings are those, exactly?" Louise said, but when he didn't answer she softened. Gently running her fingers up and down the lapels of his coat, she said, "Don't ever allow yourself to believe such a dangerous idea."

257

Inside the dome, the same taped Gregorian chant played on; the golden piers, empty of the deities but not of their presence, shone with unnatural, dusky light. Through the oculus, the sky began to boil. Then it began to rain, and once again the cylindrical cascade of water seemed suspended in the oculus. They sat together on a stone bench, looking up.

"But you loved her, didn't you?"

"No. Maybe. Who knows?"

"What will you do? Go back to your business in London?"

"I don't know about that."

"Come stay in Chicago with us. We'll fix you up."

"Think I need fixing up?"

Louise smiled but she didn't answer. Instead, she snuggled up to him and leaned her head on his shoulder, and they both looked up at the silver rods of rain coming in through the ceiling. They watched for a long time, and in the oculus—in the eye of the ceiling and in the presence of old gods—a shadow moved from blue to violet, and then to some mystical color in between.

ABOUT THE AUTHOR

Graham Joyce lives in Leicester, England, with his wife and two children. He is the author of *Requiem, The Tooth Fairy,* and *Dark Sister,* and is a three-time British Fantasy Award winner. *Indigo* is his first suspense novel.